MICHAEL'S SONG
When the love for his mother hurts more than the abuse

Pernitha A. Tinsley

Copyright © 2017 by Red Moon Publishing Group

All rights reserved. No part of this book may be reproduced in any form or by any means without prior written consent of the publisher, except for brief quotes used in reviews.

This is a work of fiction. Any reference or similarities to actual events, real people, living or dead, or to real locales are intended to give the novel a sense of reality. Any similarity in other name, characters, places and incidents is entirely coincidental.

Library of Congress Cataloging-in-Publication Data

ISBN-13: 978-0-9858727-2-4
ISBN-10: 0-9858727-2-1

First Printing February 2017

10 9 8 7 6 5 4 3 2 1

Manufactured in the United States of America

Dedication

Dedicated to the children who have suffered physical, mental, and emotional abuse at the hands of those who are supposed to protect them.

Acknowledgements

I would first like to thank God for blessing my pen, and for allowing me to create works of art to be shared with the world. I humbly thank my supporters and everyone who has, and continue, to encourage me to push beyond the limits that I tend to place on myself. Lastly, and I have saved the best for last.

Joy, if it had not been for your constant presence in my life, I would not be where I am today. You put my pen to many tests. You helped to take my writing to new heights. The valuable "jewels" that you have shared with me have placed me in a position to be in demand by many authors, as well as producers in the movie industry. Thank you.

Chapter 1
Lullaby
Saturday @ 11:00 p.m.

I lie in bed listening through my open bedroom door to Mama and Uncle Robert stumbling inside of our apartment. Their stammering was so loud that it could have disturbed the cockroaches that cowered in scattered cracks until a switch turned light into darkness and ignited their party, or self-reproduction process.

"Watch where you kicking them heels," Uncle Robert told Mama. "Almost put my eyes out."

I stared up at the paint chipped ceiling wondering how high Mama was kicking her heels. It had to have been pretty high if she 'bout took Uncle Robert's eyes out. Uncle Robert was a tall, bulky man with a belly that looked to be filled with barrels of beer. If he was ducking and dodging Mama's heels at his height, Mama must have been trying to kick a field goal over his head. Maybe Mama had cut off the lights after they entered our chariot of a roach motel, and could not see Uncle Robert. After all, Uncle Robert's skin complexion was as dark as rich soil. His eyes were as tight as the extra small shirts he insisted on squeezing into.

Mama's bare feet against the cheap hardwood floor resounded through the apartment like Sister Collins and her fake rendition of the Holy Ghost during Sunday morning service.

Uncle Robert tried to hush Mama. "Shhh, you gon' wake that boy," he told her.

I wanted to say, "I'm already awake," but knew to keep my mouth shut. Mama would have beat me to a pulp had I intruded on their faux privacy. Instead, I simply practiced hush mouth grace and laid there with my plaid blanket pulled up to my chest, and my hands folded over the blanket. My eyes were still set on the ceiling while my ears were tuned to Mama and Uncle Robert.

"Get in the room, girl," Uncle Robert said in a drunken voice. His words were slurred. His laughs were loud and dry. He had tried to silence Mama, claiming her voice would wake me from whatever nightmare invaded my dreams, yet he was just as loud as Mama.

"Carry me to the room." Mama laughed. Her words were slurred like Uncle Robert's.

Mama was as light as a feather thanks to the drugs that ate the meat from between her skin and bones, leaving her as fragile as a newborn baby. Uncle Robert could have picked Mama up with one arm, tossed her over his shoulder, and carried her effortlessly into the room.

"If carrying you will get you out these clothes, I'll do it." Uncle Robert chuckled with strain in his voice.

Their feet met the floor with a flurry of stomps. Their voices suddenly grew silent. I could hear wheezing and loud puffs. The wheezing was coming from Mama. I recognized the passion in her voice. It was no different than any of the other nights when Mama and one of my uncles killed the silence in the house with their lust.

Uncle Robert, Uncle Patrick, and Uncle Nard all sounded the same during their sexual rendezvous. I had a lot of uncles.

Every man Mama brought home with her was my uncle.

My right ear burned to hear their libido. I was only seven, but having to hear my mother's lovemaking almost every night of my young life had become music to my ears. Her light screams and my uncle's groans were like a sweet lullaby, only they kept me awake at night instead of putting me to sleep.

Mama's bedroom was to the right of mine. A thin wall separated the headboard of her bed from my dresser. It's a good thing I had taken a nap after school, because what followed next kept me up until four in the morning.

"Ugh." Mama breathed between my uncle's thrust. The eroticism gave me 'eargasms.' Please don't call me sick. I was young; born into Mama's erotic life. I was as dependent upon her pleasures as she was her drug addiction.

"Crystal." Uncle Robert heaved. "You want to make a baby tonight? Let me know now, because I'm holding back Jr. or Charles, my great uncle's name. Hurry up, girl, say something."

A baby? I thought. *A new brother or sister for me?* Mama was only twenty-eight. She could produce a dozen babies, but not without her drugs' permission. Would Mama birth a child with missing limbs, a learning impediment, deaf or mute, or even worse, another dead child? The drugs did have the last word.

Mama had birthed two stillborn babies before God finally decided to bless her with me, the nappy head child, as Mama called me during her rants. The thought of a brother or sister did sound nice, but death over life in Mama's presence was the best option.

Mama was no mother to me. She was just there, and at times, so was I.

Mama never missed my absence when I was at my Big-mama's house. Big-mama was my grandmother. Every kid in the ghetto called their grandmothers Big-mama no matter how big or small she was.

When I was home, a belt, switch, extension cord, or the front and back of Mama's hands welcomed me before I received even the slightest ounce of love.

"Are you crazy?" Mama cackled like a swarm of drunks in front of a liquor store. "I'm not having no more kids. Can barely take care of that nappy headed child I got here now. Little bastard. Been thinking about sending him to live with my mother since he loves her so much."

Bastard? That was a new one. Dummy, little piece of shit, nappy headed, dirty tail, and now bastard? I was everything but Michael, the name Big-mama had given me after I was born and Mama's lips were glued together in a coma. The hospital had to do an emergency C-section after Big-mama found Mama passed out from a drug overdose on the living room floor.

With all of the drugs that owned Mama's body, I'm surprised I was born without any deformities, unless you consider a broken heart a deformity. I'm what Big-mama calls, when she's talking to the church folks, a miracle baby. Touched by God Himself.

The loud booming sounds against the wall didn't startle me like they used to. Mama's headboard beat the wall like she beat me when she was high on OxyContin, liquid cocaine, or powder cocaine. My dresser rattled. Their lovemaking threatened to knock the small fish tank that Uncle Nard had given me for my sixth birthday off the dresser. Thank goodness the plastic cup that once held cherry soda was empty. It toppled over onto its side, and then rolled off the dresser onto the floor.

The pen and pencil holder rattled. The purple 1966

Chevelle model antique car that Uncle Robert had given me came to life. Mama and Uncle Robert's sex started its toy engine. The Chevelle moved across the dresser like a car equipped with hydraulics.

For a minute, I thought Uncle Robert was killing Mama. Of course I knew he wouldn't hurt one hair on Mama's head. That's still what it sounded like as her headboard beat the wall.

"Awe!" I heard Mama scream. The fish tank moved with a jolt. "Oh God." She exhaled deeply. Seemed like the only time she used God's name was during her sexual immorality. "Robert. Robert, stop! Robert, it hurts." Mama gasped. I could tell by her groans and ahhhs that she didn't really want Uncle Robert to stop. There was still a hint of passion in her tone.

"You like that?" Uncle Robert grunted.

The pen and pencil holder finally succumbed to its fate and fell on its side. Two markers and a pencil fell out and rolled back and forth over the dresser. A picture of me and Big-mama bounced with each thrust.

I jumped up in bed when I noticed my car moving closer and closer to the edge of the dresser. *Not my car!* I was young, but very mature for my age. I knew quality, and the Chevelle was quality.

I leaped out of bed and hopped over my football and backpack. I tip-toed over to the dresser and caught my car as it was falling to the floor.

"Are you ready?" I heard Uncle Robert ask Mama.

I didn't know what he meant by his question. I must have missed something in between their heaves, groans, and me hurrying to the dresser to stop my car from meeting the floor.

After thirty minutes of constant groans and screams, the headboard gave the wall a rest. It was no longer chipping at the paint on the wall. You should have seen Mama's bedroom wall and all of the scattered areas of missing paint. It looked like someone was desperately trying to escape their captives by clawing at her cheap wall in an effort to break free.

My music stopped. Mama and Uncle Robert turned off my favorite song without first consulting with me.

I cradled my car in my arms and pressed my right ear against the wall. I closed my eyes and prayed for them to push play on their bodies so that I could wrap myself in their music again.

"Are you tired, because I can go another round?" Uncle Robert asked Mama.

Yay! I was happy. Uncle Robert was about to turn the music back on.

I backed away from the wall and smiled. Every beat of my small heart anticipated the music. It could have been loud, medium, low, or soft. I did not care as long as it returned.

"Are you going to feed me when we're done?" Mama asked with an attitude.

"Don't I always?" Uncle Robert sighed. "And don't be coming at me with that 'I'll do for you, if you do for me' mess. I take care of you and Michael, and he ain't even my son."

"You're right. I'm sorry," Mama said seductively. "Come here."

The music returned, only it was short-lived. It only lasted for five minutes, but I was grateful for every minute. It was better than nothing.

"Lock the door behind you," Mama said in short breaths.

"I'm not going nowhere," Uncle Robert grumbled.

I heard the springs on Mama's mattress crying. I assumed Mama and Uncle Robert were crawling around on the bed. I remember hearing those same springs when I used to crawl into bed with Mama and lie down next to her whenever the drugs held her in a deep sleep. Sometimes she'd stay sleep for a whole twenty-four hours. I don't sleep with Mama anymore, though. Once my uncles started arriving, Mama made me sleep in my own bed. I blame them *and* Mama for the raggedy bed spring that pierced through Mama's mattress and sliced my ankle.

I placed everything back onto the dresser. I looked my car over and placed it on the floor, far away from the dresser, just in case Mama and Uncle Robert decided to make more music while I was asleep.

I crawled into bed and lay on my side. I stared at the clock on the nightstand. It was five in the morning. I had three hours before it would be time for me to get ready for church.

I slipped beneath the blanket. My weary eyes watched a cockroach crawl across the ceiling. I wasn't afraid of insects or animals. Big-mama used to always tell me not to fear anyone or anything but God. I tried not to fear Mama, but I couldn't help it. Her hands and my uncles' belts were hard.

I closed my eyes and said a silent prayer for Mama. I prayed for Mama to always wake up from her dreams. Lord knows them drugs held Mama captive and controlled everything about her, including her breaths.

Chapter 2
Sinful Forgiveness
Sunday @ 7:30 a.m.

I rose to the sunlight piercing my bedroom window and burning my face. It was a beautiful Sunday, and as usual, Mama was still sleep. I didn't expect her to be up at eight in the morning anyway. Sometimes Mama stayed in bed until me and Big-mama got back from church, which was between twelve-forty-five and one o' clock in the afternoon.

I woke up hungry. My stomach growled like two puppies after an afternoon of play. I wanted cereal, but we were out of milk. I thought about a peanut butter and jelly sandwich, but Mama had used the last of the bread for her sugar sandwich. You know when you sprinkle sugar on top of a slice of bread and fold it like a hotdog bun? That's what Mama did when she ran out of money to feed her drug addiction. The sugar calmed her nerves until one of my uncles showed up to refill her street prescription.

I ran to the pantry to get a Pop-Tart, but they were all gone too. I ended up stirring up a bowl of pancake mix. Big-mama taught me how to cook like her. I didn't know how to cook the big food like fried chicken, spaghetti, pork chops, or anything like that. Making pancakes was simple. Since I was only cooking for me, all I needed was one egg and two cups of water. I hated to have to use water, but since we were all out of milk, I had no choice. Water made the pancakes flat, while milk made them fluffy and moist.

I stood in front of the stove trying to be like my uncle Nard. My hands were tucked into my pants. I toyed with my penis as I watched the hot grease in the pan turn the watery batter into something edible. The tiny bubbles of grease that lined the pancake reminded me of Mama and the cloudy bubbles that formed within the liquid cocaine in the center of the spoon in her drug lab. Mama moved the spoon over the fire until her medicine, as she called it, was nice and pleasing to the eye of its beholder.

I don't know why Mama liked getting high. She didn't remember nothing when she woke up, and she was always falling out around the house, or even peeing on herself.

I turned off the fire beneath the skillet. I picked the plate of pancakes up from the center of the stove and set it on top of a placemat on the kitchen table. I stood in front of the microwave, looking up at a closed cabinet door. I was too short to reach the cabinet, which held the Aunt Jemima syrup. I don't know why Mama put the syrup so high up there, especially since I was the only one who used it. It wasn't like she ever cooked breakfast for me. Mama didn't cook dinner either. I cooked for myself, washed my own clothes, and walked myself to school. The county allowed Mama to sleep all day and have sex all night. The government gave her no reason to leave the apartment.

I looked down at four drawers in front of me. I was tempted to pull open the last two drawers and use them as a ladder to reach the cabinet. Those thoughts were crushed when a vision of the welts that one of my uncle's belts left on my legs popped in my head.

It had been a dark, rainy night, and the house was as cold

as ice. The heat had been cut off after Mama used the money that one of my uncles had given her to buy drugs instead of paying the bill. I searched the cabinet for the box of hot chocolate that my uncle Robert had bought for me for rainy days. He told me the hot chocolate would warm me up, and I believed him.

After my eyes roamed the pantry for close to thirty minutes, I turned my attention to a cabinet, where I noticed the hot chocolate sitting on the edge of a top shelf. The hot chocolate was beyond reach, but I could almost hear it calling out to me.

I pulled open two drawers and used them as a ladder. Mama stormed into the kitchen with a belt in hand and beat every obscenity into me.

I could still see the evidence of the welts months after they'd healed. Mama beat me so bad that she kept me home from school for three days.

An abusive parent never wants the school to see marks on their child, even if their hands were not responsible for them. All it takes is one call to DCFS, Department of Children and Family Services, by the school, and the police would be knocking at the parent's door, ready to arrest them. It's ironic how if the school calls DCFS on the parent, there's a knock at the door and the child is removed if the claims are found to be true. But if family or friends call DCFS, a statement is taken and everyone is allowed to go on with their lives, at least that is how it was in the ghetto.

My uncle Patrick had come over after Mama's brutal attack on me and found me curled up beneath the dining room table. Mama lied and told him that she accidently got carried away and left welts on me with a belt. It was no accident. Mama knew exactly what she was doing. She did everything in her power to hurt me, and probably would not have shed one tear had she killed me.

The beatings, the tears, and my young life being owned and operated by a dope fiend mother was getting the best of me. I was tired. My mind, body, and soul were tired. But I had no voice and absolutely no freedom over my own livelihood.

Fearing another episode of Mama grabbing me by my arm and beating me as I circled her while trying to get away from the flying belt, I decided to use a chair to reach the cabinet.

I walked over to the table and stood behind a chair. I slid the chair back with ease. I winced at the noise that the legs made as they grazed the tiled floor. I jumped back from the chair, praying that I didn't wake Mama. Gripped by fear, I raised my shoulders as high as they could go. The muscles in my face pulled the corners of my lips down into a frown. I stood motionless and listened for Mama's screams that were sure to come. Mama hated to be woke up from her sleep, especially if there were no drugs at the end of the rude awakening.

Mama finna yell, 'Stop scratchin' up my GD floor,' I thought to myself. I couldn't say the cuss word, not even in my thoughts, so I said GD. The 'G' was for God, and the 'D' was for damn. Big-mama would tell me that when Mama said that word, she was using God's name in vain. At the time, I didn't know what Big-mama meant, but now I do.

I continued to listen for Mama. Her empty voice never came. Guess Big-mama was right when she said drugs and alcohol made Mama sleep as hard as a horse.

With my eyes glued to the doorway that separated the kitchen from the hall, I crept back over to the chair and stood behind it. I held my breath and lifted the chair by its arms. When I exhaled, the front of the chair toppled forward and the legs slammed against the floor. I knew right away that I had awakened the sleeping dragon.

"Michael!" Mama screamed. Anger carried her voice from behind her closed bedroom door into the kitchen. "What the hell are you doing?"

My heart dropped down into my stomach. "I'm fixing something to eat before Big-mama picks me up for church." My voice quivered in fear.

"Stop making all that noise," Mama continued to scream. "Me and your uncle is in here trying to sleep."

I hung my head in sadness. My eyes stared at the dirt on my socks. "Okay, Mama." I dropped my shoulders.

I was tired of Mama being mean to me when all I wanted her to do was love me. If her constant screams and threats to beat my butt was her way of showing me love, then I would have chosen for her to hate me. It couldn't have been any worse than what I was already experiencing.

I gave up on the syrup. I wasn't about to get beat over no syrup. I gently opened the refrigerator door and took a jar of strawberry jam off the door. Being careful not to make any noise, I eased the door closed. I placed the jam on the table next to my plate. I was about to sit down when I realized that I'd forgotten a fork. My eyes roamed the cluttered dishrack. When I'd washed the dishes the night before, instead of placing the plates and glass cups neatly in the dishrack, and the silverware in the plastic cup that we used for a holder, I placed all dishes and silverware wherever they would fit in the dishrack. It was late and I was tired, but I knew if Mama came home to a dirty kitchen, it wasn't going to be good for me. In order to get a fork without making noise, I would have had to remove all plates and cups to get to the bottom of the rack where the silverware lay stacked on top of each other. The plates were too heavy for me to try to be all fancy with the stack, and it took both hands for me to pick up my uncles' glass beer cups.

If only I had a real mama. Mama should have been the one washing dishes, not me. Her laziness forced me to be a man eleven years before my time. I tried to keep the apartment clean, but Mama would go right behind me with her dirty gowns and underwear, and just slip out of them wherever she was standing.

The clothes would then lay there until one of my uncles went off on Mama about leaving her dirty clothes around the house. It's interesting how they would fuss at Mama about her clothes, yet could spend hours in Mama's dirty, stinking bedroom.

The house stayed dirty and stinky. I don't understand how Mama could sit in the house all day with a trashcan that smelled like the streets on trash day.

I managed to slip a knife and fork from the dishrack without making a lot of noise. I walked back to the table. My eyes moved from one chair to the next. I eyed the three chairs that surrounded the table before turning my attention to the forth chair that sat in the middle of the floor where I had left it. I was trying to decide which chair to sit in. All chairs had to be moved in order for me to sit down, and I did not want to have another episode of Mama screaming at me for making too much noise.

To keep from cutting into Mama's and Uncle Robert's sleep, and face being beaten with a belt, hand, or even her high-heel shoes, I stood and ate my pancakes.

I started for the jar of jelly when I thought I heard Bigmama's voice calling my name from somewhere in the house. At first I thought I was hearing things. She hadn't spent the night, and my mind was so tuned to Mama, that I did not hear her come in.

"Michael, where are you?" This time I knew it was Big-mama for sure.

I stood frozen, listening to her yell my name. I was too afraid to answer her. Both the mental and physical abuse from Mama traumatized me.

If there was such a thing as a perfect child, I would have fit the mold. I tried my hardest to be perfect. I feared the ground Mama walked on. I walked a straight line, while other children my age were free to make mistakes. Their discipline did not leave bruises on their arms and legs. They were not forced to stand in a corner with a bar of soap between their teeth as punishment for being a child.

Then there were the threats. Mama threatened to send me to juvenile hall if I ever told anyone about her abuse. Mama told me that I'd have to share a bedroom with boys three times my size, and that they would beat me worse than she ever did. Mama comparing what the boys in juvenile hall would do to me to what she was doing to me was enough to scare my mouth shut. Mama dang near killed me every time her hand or one of my uncle's belts came down on me. If her abuse placed me near death, I could only imagine what the boys in juvenile hall would do to me.

Big-mama's breaths found their way into the kitchen before she did. "Didn't you hear me calling you?" Big-mama asked, storming into the kitchen.

"Yes, Big-mama," I mumbled.

"So why didn't you answer me?" she asked. Her neck snapped back so quickly that I thought her head was going to fall off her neck.

The corners of my mouth were turned down into a frown. My wide-eyes looked innocently into Big-mama's eyes. I loved Big-mama more than I loved Mama, and never wanted to disappoint her.

"Because Mama and Uncle are sleep," I wept. "Mama told

me to be quiet."

"Uncle?" Big-mama questioned. She placed her balled fist on her thick hip. She ran the palm of her other hand over her hair. She held on to the black rubber band that held her hair together. She then wrapped a hand around the loose hair and brought the ends of her hair over her shoulder. I loved when Big-mama wore her hair back into a ponytail. It made her look even younger. "You don't have no uncle. Your mama is the only child to come out of this here." Big-mama pointed to her stomach.

Big-mama was a young forty-two-year-old grandmother, and she was real cute. She was fourteen years older than Mama, but looked younger than Mama. Mama was twenty-eight, but she didn't look anything like my friends' mothers that were either her age, or no more than a year younger or older than she was. Mama reminded me of one of my friend's grandmother. The drugs left Mama looking two times her age, or even more.

Big-mama was as dark as me. She wasn't big and she wasn't small. She was thick. One day when Mama was talking to herself in the mirror, she told herself that she was five feet and six inches tall. Big-mama was a little taller than Mama, so I think Big-mama was around five feet seven or five feet eight.

"And why aren't you dressed for church?" Big-mama fussed through gritted teeth.

I glanced back over my shoulder at the clock on the microwave. "It's eight-thirty. We leave at nine-thirty," I answered.

"Your mother didn't tell you I said for you to be ready by eight?"

"No." I pouted. Big-mama was scaring me. I had never done anything to make her mad before. I was her only grandchild, just like my mother was her only child, so she spoiled me rotten and had never raised her voice at me. Then again, I never gave Big-mama a reason to be anything other than loving toward me.

"Figures," I heard Big-mama say under her breath. "Go on to your room and get dressed. We going to breakfast with some of the sisters before church."

"Okay," I said. As I spun around to run out of the kitchen, I accidently bumped one of the chairs. Its legs grazed the floor, but I wasn't worried about waking Mama. If she flew out of the bedroom in a fit of rage and came after me, as soon as she saw Big-mama, she would withdraw into her own skin.

Mama knew her limits. She'd never hit me in front of Big-mama. Big-mama would have caught Mama's arm before she could strike me a second time, and probably beat Mama with her own fist.

Mama feared Big-mama, but not Big-mama's fist. Mama would hit Big-mama back in a heartbeat. Big-mama calling the cops on Mama was what worried Mama the most. All Big-mama had to do was mention the abuse and Mama straightened up quick.

I ran around Big-mama and out of the kitchen. She followed closely behind me, prompting me to say, "I can get dressed by myself."

"Boy, I'm not thinking about you." Big-mama laughed. "I'm about to see what your mama in here doing."

At the sound of Big-mama checking up on Mama, I said to myself, *Uh ohhh*. Mama was about to get it. Big-mama had told her time and time again about letting different men lay up in the apartment while I was there.

I ran past Mama's closed bedroom door to my room, slamming the door behind me. I knew what I was doing by slamming the door. I was hoping Big-mama would catch

Mama yelling at me for being loud and go off on her. I wanted desperately for Big-mama to take me away from Mama so that I could live happily-ever-after.

I begged and pleaded with Big-mama to take me away from Mama more times than I can count. Each time I asked, Big-mama either rubbed my head, or planted a kiss on my cheek and said, "One day, baby, one day."

One day. It was always one day. But in the middle of Big-mama and Mama arguing, Big-mama was quick to threaten to take me away from Mama.

"I don't even know if I'm prepared to see what's behind this door," I heard Big-mama say.

I stripped out of my pajamas and hurried into my black slacks and white dress shirt. I snatched the dirty socks off my feet and slipped into my black dress socks. Without untying my shoestrings, I forced my feet into my black dress shoes and rushed into the closet. I pulled my black blazer from a hanger. Shoving an arm into a sleeve, I ran out of the bedroom with the other half of my blazer shining the floor.

While running, I slipped my other arm into the blazer. I was running for the bathroom to brush my teeth when I noticed Big-mama standing in front of Mama's bedroom door with her hands on her hips. The door was still closed. Big-mama's facial expression might have changed three or four times, like she was trying to decide if what was behind the door was worth her losing her religion on a Sunday morning.

Big-mama reached for the doorknob, but then drew her hand back. She reached for the doorknob a second time, and drew her hand back again. I could tell by the look on her face that there was a fight going on inside of her.

I crept behind Big-mama and stood even with her joined legs so that Mama couldn't see me when Big-mama opened the door. I wasn't allowed in Mama's room, or anywhere near it. Other than passing by her room to get to the bathroom, I was to stay as far away from it as possible. Drawing an imaginary line on the wooden floor and telling a young child not to cross it was like telling a child not to touch something, and five minutes later their handprints were all over it. Not me. I took heed to Mama's warnings. That is, when I wasn't praying for her, or when she was gone.

Mama stayed so strung-out on drugs that when she misplaced something, she automatically accused me of taking it. Her bastard child took her bag of weed, bottle of liquid cocaine, a cigar wrapper that she used to roll her weed in, a wrinkled one dollar bill . . . According to Mama, I took everything in her room that wasn't nailed down to the floor. Even though I was standing there next to Big-mama, who would have readily been a witness to my innocence if anything came up missing in Mama's room, Mama would have still found some way to blame me for it.

Big-mama didn't know I was behind her. She turned the doorknob as fast as she snapped her neck around when Mama got under her skin. She pushed open the door. Together, me and Big-mama watched Mama and Uncle Robert jump up in bed.

"Mama, get out!" Mama screamed.

She swept hair out of her face. She had forgotten to cover her left breast when she pulled the sheet up to her neck to hide her guilt. Her skin clung to her bones. Mama's complexion had lost its flavor. Although she was dark, her veins could easily be seen. They traveled beneath her skin like roots from a tree that was a flood away from being uprooted by nature. Her lips were white. I don't know if they were chapped or glazed with fornication. But if asked, I would have chosen the latter.

The whites of Mama's chestnut shaped eyes were

bloodshot red. Dark spots covered her cheeks like freckles. Mama resembled a character from the television series, *The Walking Dead*. Years of shooting, sniffing, and swallowing had prepared her for death.

Mama was no longer the Dark & Lovely model that Big-mama just *knew* she would be, but could have easily passed as a spokesperson for the Drug Abuse Resistance Education program, also known as the D.A.R.E. program that most children learn about in elementary school.

The sheet covered Uncle Robert from the neck down. His round, bald head rested against a pillow. He stared at Big-mama like he didn't have a care in the world, and probably didn't.

The bedroom was a mess. Red plastic cups covered the floor. Mama's and Uncle Robert's clothes were on the floor near the foot of the bed. On the nightstand next to Uncle Robert was a silver spoon with a dark circle in the center of it. A green, clear lighter lay next to the spoon. On the floor next to the nightstand was a needle. It was partially covered by a sock with a long rubber tie lying next to it.

I stood up straight and pressed my back against the back of Big-mama's legs. I was surprised she did not whirl around and look down on me in anger. She was probably so engrossed—and possibly grossed out—by the filth before her, that she did not feel me pressing against her.

"Get the hell out!" Mama yelled at Big-mama.

"You bring these different men up in here, disgrace your temple, and don't worry about hiding it from Michael." Big-mama fussed. "Crystal, what's wrong with you? You've lost all respect for yourself. This is the third man in a month's time I done seen you lying up in here with."

Mama looked fearfully at Uncle Robert. "That's a lie." Mama's voice was rattled with fear. She turned her devil filled eyes back to Big-mama and lied. "You ain't seen me with nobody."

"The hell I haven't." Big-mama grunted. "Them drugs got you sleeping for days at a time. I come in this room every Sunday morning. You don't know it 'cause you be as high as a kite and don't hear the door opening. You be so drugged up that you don't know when me and Michael coming or going."

"Y'all need to go!" Mama yelled, pointing her finger at the door.

"I swear one day I'm going to take Michael away from you," Big-mama said in a threatening tone.

I secretly prayed that she meant it. I honestly wished for her to take me right-then-and-there.

Big-mama spun around so fast that I fell forward. "Boy, what you doing?" she said, looking down on me with anger written all over her face. Big-mama was not mad at me. She just hadn't had a chance to relax the muscles in her face after going off on Mama.

I looked up at Big-mama and smiled. I was as scared as a child lost in a grocery store, but I tried not to show it. My smiles always hit a soft spot with Big-mama, so I showed her a huge smile in hopes that it would wipe away her mean face.

Movement in the room caused me to look away from Big-mama and between her legs at Mama. Mama crawled out of bed just as naked as the day she was born. She threw on her robe and walked over to the door. Mama stood in back of Big-mama. Mama looked down on me and cut her eyes at me. She reminded me of Darth Vader from the movie, *Star Wars*. Her hair was all over her head like the hair that surrounds a lion's face.

I looked fearfully away from Mama and up at Big-mama again. "I was going to the bathroom to brush my teeth and hair," I mumbled in a low voice. My eyes continued to move from Big-mama to Mama. Big-mama didn't know Mama was standing right behind her until Big-mama noticed me looking in back of her while talking to her.

Following my gaze, Big-mama glanced over her left shoulder at Mama. "Girl, back away from me. I smell hell all over you." Big-mama turned up her nose. I didn't know a person's body could smell like hell. I only knew that they could go there if their honor to the big man upstairs was not enough to send them to heaven.

"Michael, go brush your teeth," Big-mama said, sternly. Her chin remained fixed on her shoulder. Her eyes were on Mama as she spoke to me.

I ran to the bathroom, and while brushing my teeth, listened to Big-mama and Mama exchange insults.

"Give me my key," Mama demanded.

"I'm not giving you nothing." Big-mama's words were short and sharp.

"Give me back the key to my house," Mama repeated.

I heard grunts that sounded like a man, but I could tell it was Big-mama. Big-mama had a habit of grunting when she wasn't pleased with something. It was also her way of saying, "Over my dead body."

"Girl, are you crazy? Get off me!" Big-mama screamed.

Mama's hurting Big-mama.

I hurried and brushed my teeth. I missed the toothbrush holder when I tossed my toothbrush and ran out of the bathroom. If Mama was hurting Big-mama, I would be the one to save her.

When I got to the hall, Mama was on Big-mama's back with her left arm wrapped around Big-mama's neck. I couldn't believe my eyes. Mama was riding Big-mama like two children giving each other a piggy-back ride. It was unreal.

Big-mama drew back her left elbow and knocked Mama

on the left side of her face. Mama flew off Big-mama's back and staggered in circles before her legs folded beneath, sending her crashing to the floor. Blood poured from Mama's mouth like water from a tea kettle into a cup. Mama ran a finger along the inside of her mouth before releasing an ear-piercing scream.

"Awww," Mama yelled at the top of her lungs.

Big-mama grabbed me by an arm and dragged me out of the house. She slammed the door behind us and continued to drag me to the car. "Your mama gon' learn. She not going to be happy until God saves her from herself."

"You manly looking devil." Mama's voice echoed from the open apartment window. "Today is the last day that you see my son."

Chapter 3
Amen
Sunday @ 10:00 a.m.

Me and Big-mama hugged our way through church. There was no getting around the deacons, who appeared to be programmed to shake hands and kiss the faces of every woman in their path. Their lips greeted Big-mama's cheeks before she could finish laughing with Sister Savage. I don't think Big-mama even paid attention to the kisses. Every Sunday I counted about ten of them. There was much more, but my small mind got tired of counting after the tenth kiss.

Then there were these two old women who sat in front of the church dressed in their signature white. I do not recall ever seeing them dressed in any color other than white. Their white, wide-brim hats blocked the view of the Amens behind them. One of the women seemed more talkative than the other. She was also the leader of the two. Whatever she said, the other woman said. If she shook someone's hand, the other woman shook their hand too. Both women always approached me and Big-mama with spots of bright red lipstick on their teeth. They'd each give us a big hug and a kiss on our cheeks.

I hated those kisses. By the time we made it to the seat that Big-mama had been sitting in for the past thirty years, my face was decorated in red lip prints. Big-mama would pull a small pack of tissue from her purse and wipe the love from my face. She did not bother with her own face. I guess she loved the love. I know I was happy to have the red paint wiped from my face.

"You go up there in that choir and you listen to them folks, you hear me?" Big-mama engraved those orders in my mind every Sunday. Her eyebrows bounced up and down with every other word. "If I hear you been acting up, Big-mama gon' take a belt to you. Now go on up there."

I leaned my head to one side and said, "Yes, Big-mama." It was the same lecture every Sunday. Big-mama shook a finger in my face before ending her warning with, "Now go on up there." She pushed me in the back of my head, and I took off running. I knew Big-mama was trying to scare me. Big-mama would never lay a hand on me, because I was her baby.

I ran around and between small, medium, and large legs on my way up to the choir stand. I started to pass Pastor Kidd, when he reached down to shake my hand.

"Good morning, Michael," Pastor Kidd said as he held a hand out to me. "You ready to sing?"

I placed my small hand in the center of Pastor Kidd's hand. "Yes," I said, while shaking his hand.

I walked slowly to the choir. I sat in the middle of the first row between two big women with big arms. When we sat down, you could barely see me. Their arms covered my small chest and the sides of my face. I looked like a child peeping out of his hiding place during a game of hide-and-go-seek. I smiled at Big-mama, and before I knew it, I was fast asleep.

***

Please Big-mama don't leave me
Sunday @ 1:30 p.m.

After church, Big-mama drove me home. She stayed in the car like she always did and watched me go into the house. She said she didn't want to deal with Mama after what had happened that morning. Big-mama and I were filled with the Holy Spirit, and she feared Mama was going to mess hers up with her rants. I looked into Big-mama's eyes through my puppy dog eyes and thought, *but what about my Holy Spirit? I don't want Mama to mess mines up either.*

I hated to see Big-mama go. I cried on the inside every time she left me. When Mama was high, she was like the devil. Every day Mama was the devil.

I jumped out of Big-mama's car before she could kiss my cheek. I was mad at her for leaving me with the monster she created. She birthed Mama, and I was forced to deal with her.

"Michael, where is my kiss?" Big-mama yelled out to me.

I turned and looked sadly into her eyes. I wanted to cry, but refused to cry in front of her. Big-mama used to always tell me that big boys don't cry. I was her big boy and could not let her see me cry.

Holding in my emotions was making it difficult for me to breathe. I needed to release at least a little of my sorrow, but I couldn't ... not in front of Big-mama.

I prayed for Big-mama to leave so that I could stand on the porch and cry out to God to save me from whatever awaited me inside of the house. I could rush into the house, bury my face in my pillow, and cry my heart out, but my whimpers would have awakened Mama's anger, that is, *if* she was sleeping.

Shedding tears in front of Mama over Big-mama leaving was like begging for a beating. Mama would have slapped me for crying. It was no secret that Mama despised her own mother, and hated anything or anyone that reminded her of Big-mama.

Big-mama noticed my hesitation. She blew her horn, which scared the heck out of me. My shoulders jumped as I spun around to Big-mama yelling, "Boy, get in that house."

I hated that house and the demons that lingered within it. Plus, it wasn't a house, it was an apartment. Big difference, but of course I would have never corrected Big-mama. If she called it a house, I called it a house. Plus, she already knew the difference. Big-mama was quick to correct Mama when Mama referred to our little hole in the wall as a house. Big-mama reminded Mama of her apartment status; how broke Mama was, relying on different men to pay her bills while Mama spent the county checks on drugs.

I took my only key from my pocket and unlocked the door. I used both of my small hands to turn the doorknob. That heavy door reminded me of those dungeon doors that I saw on the Saturday morning cartoons.

I pushed open the door, and I swear I almost fell back onto the porch. The scent of Mama's drugs hit me right in my face and ran up my nostrils. It smelled like plastic burning, or burning sulfur. I recognized the smell right away as burning liquid cocaine. It was the same scent that spilled through the house like ghosts in a cemetery when Mama stayed in her room getting high.

I waved bye to Big-mama and then she blew me a kiss. I tried to catch it, but my head was spinning from the fumes in the house. It felt like I was getting high from the second-hand smoke.

As soon as Big-mama pulled off, I opened the door as wide as it could go and stood there snatching air from outside until my head stopped spinning.

"Michael, why the hell you got my front door wide open?" Mama came walking out of the kitchen with yellow crumbs all over her mouth.

I jumped in my suit at the sound of her hoarse voice. Her hair was scrunched up in different directions. She looked like a ragdoll with her short, pink gown hanging off of her shoulders. I could see the sides of her flat milk jugs where they met in the middle of her chest. It was a nasty sight to see. Light brown and cream colored stretch marks were engraved in her breasts like the lines on the elderly women's faces at church. Mama's breasts appeared empty and dead.

"I feel sick," I complained. My heart gave my chest a beating. My eyes could have shot out of my head; I was so scared of Mama. In no way was she going to sympathize with me. I knew not to expect a bowl of Campbell's soup or orange juice to make me feel better. That would have been showing me too much love. Love was not an emotion that I expected from Mama.

"Close my damn door!" Mama screamed.

I ran for the door and slammed it.

"Now lock it." She scowled.

As I was locking the door, I heard something in back of me that sounded like a cat clawing at glass. I turned around and almost chocked. Mama was scratching between her legs and I could see everything that I was not supposed to see. I closed my eyes and held the palms of my hands against them.

"Why you covering your eyes?" Mama asked me.

I didn't want to see what she was doing, so I kept my hands over my eyes and said, "I'm not supposed to see that."

"See what? Move your hands and get over here." Mama controlled me through her teeth.

Sometimes when she screamed at me, she did it through her teeth. That scared me more than if her mouth was wide open. A slap or one of my uncles' belts followed behind it. Bruises on my legs, butt, arms, and face were the end result.

"Why you screaming at that boy?" Uncle Nard walked

out of the kitchen and stood behind Mama. His big stomach bumped her back and knocked her off her feet. Mama stumbled forward. She was about to meet the floor face first. Uncle Nard wrapped his three-layers of fat covered arms around her small waist to break her fall.

I was surprised to see Uncle Nard. And while he was talking to Mama, I was thinking to myself, *What are you doing here? Uncle Robert was still here when Big-mama and I left for church this morning.* Then again, that's how Mama got down. When one uncle left, another one showed up to replace him.

"Nard," Mama said in a seductive voice. She turned on the crust of the balls of her heels and punched him in his stomach.

I sort of jerked my head back and looked at them in a weird way.

"I'm not screaming," Mama said in a little girl's voice. "I walked in here and he had my door wide open, letting flies all in my house." Mama put extras on it. Despite our living conditions, there was not one fly in the house.

"I done told you about screaming at him," Uncle Nard told her. "Kids remember that stuff."

They remember sex, drugs, and a dirty apartment too, but you couldn't tell Mama that and expect her to care.

Uncle Nard kissed the left side of Mama's face. When he peeled his lips from her face, he left a big, wet circle of spit or something white and creamy behind. It turned my stomach.

"How you doing, Michael?" Uncle Nard wobbled over to me and rubbed my head. He must have noticed the frown on my face, because the next thing I knew, he asked me, "Why the sad face?"

I wasn't sad. I just didn't expect to come home and be greeted by a big man in skintight boxers and no shirt. I wanted to twist my head out from beneath his hand, but Uncle Nard was always giving me stuff. He could rub my head all day, just as long as the gifts kept coming.

"You eat?" he asked me.

"This morning," I uttered. My stomach suddenly started growling. I wasn't hungry until Uncle Nard asked me if I had eaten.

"That's good enough, he can eat later," Mama cut in. She didn't even know how I was feeling. Little kids stay hungry. Even when they're not hungry, they eat.

Uncle Nard looked back at Mama. "Carry your nappy headed tail to your room. I'm talking to my son."

My eyes lit up when Uncle Nard called me his son. I was now a normal little boy with a mother and a father. On Monday nights and Sunday evenings, instead of my now father going home to watch the NFL football games, because Mama's loud mouth and demanding tongue wouldn't allow him to enjoy the games here, me and Dad could sit in the luxury of our hell hole and enjoy the games, while tuning out Mama's lying tongue. I was happy and excited all at the same time. I thought Dad was just another uncle. No, all this time he'd been my father disguised as an uncle. At least for a second he was, because Mama quickly killed that joy.

"He ain't none of your son," Mama said to Uncle Nard. "And don't be telling me what to do in my house."

My heart dropped into my stomach when Mama snatched my dream away just that quick. I used to pray every night for my father, whoever he was. I had all those uncles but no father. And for one quick second I thought I had a daddy. I'll never forget that feeling, as short-lived as it was.

"Me and my *son* going into the kitchen to cook and have a man-to-man talk." Uncle Nard was still calling me his son.

I went along with it. He treated me nice. He bought me games and clothes. He took me to baseball games and football games. He was the only one of my uncles who spent time with me. If he wanted me to be his son, I would be that, and he could be my dad.

"Whatever." Mama shrugged. She threw her skinny neck back, turned her back to Uncle Nard and me, and made her butt jiggle like them girls in those videos.

Yes, I knew all about those videos. I watched them on TV. Women in bikinis dancing around cars, on boats, and around swimming pools as guys rapped about sex, guns, and drugs.

When I was five, me and Mama had to leave our apartment for a few months while the landlord made repairs. The roof was so brittle and old that rain found its way into our apartment and destroyed everything. The landlord paid for us to live month-to-month in a one-bedroom apartment—which was just as run down as our apartment—while he hired contractors to fix the roof before the real storms moved in.

Mama kept the bedroom for her and my uncles, and I slept in the living room on the couch. When one of my uncles spent the night, Mama turned the television in the living room to BET, a television channel that played rap, hip-hop, and R&B music videos. She raised the volume on the television as loud as it would go so that I could not hear her, and whichever uncle she was with that night, engage in dirty sex. Mama was so loud with the sex that I could still hear her over the top of the "Drop It Like It's Hot" rap song that spilled from the television speakers.

Mama stormed out of the living room to her room and slammed the door. Uncle Nard turned and headed for the kitchen with me following him.

"Burgers and French fries okay with you?" Uncle Nard asked while pulling open the freezer door.

"Y-e-a-h, Daddy," I sang. Burgers and French fries was my favorite food.

Uncle Nard pulled a bag of turkey burger patties and a bag of French fries from the freezer and tossed them on the counter.

I was surprised to see the food. Mama shopped for food every blue moon, and the moon had not been blue in at least two months. Whenever I searched the kitchen for food, I did not bother to look in the freezer. I assumed that the same old food that had been sitting in the freezer for months, with ice covering it, was all that was in there. Uncle Nard had to have bought the food within the last few days, or even the day before. The packaging was free of ice and the hamburger patties were not all stuck together in the bag.

I enjoyed being around Uncle Nard. It was always fun. But that day he kind of spoiled the fun with them boxers. And to be in the kitchen cooking lunch like that? He reminded me of the movie *Baby Boy*, when actor and singer Tyrese Gibson walked into the kitchen with food on his mind, only to find his mother's boyfriend standing in front of the stove naked while preparing breakfast.

While seasoning four turkey patties, Uncle Nard looked back over his right shoulder at me. "Pull out a chair and sit down."

I walked over to the table with my neck stretched as far as it would go, trying to look into the skillet at the patties.

I pulled out a chair and sat down. I was so ready for the burger and French fries that I sat like a soldier with my back straight and my hands folded in front of me.

"You know I love your mama, right?" Uncle Nard said out of the blue. "I love her a lot, and that's why I come here and take care of y'all. Ain't no man gonna treat your mama the way I do. I put the furniture in this apartment. I buy all the food. I keep gas in your mama's car. She may not drive it, but I do."

Mama did not drive because she stayed so drunk or high that she could not see straight.

"That little eight hundred a month the county gives yo' mama ain't nothin'. She runs through that like water." Uncle Nard nodded through an ugly grin.

Mama's drugs take all of her money, I thought.

"That's how you treat a woman, you hear me?" he smiled. You should have seen his teeth. The tip of each tooth was missing or shaved as low as they could go, without denying him the right to eat.

"You give a woman what she wants, when she wants it, and how she wants it." Uncle Nard's lips never lost their smile. His grin was mischievous, with a hidden message.

I realized what "when she wants it and how she wants it" meant. Uncle Nard was talking about sex. This, of course, was not foreign to me.

"You won't always agree with everything that comes out of a woman's mouth, but you make sure you take note of what means the most to her." Uncle Nard continued schooling me.

He was talking to me like I was a grown man. He was standing there cooking in his tight boxers, spilling his heart out to me about loving Mama, when Uncle Patrick and Uncle Robert claimed to love her just as much as he did, or even more.

What Uncle Nard was doing for Mama, they were doing too, only they put the money in her hands instead of taking the bill to the gas company and the light company, or taking the rent money down to the manager. Now that I think about it, I don't see how Mama was ever broke. My uncles kept money in her pockets.

Uncle Nard took three paper plates from a cabinet and placed one in front of me, a second to the right of me, and the last one in the center of the table. He removed a bag of bread from on top of the microwave and put two slices of bread on each plate. Uncle Nard had to have recently bought the bread too. The last time I'd went searching for bread, we were all out.

Uncle Nard took the mustard and ketchup from the refrigerator and closed the door. He turned and headed for the table, but stopped as if he was forgetting something.

Uncle Nard wedged the mustard and ketchup between his arm and chest. He then opened the refrigerator door and scanned the bottles of alcohol and salad dressings on the door.

"Y'all got any relish around here?" he asked me.

"I don't know, Daddy," I replied. And I didn't know. I just knew I never touched the relish . . . ever. If we were out of relish, Mama and my uncles were responsible for having used it all.

From a distance, I stared at the shelf on the open refrigerator door. I immediately noticed the top of a green container slightly hidden behind a tall bottle of white wine and a jar of pickles. I believed it was the relish, but was not sure. "I think it's right there." I pointed to the shelf.

"Where?" He looked back at me and said, "I don't see no relish."

I leaped out of my chair and ran over to the refrigerator. I walked around Uncle Nard and stood in front of him. I bent down and stuck my hand between the wine bottle and the jar of pickles and pointed to the green container. "Right there," I said and smiled.

"Oh, I see it. Good boy." Uncle Nard thanked me like I had just fetched a ball. It sounded like something a person would tell an obedient dog.

Uncle Nard slipped his big hand between the wine and pickles, and took the relish from the door. He bumped the refrigerator door closed with his stomach, walked over to the table, and stood next to me. He placed the jar of relish in front of me, but the look on my face let him know that I did not like relish.

Uncle Nard moved the relish and placed the mustard and ketchup on the table where the relish once sat. I guess he'd spent all of that time searching for the relish for me, because he put the relish back into the refrigerator and went on to make our plates.

I watched him move around the kitchen like a child wearing skates. To be as big as he was, boy did he move fast. I don't remember seeing him put the French fries into a skillet, but I do remember him removing them from the skillet and putting them on my paper plate, grease and all. The hot grease from the French fries put small holes in my paper plate as it made its way to my makeshift hamburger bun. When I picked up my sandwich, the bottom bread was so soggy from the grease that it split in two.

Uncle Nard walked to the doorway and looked down the hall. "Crystal, come eat," he yelled out to Mama. He sat in a chair across from me, grabbed a handful of fries, and forced them into his mouth. He then picked up his hamburger and held it in both hands while waiting to break down the fries in his mouth.

"I'm not hungry for no food," Mama yelled back. I knew exactly what she was hungry for, and I'm not talking about sex either. The monkey was riding Mama's back. "Get in here and feed me," she ordered.

Mama had total control of my uncles' hearts. She could talk trash to them all day long, and they still wanted her. I've never heard any of them tell her no. There was something about Mama that made them want to submit to her. I did not understand. Mama and my uncles were connected by alcohol and drugs, while bound by sex. Maybe that was it.

"I'm eating," Uncle Nard told her. He forced half of the burger into his mouth and dropped the other half onto his plate. "I'll be in there in a minute," he said through the food in his mouth. "And don't touch my setup. Mess around and kill yourself."

Hearing Uncle Nard mention Mama killing herself scared me. She couldn't leave without me. Yes, Mama was abusive and kept me in tears, but I still loved her and would have never wished death upon her. I just wanted God to change Mama's heart.

I wanted to go live with Big-mama, but I did not want Mama to die for me to go there. Mama could have given me to Big-mama, with me visiting Mama every weekend. But that was too much like right, and Mama was not trying to do anything right.

Mama and death in the same sentence caused my heart to beat fast. I wasn't hungry anymore. The food in my stomach ran up my throat and stayed there. I dropped the fry that I had been holding onto my plate. I looked into Uncle Nard's eyes. He did not look worried. The way he downed that first burger and then moved on to the next one, I suddenly felt like he did not care about Mama. In my mind, Mama was in the room killing herself while Uncle Nard sat in the kitchen putting food before her life.

Uncle Nard left a piece of burger on the plate about the size of my hand. He pushed the plate to the middle of the table. "Let me get in there and feed this woman," he said, shaking his head.

He held on to the back of the chair with one hand, grabbing the edge of the table with the other. He dang near flipped the table over on the both of us as he strained to stand. One side of the table rose up from the floor with our plates and everything else on the table sliding to one end.

"Grab the plates," Uncle Nard said quickly. "Get the ketchup. Stuff 'bout to fall off the table."

I grabbed for the ketchup and mustard as Uncle Nard grabbed for the plates. Before anything could fall onto the floor, the table snapped back into place.

"I'm about to put yo' mama to sleep." He laughed under his breath. "After you finish eating, take a bath and go play in your room until it's time for bed." Uncle Nard headed out of the kitchen, but stopped in the doorway. "Get your school clothes out too," he said, looking back at me. "I'm not staying tonight. Gonna put your mama to sleep and leave."

"Okay, Dad," I whispered.

"Dad?" he said with a confused look on his face.

I had been calling him Dad for the past two hours, but he reacted as if he were hearing it for the first time.

Earlier he referred to me as his son. Then when I called him Dad, he appeared confused, as if he had no idea that he was my father. Like talk show host Maury Povich had just read the results of Uncle Nard's paternity test and told him, "In the case of seven-year-old Michael Tyson, Uncle Nard, you are the father."

Uncle Nard's eyebrows looked glued together. He did not look mad, maybe a little confused, but not mad.

He leaned his head to one side and stared at me.

"You call me son, I call you Dad. You're my dad, right?" My closed lips held my next breath hostage as I waited for his answer.

With my eyes on Uncle Nard, I picked up a fry and nibbled on one end of it. I wanted to cry, because it meant so much to me to hear a man call me his son. Mama tried to take that joy away from me when we were all inside of the living room. I prayed that Uncle Nard was not in on it too.

Uncle Nard smiled at me and went on to Mama's room. I took his smile as a confirmation that I was his son.

I ate the rest of my fries while eyeing the mess Uncle Nard had made in the kitchen. The bag of French fries was still on the counter. The bag of turkey patties was sitting next to it. The ketchup and mustard were sitting in the middle of the table next to Uncle Nard's abandoned plate. The plate he'd made for Mama sat untouched.

Since I was the only one who kept the house clean, I got up and sprang into action. I did not wash the dishes, because I was full and tired. I put everything away and put all of the dirty dishes into the sink.

My lunch tickets, I suddenly remembered. My lunch tickets, or county tickets as the kids in school called them, were in Mama's room. Normally she gave them to me before I went to bed. By the way Uncle Nard was talking, it sounded like I wasn't going to see Mama until after school the next day. Whatever he was feeding Mama was going to put her to sleep, and I already knew I wasn't going to see her in the morning when I got up. Mama never got up to see me off to school. There were times when she stayed in bed until I got out of school.

I ran out of the kitchen and straight to Mama's bedroom. Any other time I would have knocked before wrapping my hand around the doorknob and shoving open the door. But on this night, I honestly forgot. I think I was so happy about being able to call Uncle Nard my dad that I wasn't thinking about what happened the last time I barged into Mama's room without knocking.

"Don't you ever bring yo' ass in my room without knocking first," Mama had scolded me while she was on her knees before one of my uncles. And she was not in prayer.

I ran into Mama's room with my lips formed to say,

"Mama," but her eyes stopped me dead in my tracks. My little heart was in distress. Every other beat was like a drum to my ears. I was breathing like a kid after a beating. I wasn't crying and I didn't feel like crying. Seeing Mama, I was shocked. I didn't know what to say or do.

My body would not move. I probably looked like a mannequin to Uncle Nard and Mama, if Mama could see me. Mama's eyes were wide open, yet blind to her surroundings. She probably didn't even know that I was in the room. Her pupils were not centered the way one's eyes would be if they were staring straight at a person. Her pupils were rolled up to the top of her eyes.

Mama's mouth hung open with spit running down the corners of her lips. Her head was sideways on my uncle's pillow. Her body stretched from the right side of the bed to the left side of the bed like one line on the letter X.

Uncle Nard was sitting on the edge of the bed nearest her chest with Mama's left arm lying across his joined thighs. A needle pierced her arm with Uncle Nard's hand behind the needle. His thumb was pressed down on one end of the needle, easing poison into Mama's vein. Mama appeared to be dead. And if she was, Uncle Nard had killed her.

"I'm taking care of your mama like I told you I was," he said with a wicked smile on his face. The corners of his mouth stretched from ear to ear, exposing all of his crooked and rotten teeth. "What do you need, son?" he whispered.

My eyes were on Mama's eyes, while my ears were turned to Uncle Nard. "I . . . my lunch tickets," I uttered. My mind was so focused on Mama that I could not collect my thoughts. "My lunch and breakfast tickets."

"Tickets?" Uncle Nard said in a low, scratchy voice.

"Yes, I can't eat lunch without the tickets or money."

"Get my pants off the floor over there and bring 'em to

me." He jerked his head toward the dresser where his jeans lay on the floor next to the dresser. It looked as though he'd unbuckled his belt, unfastened his button, and allowed his jeans to slide down his legs. They were scrunched up, but sort of standing, like he'd walked right out of them.

I held his pants by the belt buckle and dragged them over to him.

"Check the front, right pocket. Whatever you find in there, you can have for your lunch tomorrow."

I went on to search his pockets.

As I was pulling my hand out of the empty right pocket, Uncle Nard was removing the needle from Mama's arm. He put the needle on the nightstand. I stuck my hand in the left front pocket. When Uncle Nard crossed Mama's dead arm over her chest, I realized that she was still alive. Mama's arm moved up and down with the rising and falling of her chest. I smiled on both the inside and the outside, and then pulled a wad of bills from the left front pocket of his jeans.

Uncle Nard looked briefly at the money "Take that and go on to your room," he said while cleaning up the evidence of the devil's work.

Uncle Nard gathered a needle, a spoon, a lighter, and a small plastic bag with white powder in it into his hands. He then placed them on top of a pile of napkins on the nightstand.

"But I need my lunch tickets," I said through whiney breaths. I struggled to hold the wad of folded bills in my hands. There had to have been at least five hundred dollars in twenties trying to flip out of my hands onto the floor. I don't think Uncle Nard knew exactly how much money he was giving me. There was no way that an adult in their right mind would intentionally give a seven-year-old child over five hundred dollars.

"Son, with all them bills in your hands, you can buy breakfast and lunch for every kid at your school." Uncle Nard laughed. "Bring that money over here. You don't know nothin' about that."

I walked slowly over to Uncle Nard and handed him the money. Uncle Nard counted out fifteen twenty dollar bills and five one hundred dollar bills.

"Oh no, this is way too much for a boy to be taking to school." He chuckled as if he hadn't known how much money he had in his pocket. He knew how much money he had, just like he knew he was not about to let me walk away with all of it. Uncle Nard was just teasing me.

"I must have left the ones in the car," he said. "I meant to leave this here in the car and bring the ones in. Your mama can't be trusted around this kind of money. You know she goes in my pants when I'm sleep and steals everything in my pockets, including the lent." He glanced around the room. "Where does your mama keep your lunch tickets?" he asked.

"Under the mattress," I told him. I was a little sad that he took the money away from me.

"Between these mattresses here?" Uncle Nard pounded the mattress with his fist.

"Yes," I whispered. I pointed to the end of the bed. My eyes moved back to the money. I wanted the money *and* my lunch tickets.

The bills started flipping back in Uncle Nard's hands. He pressed them against his chest. He smiled at my eyes, which were glued to the money, before following my eyes to the money. He then pulled a twenty-dollar bill from the wad and handed it to me.

Uncle Nard picked his pants up from the floor and stuffed the rest of the money into the front right pocket. He leaned to his right, slid his left hand between the mattresses, and pulled my lunch tickets from underneath the mattress.

The yellow and blue packet of tickets that were stuck together like a book of postage stamps covered the entire month of January. Uncle Nard snapped off the tickets that read "Monday, January 2, 2017" and handed them to me. He shoved the rest of the tickets back beneath the mattress. Mama didn't dare give me all the tickets for fear I'd lose them. "Go on to your room. I'll come see you before I leave."

"Okay." I walked to the door and stopped right before I crossed the threshold. I turned and tried to take one last look at Mama. From where I was standing, I could not see her face. Uncle Nard's body was so wide that all I could see was Mama's legs from her knees down. Uncle Nard could tell that I was trying to see Mama. He turned and looked at Mama. When he turned back around to face me, I could now see Mama's hair, but that was it.

"Go ahead and go to your room. Your mother is okay. She's just in a deep sleep." He smiled that ugly smile again.

After Uncle Nard assured me that Mama was okay, my face moved into an instant smile. My mother was not dead. I had my lunch and breakfast tickets, money in my pocket, and a father who loved me. I was on cloud nine.

I ran to my room and stripped down to my Batman briefs. I left my clothes in the middle of the floor and jumped in bed. I wasn't feeling up to playing like Uncle Nard had told me to do. I didn't even bother to pull the blanket over me. I just lay there, glancing around the room as I waited for sleep to creep up on me. My eyes wandered to my knees and the book that rested at the foot of my bed; *A Mansion in the Hills of Heaven* by Pernitha A. Tinsley. I loved that book. Big-mama bought it for me, because she knew that I loved to read.

That book slept in bed with me every night, I loved it so much. I can't even count on both hands how many times I'd read it.

I pushed myself up in bed and grabbed the book. I flipped open the book and read until I dozed off.

"Michael, why didn't you wash them damn dishes?"

"I was sleepy."

"That ain't no excuse for leaving my sink full of dishes. Think you gon' crawl up in this bed and go to sleep with my kitchen looking a mess? You know I don't play that. Carry your tail in that kitchen and wash them dishes!"

"Ouch! Mama, no!"

"Move yo' hand before I miss your head and get your face. Bet you won't fall asleep again without cleaning my kitchen."

"A-w-w-w, Mama!"

CHAPTER 4
Prayer Time
Monday @ 4:00 a.m.

The alarm clock snatched me out of my dreams right before the leaf that I was floating on met the ground.

After Mama burst into my dreams and bashed me in the head for not washing dishes, an angel carried me to a leaf that was blowing in the wind. The angel then dropped me onto the leaf before vanishing into thin air.

The leaf dropped from the sky like a feather. Right before it hit the ground, my alarm clock saved me.

It was prayer time, and if I would have slept any longer, I probably would have died in my sleep and failed Mama.

Since Mama refused to pray for forgiveness and deliverance from the drugs and sexual immorality that she and Big-mama used to always argue about, Big-mama taught me how to pray for Mama.

"Pray for your mama's strength," Big-mama told me. "Pray that when her veins crave the drugs, her spirit will resist it."

Crave drugs? Spirit will resist? Huh? To a seven-year-old, Big-mama was speaking a foreign language. But I prayed exactly what she told me to; no questions asked.

I prayed for Mama using Big-mama's exact words. I did not know what I was saying, but whatever it was would save

Mama from hell; at least that was what Big-mama told me.

I kicked the blanket off of me. I didn't even remember covering myself with it. As a matter of fact, I know I didn't. Uncle Nard must have come into my room while I was asleep and threw the blanket over me.

The house was a deathly silent. Normally, at this time of morning, Mama's TV in her room was turned up real loud, or the music that she and my uncles' bodies made when they connected like an easy puzzle was playing past the neighbors' snores. Not this Monday morning. The house was silent, which almost caused me to stay in bed and save Mama's prayer for Tuesday morning.

I pushed myself to the edge of the bed and dropped my feet to the floor. I crept over to my closed bedroom door and opened it. I stuck my head out into the hall and listened for snores and the sound of snot trapped in Mama's nostrils from her heavy breathing. But again, the house was silent.

I walked on my toes to Mama's room. The door was cracked and I could see that my uncles' side of the bed was empty. I pressed the palms of my hands against the door and pushed it open a little further. I prayed for the door not to squeak and wake Mama from her sleep.

The door opened wide enough for me to slip inside without touching it. I planted the heel of my feet on the floor and crept over to Mama's bed. Mama was in the same position that she'd been in when I walked into the room during her feeding time, only this time her eyes were closed. She was on her back with her left arm crossed over her chest and her right arm down at her side.

I kneeled at the foot of the bed, away from Mama's face, just in case she woke up and caught me in her room. I dug my elbows into the bed. I pressed the palms of my hands together, leaned my forehead against the sides of my joined hands, and closed my eyes.

"I pray when Mama's veins crave the drugs, her spirit will resist it," I said. "Big-mama said the drugs make Mama sick, and that when Mama screams at me, she does not know what she is doing. God, please tell Mama to stop hitting me. Big-mama says if Mama don't stop hitting me, she's going to hell. Big-mama said if anybody has earned a one-way ticket to hell, Mama has. I don't want Mama to go to hell. I want Mama to come to heaven with me and Big-mama.

"Tell Mama the drugs are not good," I continued in prayer. "Big-mama said you can put a taste in Mama's mouth and make the drugs taste nasty to her. Then Mama won't want them anymore. Big-mama says Mama likes her drugs like I like my candy, but my candy don't hurt. The drugs hurt Mama.

"I have to go now." I swallowed hard. "I will talk to you tomorrow morning. In Jesus' name, Amen."

***

Words Do Hurt
Monday @ 7:00 a.m.

I stood on the corner with several kids from my school, waiting for the crossing guard to walk us across the street. I could have led myself through the double white lines, but after a crazy driver barreled through a stop sign the year before, nearly running down a third grader, the city placed a crossing guard on the corner to serve as our shield.

The crossing guard was a sweet, old lady who should have been sitting around a table playing Bingo instead of serving as a grandmother to the children of Martin Luther King Elementary School. Her back was bent like she once carried the weight of ten men on her back. Dark veins were shown through her pale skin. She graced the street with her frail smile and with excitement said, "Good morning." It was evident that she loved her job, and would remain there until her feet could no longer maintain the same pace as her heart and smile.

The crossing guard stood on the corner and held up a stop sign. She waited for the traffic that traveled east to stop before stepping out into the street. She stopped walking and stood in the middle of the street, holding one hand out to us children, signaling for us to wait.

As I waited for her to signal for us to cross the street, my eyes moved from one child to the next in admiration. Nike tennis shoes protected their feet from the street; Michael Jordans, Nike Shox, Nike Free Runs. Their long shirts or jackets kept me from seeing the labels on the back of their jeans. But since their shirts were name brand, I guessed their pants were name brand too.

Did it bother me? Yes, I was bothered. All of the children that surrounded me were returning to school from Christmas break with new clothes and shoes on, and there I was, dressed in the same old clothes that Mama had bought me at the end of the summer, two years before.

My clothes were faded and spotted with bleach thanks to Mama believing she was standing in front of the kitchen sink with a bottle of dishwashing liquid in hand, when in fact she'd been standing in front of the washer, pouring bleach all over my colored clothes. If only Mama would have stopped with the drugs.

My jeans had big holes in the knees. Strings of thread hung from the bottom of my pants legs and grazed my worn tennis shoes.

I remember about a week before school was about to start back up, Big-mama had asked Mama if I needed any clothes for school. Mama was high on the devil and angry with Big-mama for always taking care of me and showing me the love that my own mother either felt I didn't deserve, or she just didn't know how to give. Mama lied and told her that she had bought me, "A whole lot of clothes and three pairs of tennis shoes." Mama had lied with a straight face, knowing she hadn't bought me nothing.

I was standing between them during their conversation. Mama was in the kitchen doing whatever, and Big-mama was in the hall near the entrance to the kitchen. I was leaning back against the doorway that separated the kitchen from the hall with my eyes darting around in my head as I looked from Mama to Big-mama.

When Mama lied and said that she bought me school clothes and shoes, I wanted to cry and say, "That's a lie." I didn't dare allow those words to come out of my mouth, though. Mama lied, and I had to suffer.

The crossing guard motioning with her hand for the kids to cross the street jogged my thoughts from Mama and Big-mama's past conversation. Some kids ran, some walked, and these two boys who thought that they were being cute decided to walk backward, despite the crossing guard's pleas for them not to.

"Walk right." Her dry, soft voice yelled for them to turn around, but the boys insisted on being disrespectful.

Unfortunately, a lot of children from broken homes have broken, disrespectful attitudes toward their elders.

Once the children and I made it across the street, we took off running to school. Breakfast was being served, and everyone was rushing to be one of the first in line for breakfast.

Breakfast ended at seven forty-five, sending all of us running out of the cafeteria and onto the playground until the first bell rang at eight o' clock. The first sign of a long day for our teachers would then begin. High on sugar from the unhealthy breakfast, we would run all over the yard, bypassing the designated line where each class had been meeting after breakfast, recess and lunch. We would then play around the yard until our teachers scolded us about getting in line on time.

Inside my classroom, I sat at my desk, trying to avoid looking at my classmates. Everyone was talking about their new clothes, a conversation I didn't dare try to participate in. I'd be opening myself up to be made fun of. Kids were so mean sometimes, that even my silence couldn't protect me from their venom.

"What kind of Jordans are those?" a boy seated in back of me asked someone through a smile.

I did not have eyes in the back of my head, but I could hear the excitement in his voice as he spoke to our classmate.

"Air Jordan Jumpman Kicks," the boy answered with confidence. "My dad got them for me."

"They are bad," the first boy told him.

Two girls seated to the right of me giggled about how cute their hair was, and how long it had grown over the Christmas break. But if you were to ask me, I'd have to say that their hair got shorter.

The girls were dressed in sundresses with open toe sandals to match their dresses. One of the girl's toenails were painted a pinkish-orange, while the other girl's toenails were yellow.

I turned at an angle in my chair and held on to the back of it. I rested my chin on the back of my chair between my hands and stared at my classmates in envy.

I was so sad, that my eyes were slightly closed and my insides were filled with tears. The entire time the children were gloating on their new clothes and shoes, I was thinking, *I want new shoes. I want new clothes.*

No one spoke to me. Some glanced in my direction as

they turned in their seats or got up to talk to their friends, but no one said a single word to me. They treated me like I was contagious or something. Invisible even. In my mind it was because I did not have on anything new to talk about. What hurt the most was that these were the same children that I had played with every day at school before Christmas break. The kids that I played super hero with just weeks earlier during recess and lunch did not want to have anything to do with me because of my ragged clothes. Maybe when their clothes weren't new anymore they would talk to me again.

"Okay, children, have a seat." Mrs. Dillion clapped her vanilla, wrinkled hands as she glanced around the classroom at my used-to-be friends and me. The bags beneath her aged eyes appeared to have deepened since the last time I had seen her. Her swan's neck jiggled and her voice quivered as she spoke. Her snow-white hair was held back by a beautiful butterfly clip that matched her butterfly earrings.

I loved Mrs. Dillion, almost as much as I loved Big-mama, and always volunteered around the classroom just to be under her wings.

"We will not be doing any work today," Mrs. Dillion said through a crooked smile.

"Yay!" the class yelled.

Some of my former friends jumped out of their chairs and did a silly dance, while others banged on their desk, shook their heads wildly, or used that joyous moment to play with each other.

"We have teacher's meetings all week, so school will let out at twelve-thirty every day," Mrs. Dillon said.

"My brother has to stay in school until three," a blushing Bridgette Collins, the sweetest girl in the class, shared with us.

Bridgett was always full of joy. So when even she didn't speak to me, I knew right away not to expect anyone else to acknowledge me.

"What school does your brother attend, Bridgett?" Mrs. Dillion asked.

"Westchester High School," Bridgette answered proudly. "He's in tenth grade."

"All elementary schools in the Los Angeles school district get out early after returning from a holiday break," Mrs. Dillion told her. "Your brother attends school in the Westchester, California district." Mrs. Dillion peered out over the classroom. "We will resume our regular schedule next week. Today, each of you will share with the class what you did over your Christmas break." Mrs. Dillion held her left hand in her right hand.

At the sound of getting out of school early that week, every child, except for me, jumped to their feet in excitement. Toys, fun, family time, video games, bikes, and simple laughter awaited them when they returned home. Not me. I felt cheated by time. Getting out early meant more hours with Mama and her abuse.

"Take your seats," Mrs. Dillion said in a soft voice. I used to wish Mama's voice was as soft as hers. "We are going to start over here." Mrs. Dillion pointed to the right of her to a double desk next to the wall. It was the first double desk in the row of six desks. All three rows of desks had two kids sitting at each desk. "Each student will stand up and tell us what they did over the break. If you get carried away, I'll have to stop you, okay?" Mrs. Dillion continued to smile.

A girl dressed in a green, sleeveless, flowered dress stood with smiling eyes. She tugged at her two shoulder-length pigtails like she was nervous. Her pink fingernails moved along her left arm and added white streaks to her butterscotch complexion. She was scared out of her white sandals, and I was laughing on the inside.

"Me, my mama and daddy, my big brother and little sister took the plane to Florida to see my grandma," she finally said. "We went to Disney World and got on lots of rides and won a lot of toys." Wearing a big grin on her face, she flopped back down in her chair. She then covered her face with her hands as Mrs. Dillion led us in a clapping session.

The whole class clapped for the excited little girl. It was as if she was re-living her Disney World adventure.

The boy seated next to the girl jumped to his feet. He rubbed his hands together and scanned the class. He seemed to be looking around to ensure everyone's attention.

"My dad took me fishing," a loud, squeaky voice erupted from behind the boy's smile.

At the sound of fishing, my heart jumped in excitement. It then slowed to a sad beat. I had always dreamed of going fishing like the kids on some of the Saturday morning specials, and there he was living out my dream.

"Me and my dad cut the fish open and cleaned them for Mama to cook," the little boy said. "Um . . . another time we went camping for two whole days." He grinned. The more he shared with the class, the more I wished for his shoes, or at least to walk in them. The boy took a deep breath and said, "Then we picked up my uncle from Fontana and we all went to Circus Circus in Las Vegas, Ne-va-da." In a haste to share one of many precious moments with his father, he stumbled over the word Nevada. "We had fun, fun, fun!"

The class clapped for him, but my sorrow wouldn't allow me to join them. I was hurting. I didn't know anything about Las Vegas or Circus Circus, but I knew what a circus was. And if Circus Circus was anything like the elephants and monkeys that swept through my thoughts as he spoke, I could only imagine how much fun he had.

The boy sat down in his seat. He turned at an angle and

looked in back of him at a boy and a girl who were laughing and pointing at each other while yelling, "You go first."

"Darryl, you go first." Mrs. Dillon made the decision for them. She crossed her arms and leaned her head to one side.

Darryl sulked his way to his feet. He peered down at the girl before saying, "My sister had a baby. His name is Jacob. All of my family went to the hospital to see them. When my sister came home with the baby, my sister said she was hungry, so my mama cooked a big dinner. I got a lot of stuff for Christmas. A PS4 with five games, clothes . . ."

"Okay, that's enough." Mrs. Dillion stopped him from taking us through his entire Christmas. All that was missing was the Christmas carols. "Take your seat, Darryl."

Darryl sat hunched down in his chair with his brand-new shoes thumping the floor. He eyed the girl next to him and continued to watch her until she stood to share her story, or testimony, as Big-mama called it, with the class.

I was getting tired of hearing about Christmas. Our dreary apartment had not been trimmed in Christmas decorations. The fresh scent of pine from a beautiful Christmas tree sitting perfectly in a corner of the living room did not exist. There was no Christmas tree, and the horrible scent of cocaine burning in the center of a spoon was one of many odors that one could expect to inhale when arriving at our apartment.

I didn't get anything from Mama. Since Mama lied and told Big-mama that she bought me clothes and shoes, Big-mama blessed me with a Bible for Christmas. I was grateful for the Bible, but would have been excited about toys and clothes. I should have told Big-mama the truth when she asked Mama if I needed any school clothes. Mama lying to Big-mama deprived me of one of the joys of Christmas.

My heart couldn't take any more of the smiles and happiness from everyone else around me. The happiness was hurting my ears. I wish I could have crawled into darkness and stayed there. It would save me from having to hear about the next white Christmas.

The girl's smile told a story, a story of thankfulness. The corners of her mouth could have touched her earlobes, she was smiling so wide. The girl pushed her lips to the left corner of her mouth. Her pupils were glued to the ceiling like she was thinking of what to share first. Either that, or she was admiring the bright lights.

The girl dropped her eyes on Darryl and laughed. "I stayed at Darryl's house for Christmas break. My mother and father went out of town."

"You two were together?" Mrs. Dillion asked. Every eye in the class held a question mark. The whole class wanted to know the answer to Mrs. Dillion's question.

"Yes." The girl grinned. "He's my cousin."

Mrs. Dillion turned her attention to Darryl. "I know the two of you are cousins," she said. "Darryl, why didn't you add Christina when you were telling us about your Christmas?" Mrs. Dillion cut her eyes at Darryl. It was the same look that Mama gave me when she was high and could hardly keep her eyes open.

Darryl's eyes moved away from Mrs. Dillion's gaze. He hunched his shoulders and stared down at his lap.

Mrs. Dillion looked from Darryl to Christina. "Take your seat, Christina. If you were with Darryl, we already know what you did."

Christina pulled her chair out and sat down as quickly as a group of children playing musical chairs.

Every five minutes, one of my classmates hopped, jumped, or leapt to their feet with a story to tell. Their stories were filled with animation. Every eye was full of light. A girl drew a picture of a flower in the air as she visually took my classmates and me on a journey through the rose garden that she and her grandmother planted in their backyard.

Some of my classmates' stories were exaggerated. One boy stood and said he bumped into a man who was thirteen feet tall when he and his family went to Universal Studios for Christmas break. I knew he was lying. I knew a lie when I heard one.

The girls bragged about playing hopscotch during their Christmas break. They gloated on their gold earrings or gold bracelets that they received for Christmas. One girl held the charm from her necklace up for the class to see.

Many of the girls' stories were boring. I lowered my head onto my crossed arms on my desk and dozed off every time a girl stood to talk. Mrs. Dillion had to call my name two or three times before I pushed my head up from my makeshift pillow and used the bottom of my shirt to wipe saliva from my desk.

One girl's story was so long that I was dreaming. I guess Mrs. Dillion's attention was on someone else, because I slept for at least two minutes.

I dreamed that I was in the backseat of Big-mama's old Cadillac. We were on our way to our favorite breakfast spot, *The Serving Spoon* in Inglewood, California. I had ordered pancakes with strawberry topping and orange juice, while Big-mama switched between a cup of coffee and toast.

"Is it good?" Big-mama had asked me.

My pancakes came with a look of joy. The cook had drawn eyes, a dot for a nose, and a smile on my pancakes, all with whip cream. My food was more than good, it was delicious.

"Yes," I said with a smile as big as the smile on my pancakes.

"I'm taking you home with me today," Big-mama said through toast in her mouth. "You not going back home to your mother. It's time you came to stay with me."

"Yay!" I bounced up and down in my chair. I danced in place. My prayers had been answered.

"Michael," I heard a voice calling out to me. In my dream, it was Big-mama.

"Michael, wake up."

"Huh?" I groaned, lifting my head.

"Michael, you wake yourself up right now and get to your feet." In real life it was the voice of Mrs. Dillion. Her usual soft voice was gone and replaced with Mama's scratchy, angered-filled voice. It scared me.

I pried my rear up from the seat and eased to my feet. I glanced down at my right foot, which was leaning to the left, because the bottoms of my shoes were worn and uneven. My striped, two sizes too small shirt stopped right at the waist of my jeans. I pulled down on the bottom of my shirt to protect my ashy stomach from humiliation.

"For Christmas, my Big-mama bought me a Bible," I started, trying to muster up the same amount of excitement as all the other kids had in their voices. My body language was anything but happy, though. With one hand on the desk, I leaned to one side and kept my eyes on the floor.

"A Bible?" A boy's laughter rang out over the classroom, causing the entire class to laugh with him. "You can get a Bible for free. My church has lots of them."

"Enough, Richard," Mrs. Dillion scolded. She smiled at me and nodded her head. "Go ahead, Michael."

"I went with Mama to cash her check on the first, and we ate at Taco Bell. My daddy gave me some money . . ." My voice trailed off as I ran out of things to talk about. Then all of a sudden I could hear the choir singing in my head. I wanted to tell the class about Pastor Kidd preaching, but the looks on their faces showed anything but interest. The class stared at me like they could not wait for Mrs. Dillion to tell me to take my seat.

My gut was telling me no, but my heart and brain was telling me to scream and shout Jesus' name. I was young, but I knew a lot about the Holy Spirit. If going to church made me happy, the class would be happy to hear about it.

"I went to church with Big-mama," I said faster than a speed reader.

"Yeah, but why are you wearing old clothes?" a boy's voice yelled from the back of the room.

The class erupted in laughter. It was as if they'd been holding their breaths waiting to see who was going to mention the fact that I was the only kid wearing the same old clothes from before winter break.

I was so embarrassed that I wanted to put my head down in shame, but more than that, I wanted to know who it was that called me out like that. Even though I'd sat in that same class all year with the same kids every day, I did not recognize his voice. And when I turned to look in back of me, I did not know who to look for.

"His shoes are old too." A girl's voice pushed the boy's words, and me wanting to find him, out of my head. Instead, I now wanted to search for her. It had to be one of four girls that sat to the left of me, since my back was to them, and only them, when the voice came from behind me and hurt my heart.

"Enough!" Mrs. Dillion silenced the laughter in the class that hadn't died down the least bit.

I turned my attention to Mrs. Dillion. Her sympathetic eyes were filled with warmth. Her lips quivered a half-hearted smile. Her eyes moved around the classroom until the laughs, giggles, and coughs—from where my classmates had laughed at me so hard that they could hardly catch their breaths—had ceased.

I sat down and kept my eyes on Mrs. Dillion, my protector for that moment. Too bad I could not take her home with me to protect me from Mama.

My feelings were beyond hurt. If my heart was on the outside of my chest, my classmates would have probably laughed at the cracks from where it was broken.

Chapter 5
Scars, Blood, and Pain
Monday @ 2:30 p.m.

My key let me know that the front door was already unlocked. I turned it to the left, which should have unlocked the door, but instead hit a snag. Thinking that something was wrong with the lock, I turned my key to the right and puffed when I realized that I had locked the door.

Once I finally let myself into the house, I was completely shocked by the sight before me. My eyes popped out of my head. My body shook with my heartbeat. Although I was used to Mama's filth and the usual odor that lingered around the house, the mess in the living room scared me to death.

The couch that once sat in front of the living room window was flipped over with its two cushions lying beneath it. The big couch was pushed away from the wall; its cushions stacked on top of each other. Small pieces of trash, magazines, coupons from the Sunday's paper, my clothes, my suitcase, books, the Bible that Big-mama gave me, and a lampshade were scattered all over the floor.

I walked slower than a turtle to the middle of the living room. I allowed my backpack to slide off my right shoulder, down my arm, and onto a pile of magazines. I looked at the doorway that led from the living room into the kitchen. My eyes then moved to the doorway that led from the living room into the hall. I was searching for Mama, praying that she was okay. Yes, Mama had let me down my entire childhood, but I still loved her. She was my mama.

Darkness replaced the sun in the brightly lit living room, right before my body and the back of my head met the wooden floor with a hard thump. The left side of my head was pounding with pain. I could see flashes of light behind my eyelids. I tried to talk, but my brain and mouth refused to cooperate with each other. My brain cried, *Mama, what did I do,* yet my lips were paralyzed.

"You wanna start stealing from me, huh?" I could feel one of Mama's feet touch my forehead. Her spit rained down on me. "I had a small bag of cocaine on my nightstand and now it's gone. I know your Uncle Nard ain't took it, because he the one who gave it to me. Now where is it?" Mama kicked me in my side so hard that my body bounced off the floor and rolled next to my suitcase.

I could not answer her even if I wanted to. My heart was crying. *Mama, Dad put the cocaine in your arm last night. He put all of it in a needle and stuck it in your arm to put you to sleep.* But again, my lips were frozen in time.

"Michael, where is it?" Mama screamed. "I tore this house up looking for my coke. You better hurry up and say something before I beat you with my foot."

"I . . . Dad," was all that I could muster up enough strength to say. The cocaine was lost in her arm. She should have been able to feel it.

"What you say?" Mama's breath splashed against my face. "Where'd you say it was?"

"Dad." I wheezed.

"Dad? You ain't got no Daddy. Your daddy left your nappy headed tail when you was two. Left me to deal with the sorry, thieving child you've become. Now where is my cocaine?"

"Uncle Nard," I whimpered.

"You saying your uncle Nard stole from me? Is that what you're saying? You gon' lay there and lie after all the stuff he done did for you? Let me show you what I do to liars. You stay your tail right there, and you bet not get up!"

Mama's feet hit the floor like thunder during a rainstorm. Her footsteps grew further and further away, until silence filled the room. My mind slowly drifted off into a painful sleep, until one of my uncle's belts cut through my pants and broke my skin.

Not only did the belt make me talk, but I could scream. "Awww, Mama! I don't have it. I don't have it," I cried.

"Yes you do! Where is it?" For every word that came out of Mama's mouth, my butt, arms, and legs were marked by the belt.

I curled my legs up to my chest and covered my face with my hands. The pain shot through my limbs like electricity through a wire, and was released through my tears.

With Mama screaming about beating her coke out of me, the excruciating pain rocked me to sleep.

***

XXXX
Tuesday @ 12:30 a.m.

Mama beat me into a new day, with me sleeping until Tuesday morning. My whole body stung like a cut drenched in alcohol. Each time I moved, it felt like somebody had dragged me down the middle of the street. My knees, legs, arms, back, and stomach were full of pain. I don't know how Mama got my stomach with the belt. I thought I had shielded it with my knees as I pressed them against my chest, but I guess not.

I opened my eyes and tried to look through the darkness

that surrounded me. I didn't know where I was. I can't honestly say that I even knew who I was. I just lay there without understanding.

Blurred visions of Mama beating me with one of my uncle's belts played in my head like a silent film. Her lips moved, yet were absent of sound.

Mama's body language spoke for her, and it was nothing nice. Her eyebrows were drawn together in anger. Small lines creased her forehead. Her chipped nails picked at sores left on her arms from years of drug abuse. Her shoulders jumped and her head moved viciously around on her neck.

In the vision before me, Mama was in desperate need of her medicine, and none of my uncles were around to feed her.

I pried my left side up from the floor and rose slowly to a seated position. The throbbing pain had me sweating like a dog. The only parts of my body that were free of pain were my hands, face, and feet. Thankfully, my shoes protected my feet from Mama's wrath.

I sucked air through my teeth. Once my eyes adjusted to the darkness, I could see that I was in the living room next to the front door. I stared at the front door for so long that everything that happened when I walked into the house from school suddenly came to me.

While peering around the living room at the mess that Mama had made, I heard movement behind me. As I spun on my heels to confront the noise, Mama bashed me in the head. With what, I do not know. She knocked out my voice box, or at least that's what it felt like.

Mama had been hiding behind the front door, waiting for me to return home from school. She then attacked me like two ghetto mothers in the streets fighting over the same man, and beat me unconscious.

I pushed my body all the way up from the floor. When I

got to my feet, I staggered backward. I was so disoriented that I could not control my steps. I wanted to grab each part of my body that was baptized in Mama's rage, but I was hurting in so many places that I would have looked like an octopus with only two arms trying to capture the pain.

I reached for my shoulder when my stomach started growling. Hunger mixed with pain was a bad combination. I needed something to satisfy my hunger and to rid my body of pain. Then delusion set in. I worried that if I didn't stop my stomach from growling, that the noise would wake Mama, or one of my uncles and Mama, or whomever Mama was entertaining that night.

I headed for the kitchen. I didn't bother to cut on a light. We had been living in that raggedy apartment for so long that I could maneuver my way around the entire house with my eyes closed. But I forgot one thing. The furniture had been moved.

I walked right into the couch. "Ugh," I grunted.

I walked around the couch, held my hands out in front of me, and took large steps to keep from stumbling over anything else that might have lay ahead of me. For all I knew, Mama could have been passed out on the floor.

I turned on the kitchen light and stood there sulking. My first thought was to look myself over to see how bad the bruises were, and they were bad. My arms looked like a cat had tossed me around the floor and dug its claws into my skin like a ball of yarn. The belt had carved the letter X all over my arms. I pulled the bottom of my shirt up and tucked it beneath my chin. My stomach was covered in small X's as if two people had played a game of Tic-tac-toe on my stomach, minus the O's. All lines were capped with dried blood.

I pulled my shirt down and held it away from my skin. I didn't want my shirt to rub against the scars, adding to the pain. I didn't bother to drop my pants and look at my legs or turn my back to a mirror in search of X's. I think I figured that if my stomach looked like my arms, then my legs and my back probably did too.

Once I finished inspecting my body like a child does a strange rock, I pressed my hands against my stomach to silence the growls. It didn't work. It never worked. But instead of going to sleep like I normally did when I was hungry and the refrigerator was empty, I was going to find something to eat, even if it was nothing more than cheese and crackers.

I silently searched the cabinets and refrigerator for something to eat. I wanted a peanut butter and jelly sandwich, but as usual, we were all out of peanut butter. The cabinets were nearly as empty as they were the day we moved into the apartment, and the refrigerator held the basics; eggs, cheese, rotten tomatoes, and food stains all over the shelves.

After a while, my eyes stopped cooperating with my brain. They started closing on their own, even when my brain was telling them to search for food.

Weary was an understatement. My body was weak, hungry, and in a lot of pain.

I walked over to the counter where the microwave was and stared at the half-filled bag of bread. Uncle Nard had only used six slices of bread when he made our burgers the night before, yet there were only four slices of bread left in the bag. Mama must have made sugar sandwiches when she couldn't find her cocaine. The new bag of bread was wide open with five slices of bread forming a trail outside of the bag.

I took a slice of bread from the bag and placed it on the table. I then pulled open the refrigerator door and scanned the shelves, hoping Mama had not eaten up all of the sugar. Yes, we kept our sugar in the refrigerator. It was the only way to keep the roaches from making a home inside of the box of sugar.

Spotting the small box of sugar on a bottom shelf, I managed a weak smile. I reached for it when a throbbing pain, followed by flashes of light, shot through my head and sent me folded over in tears.

I locked my jaw, sealed my lips, and wept on the inside for Big-mama, God, or just anybody to make the pain go away. Tears rushed down my face and were immediately joined by saliva as they dripped down my chin onto my bruised chest.

I pressed a hand against my forehead and took the sugar from the refrigerator door. I closed the door and turned to the table when something came over me. My legs grew as still as the trunk of a tree. I couldn't move. The pain in my head then traveled behind my eyes and caused everything within my eyesight to appear blurry.

My brain cursed every bone in my legs and commanded them to move, but my legs stood firm in their decision to disobey. My knuckles dug circles in my closed eyes as I struggled to see through my blurred vision.

I stared at the piece of bread on the table. My stomach grumbled for the sandwich that curbed my mama's appetite for drugs. I had never indulged in a sugar sandwich before. But at that moment, when my body was drenched in pain and my heart stained, all in the name of a drug-addicted rage, I was willing to eat anything.

I dragged my legs to the table and poured sugar in the center of the bread. I folded the bread in two and bit into one end of it. Sugar spilled from the opposite end of the bread and formed a circle with jagged edges on the table.

My saliva moistened the sugar and made the bread stick to the roof of my mouth like glue. I used my tongue and one of my fingers to clear the roof of my mouth. I chewed, and chewed, and chewed until I broke down the lumpy sugar sandwich.

Mama must have really been thirsty for drugs to spend five minutes chewing on a sugar sandwich, because it took me forever to break it down enough to swallow without choking to death.

I took a second bite. This time the bread became wedged in my throat. I dropped the last of the bread in my hand onto the floor and snatched open the refrigerator door. While my brain was being robbed of oxygen, I searched frantically for something to drink. Other than Mama's beers, the refrigerator was absent of any type of liquids. The third rack, where I kept my Hi-C fruit drinks, was empty, another courtesy of Mama and her drugs.

I was afraid to drink the faucet water. Big-mama once told me that faucet water had mercury in it, and that I'd get real sick if I ever drank it. She always had bottled water for me at her house.

With my heart beating what felt like a hole through my chest, I grabbed one of Mama's beers and snapped it open. I didn't even bother to take a sip to see if I liked it or not. I took that eight ounce can of beer to the head and downed it like a drunk in front of a liquor store. I couldn't even remember what it tasted like. I just know that even after the beer cleared my airway, I continued to drink it until it was gone.

I shook the empty can. I tried to crush it with my hands like my uncles did, but my hands were too small.

I put the can on the counter next to Reba McCaine's bottle of Zoloft. I have no idea who Reba McCaine was. When Uncle PJ showed up like Santa Clause with a freezer bag full of prescription drugs, Reba McCaine's name was on nearly every bottle.

I turned around to bend down and pick up the bread that had fallen on the floor when I stumbled backward, bounced off the counter, and fell face-first onto the floor. I was drunk.

My mind moved slowly into perfect peace. The beer made me numb to my surroundings; deaf to Mama's screams that plagued my subconscious.

I pulled myself up to my feet and stood as still as a mannequin. My body felt as light as a feather. A sudden urge to run came over me. Where? The urge had no address, no specific destination. My feet were set to run out of the kitchen as fast as I could without stopping.

I started to run when I tripped over my own two feet and landed on my knees. I struggled to get to my feet, to set my feet back on course, when I slipped around the floor like a boxer scrambling to get to his feet after a hard punch to the face.

With the exception of the floor, the kitchen circled me. Like a blind man feeling his way around an unfamiliar home with no cane or seeing-eye-dog to guide him, I reached for the piece of bread. My hand moved over and around the bread, maybe twenty times, before I was finally able to grab it. I stuffed the bread into my mouth as sleep slowly covered me like a blanket.

I kicked off the sleep. I couldn't fall asleep on the kitchen floor. I was drunk, but not too drunk to forget Mama's backhand. Mama would have found me lying there in the morning. Once the scent of beer hit her nostrils, she would have added to the fresh bruises on my body.

I knew I was wrong for drinking her beer, but what was I supposed to do? I almost died from choking to death.

I was ready to go to my room and pass out in my bed, but the kitchen wouldn't stop spinning. I rose to my knees and held on to the table. As I was pulling myself up to my feet, I fell back down on the floor. I crawled to where I knew the doorway should have been and waited for the entrance to come back around. The counter with the microwave passed by me first, then the stove, then the table and chairs, and then the entrance to the laundry room.

The entrance to the kitchen was behind the entrance to the laundry room. I missed the entrance to the kitchen the first time. As soon as it came around a second time, I crawled out of the kitchen like a roach running from human feet.

I continued down the hall, headed to my bedroom, when I noticed Mama's bedroom door was pulled all the way open.

I came to an abrupt stop right before passing her bedroom. I pressed my back against the wall. I sobered up real quick. Someone had been up while I was getting drunk, because Mama always kept her bedroom door closed or slightly open, but never all the way open.

My heart was in a race with itself. I swallowed hard. Taking a deep breath, I got on all fours, ready to crawl as fast as I could to my room. After my first push forward, I found myself locking eyes with Mama.

Instead of looking straight ahead with my mind on my room, I looked into Mama's room and straight into her eyes.

Mama rested directly on the edge of the side of the bed nearest the door. Her head was propped up on a pillow and she was looking dead at me.

I jumped onto my knees and took a sharp, short breath. My lips trembled words that my voice refused to join in on.

"I was thirsty," I mumbled. Mama didn't say one word, she just looked at me. "I'm . . . I'm going back to my room now." Again, Mama just looked at me.

The silence made it even worse. Mama's silence was the calm before the storm. Nothing, not even God's angels, could protect me from Mama's storm.

A loud snore rattled Mama's throat and cut through the silence. Mama was asleep with her eyes open.

Mama turned over with her back to me, the only signal I needed to get as far away from her as I could, and back to my room where I'd be safe, for a little while anyway.

CHAPTER 6
If Death Knew Me
Tuesday @ 4:00 a.m.

The alarm clock buzzed my ears awake. I turned over out of my sleep. With my eyes half-closed, I read the time on the clock. I already knew what time it was. It was prayer time. Mama was in need of some spiritual healing, especially after beating me to a pulp.

Big-mama taught me how to set my alarm for school. I had been late for school one too many times and my teacher got tired of holding me after school. Back then, Mama's phone rang every morning at eight-thirty without skipping a beat. It was always the school calling, and I wouldn't be surprised if Mama knew it. Of course she didn't answer the phone. It was too early to be calling a drug addict who spent all of her nights and days getting high. Any time was a bad time to call Mama. That is, unless one had drugs or money in their voice.

After two weeks of being late for school every morning, and the school unable to reach Mama, the school started calling Big-mama. Big-mama already knew that talking to Mama was like not talking to Mama. She rushed out and purchased me an alarm clock. She then came right over and taught me how to use it. Not only did I set the alarm clock for school, I used it to notify me when it was time to save Mama's soul from hell.

I climbed out of bed and quickly noticed that my bare feet did not touch the cold floor. Groggy, and still a bit drunk, I glanced down at the shoes on my feet. I was so out of it that I'd forgotten to remove my shoes before crawling into bed.

I stepped out of my shoes and walked on the tips of my toes to my open bedroom door. I stuck my head out into the hall and looked toward Mama's bedroom. I then looked toward the dimly-lit kitchen. My exhausted heart still found room for fear. Had Mama awakened to the kitchen light on? If so, there was no telling what she'd do to me. I do know that it would involve her hand or a belt.

I hurried to the kitchen and turned off the light. I then retracted my steps back to the hall and on to Mama's bedroom.

I stood outside of her bedroom door with fear putting a beating on my heart. There was a negative energy surrounding me, telling me to back away from the door or else, but I couldn't. Mama's soul was at stake. My prayer would save her from going to hell. My prayer would eventually save her from herself. When? Only God knew the answer to that.

Any other morning, I would tiptoe to Mama's room, gently crack the door, and slip inside. The drugs placed Mama near, if not in a temporary coma. I wasn't worried about her waking up and catching me in her room. But that morning, I don't know why I was afraid to go into her room, even as she slept. It felt like something was not right. And whatever that something was, it was on the other side of her closed bedroom door.

I turned the knob real slow and thanked God that it was a silent turn. I opened my eyes just as wide as they would go and peered through the darkness at my uncles' side of the bed. There was someone there. From where I was standing, I could not see the person clearly.

A pillow covered his head. His small feet hung off the side of the bed. It was my first time seeing a grown man with small feet. All my uncles' feet were at least a size eleven. I knew right away that whoever it was that was fast asleep was new to our hole in the wall, and would later be introduced to me as my uncle, not that I needed another one.

With every new uncle came even more drugs for Mama's body to dance to. That meant more abuse on top of the abuse that I was already forced to wake up to every day.

I had never prayed for Mama when there was someone lying next to her, but I had to. Mama had beat me real bad and was in desperate need of God's forgiveness. I had already forgiven her. I forgave Mama the moment I woke up from the blackout. She needed God's forgiveness, and in a hurry. Just in case she failed to wake up from her sleep, I had to make sure that she would be joining me and Big-mama in heaven when the time came.

I got on my knees and crawled into the room. My eyes stayed on the body with the small feet until I made it to the foot of the bed. Once I made it to Mama's dreadful feet, I stood on my knees, put my elbows on the bed, and pressed the palms of my hands together. My prayers would have to be in my head. Mama was a hard sleeper. She might have felt the power of my prayers, but never heard them. However, the man with the small feet I knew nothing about, and worried that my prayers would wake him and cause him to wake Mama.

I closed my eyes and said a prayer in my head. I said a new prayer. The prayer that Big-mama had handed me was not working. Either that, or God was busy answering someone else's prayer and did not hear my cries for help.

God, Mama beat me bad. I got scratches all over my body and they hurt. Please forgive Mama. She still loves me. She was just mad. Big-mama says when Mama's mad she do things she don't mean. Mama didn't mean to hit me hard with the belt.

Please, God, bring Mama to heaven with me and Big-mama. I'm okay. I love Mama and she has to come to heaven with me. Me and Big-mama can't go to heaven if Mama don't come with us. Mama's sorry.

I was ready to open my eyes from the prayer when I remembered the beer.

God, I'm sorry for drinking Mama's beer, but I couldn't breathe.

Satisfied with my prayer, I opened my eyes to a pair of greenish-brown cat eyes staring me in my face. I was overcome with instant fear. I took a short breath and held it. I stared in horror at the set of eyes as they rose from beneath a pillow and moved toward me.

The eyes belonged to a woman who was as light as Mrs. Dillion and as naked as Mama. Her hair was dark and blended perfectly with the darkness that surrounded us. I could see the silhouette of her hair, which appeared to be a big afro.

The woman was sitting up on my uncles' side of the bed with her left leg folded on top of Mama's bare back, and the woman's right thigh pressed against her own stomach. Her right knee parted her small breasts and her chin slept on her knee. I looked the woman over from head to toe, which didn't take long, since she was folded like a picnic table.

My pulse was beating like crazy and my feet itched to run. I could feel the beer bubbling within my stomach and up my throat. It sat in my throat and was eventually met by the sugar sandwich. The beer and the sugar sandwich combined left me swallowing back vomit that threatened to send me bent over in convulsions and add to Mama's repulsive room.

Cat-eyes gazed into my eyes. The woman removed her knee from Mama's back and replaced it with her hand. With her eyes locked on me, she rubbed Mama's back. Mama stirred in her sleep, but not once did she open her eyes. Cat-eyes then ran her hands down Mama's back and stopped at the blanket that covered Mama from the waist down. She flipped back the blanket, exposing Mama's nakedness.

Cat-eyes' teeth emerged from behind her lips. No overlapping teeth and no gaps.

Seconds followed by minutes passed between our gaze. One of us had to break the trance. Either she would wake Mama, a tornado always ready to hit me, or I would find my way out of the bedroom and hope that Cat-eyes never revealed to Mama that our eyes had met.

I twisted off the bed onto all fours and crawled out of the room. I didn't even bother to close the door behind me. I just wanted to get to my bedroom, and in a hurry.

My hands and knees met the hall with ease. Like a baby enticed by a toy in front of him, I crawled as fast as I could to my room and scurried into bed.

That was the first and last time I would ever pray for Mama when a contributor to her addiction failed to click their heels and find their way home. Mama had never brought a woman to the house before, so I had no idea who or what Cat-eyes would be to me. I do know that there was something about her that scared me, and I prayed that she wouldn't be my second mother. Not even an auntie.

Two hours later I woke up drowsy after a failed attempt at sleep. The welts on my back were so painful that I was forced to lie on my sides and stomach. Sleep eventually found me, but only temporarily.

As I watched the sheep take turns jumping over the gate, sleep sent me onto my back. Again, I was met with pain just as the next sheep leaped into the air. I rolled onto my side and held on to my back until the pain subsided. My eyes then blinked slowly into sleep. I was able to smile at the sheep again. I stood by the gate, rubbing the coats of the sheep that had already taken the leap. Seconds into my sleep, I found myself sitting up in bed and sucking air through my clenched teeth after turning over onto my back again. I finally decided to accept my fate of no sleep.

I climbed out of bed thirty minutes before I normally woke up for school and started getting ready. I peeled off my blood-stained clothes and left them on the floor. I then walked out of my room and headed for the bathroom.

While passing by Mama's bedroom, I peeked inside at my uncles' side of the bed. Cat-eyes must have crawled out of the house, because Mama was lying in the middle of the bed on her back with her arms and legs spread out at her sides like an eagle. No one was next to her.

I continued to the bathroom and closed the door behind me. I slid back the shower curtain and stuffed a balled up sock that we used as a stopper into the drain.

I took my baths in the mornings instead of at night. I loved the fresh scent that the Dial soap left on my skin, and how a light breeze carried the scent into the air.

The scent of Dial masked the smell of the liquid cocaine and marijuana that lingered in the air of our apartment, and clung to my clothes before I could step one foot out of the door.

I turned on the water and passed a hand beneath the running water to see if it was hot, cold, or warm. The water splashed onto the welts on my wrist and arm and left me snatching my hand away in pain.

I spun in circles and grimaced through my clenched teeth. I put my hand between my legs and fought every muscle in my face to keep from whining.

I cut off the water. I reached down to pull the sock from the drain, but stopped just as my fingers touched the puddle of water that covered the sock. No way was I putting my arm in that tub of fire.

Mama can pull it out if she takes a shower, I said to myself.

I used the word 'if' because Mama didn't take showers every day. She sometimes walked around the house with a musty odor on her for days at a time.

"Get out so I can use the bathroom." Mama yawned behind me.

I jumped after hearing Mama's voice. I spun around to face her. I didn't hear the door open, nor was I happy to see her standing naked before me with her morning, noon, and night face on, which was always angry.

Mama's voice caught me off-guard and scared me so bad that urine ran down my legs and through the cracks on the floor. I looked from Mama to the trail of urine, while fearing her reaction to her son urinating on himself. A fresh beating over the welts would have probably sent me to the hospital.

Mama's voice always scared me. I can't even remember the sound of love, well at least not from Mama. Maybe it once existed when I was a baby, because I can remember Mama screaming at me and threatening to snatch my ear off for peeing in the bed when I was around three or four.

"What the hell is wrong with you?" Mama yelled. "Pissing all over my floor." Her hands were balled into fists. Her bare feet crept toward me.

I looked past the welts on my stomach and down at the urine on my legs. My inner thighs and legs absorbed the rest of the urine before it could run onto the floor.

"Whose gonna scrub this floor? You, because I'm not. You two feet away from the toilet, but you went and pissed on my floor. Where your face rag?" Mama's top lip trembled she was so mad.

I pointed to my Sponge Bob face rag that hung from a towel rack nearest the door, next to the sink.

Mama ripped my face rag from the towel rack and stood

in front of the sink. She turned the knob for the cold water so hard that I thought it was going to spin off its screw, into the air, and go flying across the bathroom.

"Scrub that mess off my floor," she said and slapped me in the face with my rag. "Then get your no-knowing-how-to hold-his-piss pissy butt in the tub before I knock your head in."

I caught my rag right before it dropped from my face. I was sad, but refused to cry. Crying excited Mama's anger. To cry meant that I wanted a beating, and Lord knows I didn't want that.

My legs folded beneath me and sent me to my knees. I crawled in a circle and sat where I could keep one eye on Mama while I scrubbed the urine from the floor. I feared Mama would attack me from behind, which she'd done many of times.

Mama squatted down on the toilet and watched me scrub the floor. Her knees were knocked together and her arms hung freely at her sides. The black dots on her arms, from where my uncles fed her, were very visible.

"Michael?" Mama called my name with a questioning tone. It was almost as if she was unsure of my name. Either that or her brain was so fried from years of drug abuse that she had forgotten who I was.

"Huh?" I answered with my eyebrows raised in wonder.

"Michael?" Mama was still questioning my name.

"Huh?" I responded a bit louder.

"What have I told you about saying "huh" when I call you? Get over here!" Her voice was short and sharp.

I set the rag on the floor. I kept my eyes on Mama and jumped to my feet. I didn't run over to her, but I should have after answering with a "huh" twice.

Mama shot up from the toilet. Urine dripped from her

pubic hair and stained her legs. She yanked my right arm from its socket. Morning spit splashed my face.

"My arm!" I screamed, took short breaths, and cried.

"Shut up!" Ignoring my cries, Mama continued to tug on my arm.

"My arm, Mama," I screamed. "You're breaking my arm. Let go, Mama. Let go."

"Shut your damn mouth!" Mama growled. She shoved my arm back into its socket and slapped me across the side of my head. I could both hear and feel my arm snap back into place. I shrieked in agony and cradled my arm in my hand.

Mama was a professional fighter, at least when it involved inflicting pain on me. Snapping my arm in and out its socket as she yanked me toward her, or slinging me back against a wall was a natural occurrence in our apartment that misery built.

"Next time I call you, I don't care if you're standing five feet away from me, I want you right here." Mama pointed to a dirt stain on the floor at her feet. "Do you hear me?"

"Okay, Mama." I sobbed. My arm throbbed in pain.

The physical and verbal abuse was unbearable. Yet because Mama had total control of the wind beneath my wings, she continued to torment me for the next eleven years of my life, if death didn't find me first.

I was Mama's punching bag, but loved her with the same amount of love that I was born with. That love that every child has for their parents even after being exposed to hate, drugs, and alcohol in the home. The physical and verbal abuse that's often inflicted upon the child once the drugs take effect is nothing short of a tragedy. But like any child, regardless of the pain and suffering, I loved my mama.

Mama's eyes suddenly grew wide as they examined me from head to toe.

"Who put those scratches on you?" She wrapped her bony hand around my wrist and raised my arm high above my head. She used her free hand to twist my body from left to right, and in a circle. I was a marionette being controlled by strings that were owned and operated by a drug addict.

The drugs were starting to give Mama Amnesia. First she beat me over the cocaine; the devil that smiled from her veins. Next she forgot that she had even beaten my spirit out of me and left me in complete darkness, both in my head and on the living room floor.

"You did it with the belt," I mumbled.

"What?" Mama cupped her hand beneath my chin and pulled me to her.

"You hit me with uncle's belt."

"Boy, I ain't touched you. Don't you stand in my face and lie on me." Mama dug her nails in my chest and pushed me back against the sink.

A sharp pain shot up and down my spine. My legs weakened beneath me and sent me to the floor on my side.

"Get up. You ain't going to school today. I let you go to school, look up, and the cops banging down my door putting cuffs on me cuz you done told one of your teachers that I beat you. Stay your pissy, lying butt here." Mama's anger controlled the tone of her voice like a choir director leading a choir at church. Her voice rose and fell with a pause between each level. "Better yet, you can stay your tail here for the rest of the week. Short days anyway. They won't miss you." She huffed and then scratched her arm.

"Mama come blowing up my phone at seven in the morning about you getting out of school early this week," she continued to fuss. "Phone ringing off the hook like she couldn't wait until she knew I was up to call. Always messing up my high with her nose all in my life."

My heart dropped to the pit of my stomach. Why, oh, why did Big-mama tell Mama that I was getting out of school early? Big-mama could have picked me up from school all week and let me stay with her until the time that I normally got out of school. Mama would have never known. A drug addict does not keep up with their child, let alone their child's school schedule.

Stay home with Mama? I knew right away that it was going to be a long week. All I could think about was more beatings, Mama's yelling and screaming, and her constant complaints.

Mama beat the floor with her hoofs on her way out of the bathroom. "Stay there," she yelled. She returned minutes later with a box of Epsom Salt. "Move," she grumbled.

I rushed in back of her.

Mama filled the tub with water and then poured at least half of the box of Epsom Salt into the water. Lord, was I crying on the inside. I shivered at the sight of the white crystals spilling from the box like a waterfall. The water had already set fire to my arm, but nothing could have prepared me for the excruciating pain that the Epsom Salt and water combined inflicted upon me.

Mama snapped her neck around to me. "Get in the tub." She pointed in back of her at the mixture of medication that would soon send me back into darkness.

"It hurts, Mama," I wept. "The water burns."

"Boy, get in the tub!" Mama demanded. "That water ain't even hot. You ain't put two fingers in there, but quick to say that it's hot."

"Please, Mama. No." My legs took me back toward the door. I was three steps away from making it out of the bathroom when Mama snatched me up by my arms and carried me over to the tub.

"Daddy," I yelled. I kicked my legs faster than the fastest

runner in the world. I dangled from Mama's hands. I could feel pins and needles inside of the arm that she had pulled out of its socket.

"Stop screaming." Mama was screaming her own self.

I managed to free my right arm from her grip just as she held me over the tub. By now, I was hanging by one arm over the fiery pit of hell.

"No, Mama. Daddy. Daddy. No." My cries bounced off the walls. They cut through Mama's sudden outburst of laughter.

"Daddy?" Mama continued to laugh. "You ain't got no Daddy. He didn't want me or you. Neither one of us. Took off to the store one day and never came back. Probably run off with some other woman and got her pregnant."

Mama dropped me into the inferno. Once the mixture invaded my bruises, I yelled at the top of my lungs. Darkness pulled at my feet and placed me next to the gate with the beautiful sheep.

Every time I think about what I went through that morning, I become angry with God for not saving me. He allowed me to drown in so much pain. If He really loved and cared about me, He would have just let me drown in that tub. Death would have been better than what I would ultimately endure.

Chapter 7
Domestic Abuse
Tuesday @ 2:00 p.m.

My eyes shot open. In a panic, I breathed short, fast breaths. I almost didn't recognize my bedroom. It was as bright as the sun, yet it took a while for both my eyes and my mind to become familiar with my surroundings.

When Mama dropped me into the tub, the left side of my face slammed against the back of the tub. Pain then traveled through my gums, face, head, neck, and body, forcing me into a deep sleep. I have no recollection of how I got into my room, but I'm guessing it was Mama. If she really loved me, then she would have let me drown. But like God, Mama had no love in her heart for me.

I held a hand against the left side of my face and examined the inside of my mouth with my tongue. My gums were sore and three of my teeth were loose. My teeth were so loose that I could move them with my tongue. It went without saying that soon I'd be receiving a visit from the tooth fairy, right? Wrong.

When those three teeth eventually fell out of my mouth, one after the other, I would do what I'd done with the others. I'd slip them beneath my pillow, only to wake up to those same teeth still under my pillow, which would eventually land in a small box that I kept on my dresser. My hope was that one day the Tooth Fairy would find them there.

Three voices in my stomach spoke to me. Each voice spoke a different language, which I didn't understand, but I did know the purpose of their visit. I was hungry.

There was growling on the right side of my stomach and whining in the middle. The left side of my stomach felt like it was in a fight with itself. There was thumping against the lining of my stomach along with a loud roar.

With my teeth showing, my eyes closed, and my nose and cheeks tightened, a result of my pain, I forced my head up from my pillow and looked myself over. My head flopped back down on the pillow. It took too much strength for me to sit up, but I did get to see that I was dressed in pajamas with white socks covering my feet.

"Get out of my house!" I heard Mama yell in distress.

All of a sudden I had a lot of energy. My mind was not on the pain. It was on protecting Mama.

I flew out of bed and ran for my closed bedroom door. I snatched open the door and followed Mama's voice into the living room. I found Mama and Uncle Nard standing face to chest in a heated argument. Mama was shorter than Uncle Nard. The top of her head stopped just below his neck.

Neither one of them noticed me. I was peeking out from the side of the entertainment center watching them from afar. My intentions were to help Mama, but when I saw that it was Uncle Nard, I remained where I was. Uncle Nard said that he loved Mama. Love would not allow him to hurt her, even though it always left an open invitation for Mama to hurt me.

"If I leave, you going right behind me, because I pay the bills here," Uncle Nard told her. "I bought all this here furniture when that rain seeped through this ceiling and destroyed everything. Yo' landlord didn't compensate you.

Walk in here and you got some trick lying up in the bed that I bought. Hell yeah I put her the hell out. Lucky I didn't kick yo' broke tail out." He did a sweep of the room with his arms. "I ain't going nowhere." Uncle Nard's nostrils were flared open. His words were full of rage.

Cat-eyes was still here? I thought that she'd left when I didn't see her lying next to Mama as I passed by Mama's room that morning to get ready for school. At least that had been the plan before Mama greeted me in the bathroom.

Since Cat-eyes was not in Mama's room, where had she been when Mama's lifeless body was taking up the entire bed? Maybe Mama's wild sleeping pushed her onto the floor on the opposite side of the bed where I could not see her.

Mama walked up on Uncle Nard and pushed him in his chest.

"Keep your hands off me, Crystal," he ordered.

"Get out of my house!" Mama's white robe hung off her shoulder. As she was speaking her peace, which included throwing her arms all over the place, her robe flew open, revealing everything that I was not trying to see.

"Look at you, Crystal." Uncle Nard shook his head. The left corner of his mouth was turned up into a snarl. "I been providing for you and Michael for a long time. I make sure the both of you eat. I keep that monkey off your back. If it wasn't for me, yo' landlord wouldn't have never cleaned this place up. I had to manhandle his ass." Uncle Nard laughed or said something beneath his breath; one or the other. His lips moved, but no words that I could understand clearly were spoken.

"Is this dump something to be proud of?" Mama asked with a jerk of her head. She held her arms out at her sides and twisted from left to right while glancing around the living room at the old furniture and stained walls. "This apartment looks like trash. The wood on this floor is broken and chipped. Kitchen faucet is leaking. Mildew on the shower walls. This is not exactly the Ritz Carlton Hotel. My landlord didn't do nothing but repair the roof. But I'm sure you see that, Bernard!"

"Oh you saying that it's my fault this house is tore up?" Uncle Nard placed a hand against his bare chest. He brushed his chest hairs with his fingers, set his eyes on the ceiling, and passed both hands over his face. "Crystal, we're not talking about this apartment right now. We're talking about that tramp you had lying up in there, stoned as I don't know what. You up here trickin' with Michael in the house."

Uncle Nard noted Mama's sexual immorality like it was something new. Then again, it was new to him. Uncle Nard had no idea that he was not the only person Mama was seeing.

"It's my house, mine." Mama grumbled. "I can have anybody in here that I want to. You ain't my daddy. You ain't nothing but a fat, overstuffed turkey."

"But when I'm giving you my money it's 'baby this' and 'baby that,' huh? 'I love you. Don't nobody treat me like you do.'" Uncle Nard thumped a finger against Mama's forehead. "Typical trick."

"Don't you ever put your hands on me." Mama slapped Uncle Nard's finger away from her forehead and shoved him in his chest.

"Trick." Uncle Nard laughed.

"I got your trick," Mama said. She spun Uncle Nard's face to the left with a hard slap and jumped back just in case he decided to return the favor.

"You don't want me to hit you, but it's all right for you to hit me?" Uncle Nard asked. "Keep your hands to yourself, trick."

Mama curled her fingers into a fist and walked up on

the back of the shoe and peered up at Uncle Nard.

"Put that shoe on right." Uncle Nard pointed at the shoe that I had turned into a slipper.

I kneeled down on my right knee and put my left shoe on correctly. I leaped to my feet and smiled into Uncle Nard's eyes.

"Let's go." Uncle Nard walked ahead of me as we made our way to the living room and then out of the house.

I bet Uncle Nard thought he had me exactly where he wanted me. He was preying on my emotions. Beat my mother, then offer a desperate, lonely child food and a good time to silence him. Uncle Nard silenced me all right, but it was not the bribe that did it. The image in my head of Mama lying out cold on the floor like death had knocked on our door and quickly seized her was what silenced me. I was traumatized by the look of death on Mama's unconscious face. I wanted to move my thoughts as far away from Mama as possible.

Chapter 8
A Kid Being a Kid
Tuesday @ 7:00 p.m.

Chuck E. Cheese's was like a huge game room. Arcade games, mini Ferris wheels, stationary motorcycles and cars, a children's basketball court, a Sky tube, and a stage where Chuck E. Cheese and friends performed all made up Chuck E. Cheese's.

The staff was dressed in black pants and red shirts. Their hats had an image of Chuck E. Cheese on the front of it.

I gazed around Chuck E. Cheese's in awe before looking up to Uncle Nard in excitement.

"You like it?" Uncle Nard asked, glancing around.

"Yeah." I chuckled. I sprung up and down in my seat. I was as happy as a kid in a candy store. Only this was a pizza store! Same difference.

"One large pizza and a twelve piece wing." A waiter placed our order on the table.

"Thank you," Uncle Nard said before the waiter walked away and became lost in the crowd. Uncle Nard picked up our cups and slid out of the booth. "What kind of drink do you want?"

"Fruit punch," I answered.

"Okay, stay right here and eat. I'll be right back." Uncle

Nard walked away, headed for the soda machine.

I dug right into the pizza and wings. I peeled one slice of pizza from off the platter, slapped it on my plate, and then ripped into it. My feet beat against the bottom of my seat as I peered around at the laughs, smiles, and small tantrums that many of the children called themselves throwing when they did not get their way. I pulled a wing apart and tried to stuff half of it into my mouth while still enjoying the pizza.

"Hold on, Michael," Uncle Nard said as he approached me with our drinks. "Slow down. The food is not going anywhere." That was easy for him to say. Uncle Nard could eat all day long and not worry about where his next meal came from. I was hungry. One would think that I would have been more concerned with playing the games than I was the food. I just wanted to eat.

Uncle Nard sat down in the booth and the adult conversation began.

"You know when you seen me hit your mama today?" Uncle Nard asked out of the blue.

I was having so much fun that I wasn't even thinking about Mama. "Yes," I said. My ears were tuned to Uncle Nard, but my eyes remained on the food. My legs led my body in a bounce. My head rocked back and forth.

"I wasn't trying to hurt your mama. She kept putting her hands on me after I told her to stop. I warned her." Uncle Nard shook a finger at me. The only time anyone had ever shaken their finger at me was when I was being scolded.

I didn't do nothing, was the first thought to come to mind. I thought Uncle Nard was mad at me until he continued his rant about Mama.

"It ain't never good for no man to hit a woman," Uncle Nard continued. "But at the same time, it ain't good for no woman to try a man either. Women need to know when to stay in their place. Don't nothing good come from trying a man's patience, and women need to learn that. Yes, I was taught to walk away, most men are. But these women . . . these women make it hard for a man to turn his back to their sharp tongues, revengeful ways, and small fists."

"Why you feed Mama that stuff in her arm?" I blurted out. Talking about Mama caused flashbacks to torment my thoughts of her beating me over her drugs. I finished off the slice of pizza. I picked up the other half of the wing and began eating it.

"What was that?" Uncle Nard asked me. He turned his head to the left. His pupils were stuck in the right corners of his eyes, and they were watching me. His right ear moved as he waited for me to repeat myself.

I gazed into Uncle Nard's eyes. Uncle Nard staring at me from the corners of his eyes scared me.

My forehead tightened in wrinkles. "Why you put that stuff in Mama's arms with that needle?" My gaze moved between Uncle Nard, the children at play, and our food.

The expression on Uncle Nard's face softened into a look of understanding. "It's your mama's medicine. You see how she acted today? If I skip a day of giving her that medicine, she flips out like she did today. Your mama been on that stuff for so long that her body depends on it. If she don't have it, she'll start shaking. Then sweat . . . She sweats so bad, she looks like she just stepped out of the shower," Uncle Nard said. "She'll lose all control of her muscles. When that happens, her body shakes, and she ain't had nothing to do with the shaking. It does it by itself.

"Scratches on her arms and legs from riding the monkey." Uncle Nard ran a hand along his arm. "Once life prescribes that type of medication to you, you're hooked, and there's no giving it up. Your mama is hooked. You understand?"

"Yes," I lied. I didn't understand any of what Uncle Nard had said. I was too young to know about his hood version of medicine.

"Good," Uncle Nard said with a sharp nod of his head. "Now eat."

And that he didn't have to tell me twice!

I had so much fun with Uncle Nard that I could not sleep that night. I lie on my back, staring up at the ceiling as I reflected on my alone time with him.

I'll never forget Chuck E. Cheese's, and there was no way that I could forget the *Power Rangers*. Not because it was an amazing movie, but because it was the first time I had ever been to a movie theatre.

My kid's meal came with popcorn, a small drink, and a pack of gummy bears. Me and Uncle Nard tossed popcorn into the air and caught it on our tongues. Uncle Nard licked the back of a gummy bear and stuck it to his forehead. He turned to me with his head held slightly back to keep the gummy bear from falling off. I laughed so hard that I nearly choked on the popcorn in my mouth.

I then followed Uncle Nard's lead. I licked the back of a gummy bear and stuck it to my forehead. I licked a second gummy bear and stuck it to my chin. By the time the movie started, I had gummy bears falling from all over my face. Uncle Nard laughed so hard that the sound of deep sighs and the smacking of lips could be heard throughout the theatre.

We dropped our laughs to low chuckles and fell deathly silent when the movie started.

At about 2:00 AM, sleep was all over me. I finally dozed off, only to be awakened two hours later by my alarm clock. It was prayer time; time for me to pray for Mama's sins. Dropping me into the tub would have definitely been added to my prayers had I made it out of bed.

Uncle Nard. Uncle Nard backed away in laughter.

There was anger within Uncle Nard's laughs. He kind of swayed as he stepped away from Mama's fist. His eyebrows were raised in an arch. "Trick. Trick. Trick. Trick." Uncle Nard said trick so many times, and with such speed, that he sounded like the mother of the church speaking in tongues.

Mama's fist slammed into Uncle Nard's stomach like a boxer giving a beating in a ring. She followed the blows up with a punch to his right ear.

Mama held his diamond stud earring between two fingers, and before Uncle Nard knocked her in her temple with a fist of steel, she split his earlobe into two, taking the diamond stud earring to the floor with her.

Mama's body had lost its soul, even before she hit the floor. Both her head and body teetered off the wood. First her head hit the floor, and then her body. Her feet rocked from side-to-side before her body lay motionless and appeared to lack life.

Uncle Nard hit Mama? I was angry. I was sad. He told me that he loved Mama and would never hurt her. Yet at that very moment, he showed Mama the same amount of love that Mama showed me.

"Mama!" I screamed, running out of my hiding place. I dropped to my knees and shook her legs. "Mama, wake up. Get up, Mama. You going to heaven with me and Big-mama. Mama, wake up." I looked up at Uncle Nard. I was pouting like an angry three-year-old.

"Why did you hurt Mama?" I sobbed.

"She not hurt, she's sleep. Go on back to your room. I'm going to take your mama to bed and feed her." A slight smile lingered in the corners of Uncle Nard's mouth.

"No," I cried. "You hurt Mama. You hit Mama hard." I looked away from Uncle Nard and crawled to Mama's chest. I reached for Mama's left breast to shake her awake, but I withdrew my hand, and instead, planted a kiss on her forehead. My kiss then moved to her cheek. "Wake up, Mama. Me and Big-mama still here. We going to heaven together."

My pleas fell on deaf ears. It was as if Mama was no longer in the world with us. Aside from the rising and falling of her chest, she was as still as silence.

"Mama, I love you." I slipped two fingers between her closed lips to look inside of her mouth, but her locked jaws prevented me from going any further than her teeth. I was trying to look down Mama's throat. I don't know why. I just was.

"Let me carry your mama to her room, and then me and you will go get some lunch." Uncle Nard stood, looking down on me.

Me leave the house with Uncle Nard? To go eat? Just the thought of food drew my attention back to the hunger pangs I'd felt before hearing Mama and Uncle Nard arguing. I got so excited about hanging out with Uncle Nard that I forgot all about Mama not hearing my love for her.

"We going to lunch?" I wiped away my tears and smiled. "I want to go to lunch."

I loved hanging out with Uncle Nard. Whether we were at the park tossing a football around, or going to the Science and History Museum where I could run up to a glass-incased dinosaur and look in awe at its scary face and huge body, being with Uncle Nard removed me from the presence of Mama's rage. Even if it was only for a few hours.

It's a sad life when a child does not want to be around their own mother. As much as I loved leaving the house, I didn't want to go anywhere with Mama.

Mama toted me around on the first of the month, when she got my county check. But everywhere that we went was solely about her. The check was so that she could take care of me, but I was the last person to be taken care of.

One day, Big-mama went off on Mama about spending my county check on a three-hundred dollar weave. Mama had worked hard to look good on the outside, when on the inside she was nothing short of a poisonous apple.

With Mama placing all of her weight on one foot, and with an attitude written all over her face, she listened without saying one word, which was unlike Mama. Mama was quick to cut people off and not give them a chance to say anything that involved disagreeing with her. So for Mama to stand there with her mouth shut, the world must have been coming to an end.

Big-mama had gone on to yell about Mama getting her toes and nails done. "My grandson's toes busting holes in his tennis shoes," Big-mama yelled. "Only decent shoes he got is his church shoes, and I bought those. He can't wear church shoes to play in. He can't wear his church shoes to school."

"Got to be thankful for what we have, right?" Mama had laughed. "Money don't grow on trees."

As long as I had shoes on my feet and clothes on my back—even if they were too small— and food in the refrigerator, clumpy milk, molded tomatoes and all, Big-Mama's complaints went in one of Mama's ears and out of the other. Mama was going to do her regardless.

On days that Mama felt beautiful, she spent my county check to look as good as she felt, and relied on my uncles to pick up the household expenses while feeding her drug addiction.

The needle was Mama's feeding tube, and my uncles were the doctors responsible for administering the doses. My uncles being at Mama's disposal came with a price. Beating Mama, and calling her every trick or hoe in the Urban Dictionary, was the price that Mama paid for the drugs.

"Move out the way," Uncle Nard said to me. He kneeled at Mama's side and slipped his hands beneath her. "Go on to your room and throw on something nice. We gonna spend the rest of the day together. Take you to Chuck E. Cheese's, then we gonna go see *Power Rangers*." Uncle Nard scooped Mama into his arms and rose to his feet. Her head bounced off his chest until she was nice and snuggled in his arms.

I ran to my room and shuffled through my drawers for my favorite long-sleeved shirt with a design of the universe on the front of it. Snatching the shirt from a drawer, I ran to the closet, stood on the tips of my toes, and pulled the only pair of jeans that fit me decent from a hanger.

I stripped out of my pajamas and got dressed as fast as I could. As I was tying my right shoe, I heard a door opening and closing. I panicked. I thought it was Uncle Nard trying to leave me.

I picked up my other shoe and ran out of the room into the hall just as Uncle Nard was walking out of Mama's room.

"Who was that woman lying up there with yo' mama?" Uncle Nard asked me.

"I don't know," I replied. I almost slipped up and told Uncle Nard about my encounter with Cat-eyes that morning, but quickly caught myself.

Uncle Nard shook his head and puffed. He then looked down at me. "You ready?" he asked, rubbing his head.

I dropped my shoe to the floor and watched it land on its side. I kicked it upright and stuck my foot inside. I didn't bother to untie my shoes before putting them on. I could not risk Uncle Nard leaving without me, which is what I believed would happen if I stopped to tie my shoe.

I was so excited about getting out of the house that I didn't even try to put my shoe all the way on. I came down on

Too tired to crawl out of bed, I hit the snooze button and rolled back over in my sleep. Uncle Nard had stayed the night. And after my encounter with Cat-eyes, I swore to myself that I would never go into Mama's bedroom for prayer when she had company. I don't think Uncle Nard would have made a scene if he woke up to me praying at the foot of the bed, but I was too afraid to take a chance. I was tired, and Mama was in good hands with Uncle Nard, or at least in my mind she was.

God was everywhere, so I didn't need to be in Mama's room for Him to hear me and know that I was praying for her. I closed my eyes and said a silent prayer for Mama *and* Uncle Nard. I had so much fun with Uncle Nard that day, that I was eager to mention him in my prayers. He was fill-in Dad, and I his son, regardless of what Mama said.

"God, thank you for Dad taking me to Chuck E. Cheese's. I had a lot of fun. Forgive Mama for dropping me in the tub. She didn't mean to do it. The monkey made her do it. I hope Mama is coming with me and Big-mama to heaven. She can't stay here by herself. In Jesus' name, Amen."

Chapter 9
Home Alone
Wednesday @ 8:00 a.m.

It was Wednesday, and another dreadful day with Mama. Most of the welts on my body were gone. But since the welts had turned into dark marks, there was no way that Mama was going to let me go to school.

It would have been easy to get dressed and leave since Mama didn't wake up until the middle of the day anyway. But then I thought to myself, *Mama said no.* Go to school and risk feeling her wrath when I got home, never. Plus, the only thing that awaited me at school was the giggles and finger pointing by the kids who felt the need to taunt me about my clothes and shoes. It was hard for me to learn anything worrying about the kids and their chatter lingering over my shoulders.

Staying home was my best option, not that I actually had one. Mama said no. And of course, she had the last word.

To avoid getting yelled at, the best thing for me to have done was to stay out of Mama's way on that dark Wednesday. But of course, as a kid, that was hard to do. What I was thinking about was Bible study that night and Big-mama rescuing me from whatever Mama had up her sleeves. Or should I say veins?

"Wake up!" Mama's hoarse, drunken voice stormed into

my bedroom through the closed door.

I jumped up in bed and pushed my back against the wall, since I didn't have a headboard. I watched the bedroom door burst open. I cringed at the sight of Mama.

Mama stood in front of me with a pair of red and black underwear hugging her boney hips. I knew there were breasts behind her pink bra, but a stranger wouldn't have noticed them. Mama's breasts looked to have been getting smaller and smaller by the day.

"You think you're gon' stay home all week and lay up here doing nothing?"

My lips remained sealed with drool. There was nothing to say. Mama had spoken.

"Go get that red bucket from under the kitchen sink. There's a sponge in it. Pour some dishwashing liquid into the bucket and fill it with water. You gon' scrub these walls today. Hell, you the one who dirtied 'em up."

As Mama was heading out of my room, I could not help but to notice her spine. It reminded me of a snake, the way her skin moved along her bones.

"Me and Nard leaving, so you gon' be here by yourself," Mama said from the hall. She was out of sight, yet I could tell that she was standing near the door. Her voice sounded as if she was less than five feet away. "Do not answer the door, and don't touch my phone. I don't care if it's ringing off the hook. Don't you call nobody either. Stay away from the windows, you hear me?"

"Yes," I answered in almost a whisper.

"Did you hear me?" Mama yelled.

I'd already said yes, so I didn't know why she was screaming.

"Yes," I said, a little louder.

"And I called your grandmother to let her know you ain't going to Bible study tonight."

"Nooo," I screamed. I wanted to see Big-mama. I needed to cry my heart out to her and show her all of the X's inscribed in my skin. I would plead with her for the hundredth time to physically remove me from Mama's presence for good.

The fresh marks on my body probably would have been good enough for Big-mama to say, "That's the last time you will ever touch my grandbaby, Crystal. He's coming to live with me."

Even if those were not going to be Big-mama's words, I'd never know. For the first time since being baptized by Pastor Kidd five years earlier, I was missing Bible study.

Mama walked backward into my bedroom like she was retracting her steps. "I said you ain't going to Bible study." She snapped her neck with every word. Mama's right hand was on her right hip, and only inches away from her left hip she was so skinny. "I told your grandmother Nard was taking us out."

My face lit up with happiness that took away the sadness of missing Bible study with Big-mama. Maybe Uncle Nard was taking me back to Chuck E. Cheese's. I clawed at the blanket and staggered out of bed. My feet weren't going fast enough for my mind. I was eager to wrap my arms around Mama's legs and hug her for dear life. Another day out with Uncle Nard, oh I was more than excited.

I embraced Mama's legs, when suddenly she gripped my head with both hands and shoved me away from her.

"You ain't going nowhere!" she said through drunk slurs. "I just told your grandmother that." She turned her back to me and laughed her way out of the room. "Li'l bastard. You gon' stay yo' ass right here."

To be so young, my heart was strong. All of Mama's name calling bounced right off of me. I was used to it.

"You ain't gone be s***! Dirty a**. He ain't your father.

Where the hell is my coke? Get your ass in the tub. My mama can't save you. What she gone do, beat me? You ain't getting nothing for your birthday, I got bills to pay. Damn hands off my wall . . . " Mama spoke down to me so much, all day every day, that even when she wasn't home, her voice still owned the house. I swear I could hear her in the kitchen, the bathroom, the living room, and my room, even as I slept.

Mama's evil spirit prepared its grave in our home, and it refused to give me rest.

I made my way to the kitchen and took the bucket from underneath the sink. I looked up at the faucet, trying to figure out how I was going to fit the bucket underneath it. I glanced from the faucet to the entrance of the kitchen, while my mind stretched beyond the kitchen to Mama's room. I thought about yelling out to Uncle Nard to fill the bucket with water since he was taller than me, but hearing him and Mama argue over who was the biggest drunk as they dressed for their date, immediately caused me to change my mind.

I stood on the tips of my toes, pressed my stomach against the counter, and stretched my arms as far as they could go as I strained to reach the dish washing liquid that sat in the window.

After several minutes of beating the counter and the air trying to get to the dishwashing liquid, I took a spatula from the dishrack and knocked the dishwashing liquid onto the counter. By then I was out of breath, with beads of sweat dressing my forehead.

After I caught my breath, I hung the bucket from my arm, picked up the dishwashing liquid, and headed out of the kitchen and out of the house.

Although the sun had made its presence known by six in the morning, it failed to dry the dew from the grass. It was going on nine, yet the grass was still garbed in droplets of water.

The ground was cold and wet against my bare feet. Any other time I would have skipped back into the house and put on my shoes to protect my feet from the morning elements, but not at that moment. My thoughts were on Mama and Uncle Nard leaving me, and me not being able to go to Bible study with Big-mama. Protecting my feet was the last thing on my mind.

I squeezed dishwashing liquid into the bucket. I then dropped the dishwashing liquid on the grass and picked up one end of the water hose. I reached for the knob on the faucet when I noticed trails of ants on the water hose, around the faucet, and near my feet.

I immediately dropped the water hose and jumped backward. I wanted to run, but I needed to fill the bucket with water and get to work before Mama could find a reason to go off on me.

I looked over my hands and feet to make sure that I did not have any ants crawling on me. I picked up the water hose. With my eyes moving from the ants on the water hose to the ants near my feet, I slowly turned the knob and filled the bucket with water.

I filled the bucket with just enough water to get the job done. My hands were too small and my bones were too weak to carry a big bucket of water into the house.

I cut off the water and dropped the water hose. I dragged the bucket up the three stairs that led to our small porch. I then checked my feet for ants. I banged the front door open with my hip when I suddenly remembered that I'd left the dishwashing liquid in the grass. There was no way that I was going back over there with those ants. I'd wait for them to all crawl away. I left the dishwashing liquid in the grass and headed into the house.

As I stumbled into the house with the bucket, Mama and Uncle Nard were on their way out. For the first time in a long time, Mama looked beautiful.

Mama's hair was pulled back into a ponytail and hung loose at the ends. Waves started at her hairline and worked their way back into the ponytail. The ends of her hair swept against the back of her neck with every movement of her head.

Mama was dressed in a dark brown, spaghetti-strapped, summer dress with checkered designs. The designs resembled a maze, with each turn being marked by a new color. The color continued on for three or four squares before being cut off by a new color, which switched the direction of the maze.

On the outside, Mama was the beautiful Mama that I wished for, but on the inside she was as sour as a lime.

"You leaving me?" I pouted.

"Yes, we're going to breakfast and then an early matinee or something," Mama answered. "Don't forget what I told you."

The holes in Mama's arms were very visible, and Mama was so into herself that I could tell that she didn't care. She snapped her head from right to left in confidence. Her eyes fluttered and her lips smacked. She rolled her eyes at no one in particular as she tugged on the end of her ponytail. Mama's hair had never been that smooth before, and I loved it.

Mama was dark and beautifully lovely. But that day she could have passed for being Indian, or mixed even.

"Okay." I cried without visible tears. There was hurt in my voice. I didn't expect Mama to recognize it. She ignored everything else about me, including my existence. That is, when she was not beating me.

With a heart as cold as a winter storm, Mama would never admit to the pain that she put me through.

Mama pushed past me. She spun on the front of her sandals and stared at the back of Uncle Nard's head as he spoke to me.

"You a big boy, right?" Uncle Nard asked me.

I stared into his eyes from the top of my sad eyes. I nodded in sync with the nod of his head. Uncle Nard was indirectly coaching me into agreeing that I was a big boy, and I played right along with him. On the outside, I would be his big boy if he wanted me to. But on the inside, I felt like withdrawing into a fetal position and weeping like a baby.

"I know that's right." Uncle Nard smiled. He was moving so much that the bottom of his green Polo shirt would rise to the middle of his stomach, exposing his belly button. Pulling down on the shirt proved to be useless. Because every time he moved, his shirt crawled right back up again.

Uncle Nard had grown so used to pulling down his shirt that he pulled on it even before it had a chance to rise.

"Don't mess with the stove, and stay out the windows," Uncle Nard told me. "Leave that phone alone too. Don't be calling nobody. Your mama said not to touch her phone. That means you can't even call your grandmother, you hear me?"

This time I nodded on my own, and it had nothing to do with what Uncle Nard was telling me to do and not to do. The mention of Mama's name is what made me nod. I knew that if I went against his or her strict instructions, I would be out of school for another week with fresh, open wounds.

"Go on in there and start scrubbing them walls," Uncle Nard said with a smirk on his face. His teeth appeared to have gotten darker overnight, like the color of roasted chestnuts. They reminded me of sunflower seeds. As a kid, I didn't know them as sunflower seeds. I was always told that they were poliseeds, which I later learned was just another word used to describe them.

Mama would hang out in front of the house, spitting sunflower seeds all over the ground while she, one of my uncles, and her friends would stand outside whispering, joking, and laughing about the neighborhood whore, Christine, whom Mama nicknamed Herp. Herp was short for herpes. My young ears did not know what herpes was, but I could tell by their laughs that it was nothing good.

Each time Mama mentioned the name Herp, frowns spread across faces, heads shook in disgust, and the men made threats of killing any woman who gave them herpes.

Mama always seemed to enjoy degrading Christine. And the smile on Mama's face when the men spoke of death was priceless.

"Okay," I moaned

I slid the bucket across the floor next to the coffee table and closed the door. I leaped onto the couch on my knees and started to pull back the curtain to watch Mama and Uncle Nard drive away. But as my fingers slipped between the curtains, Mama's voice started ringing in my imagination.

"Didn't I tell you not to get in the window? Just that quick you done forgot. Bet you won't forget me taking a belt to your hard-headed ass," is what I could hear Mama screaming if she caught me in the window.

The last thing I wanted was for Mama to lock eyes with me as I peered out of the window. Yet, just like any other kid, I was willing to learn the hard way.

With my next breath lingering in my throat, I edged the curtain back and watched Mama and Uncle Nard take off without me. I was sad, but I didn't feel alone. I was feeling some kind of way, but it was not alone. How could a child, who was always in the presence of pain and grief when their mother was around, feel alone?

Chapter 10
Curious Michael
Wednesday @ 7:00 a.m.

I woke up around seven that evening. My pillow was soaked with tears I was so hungry. I didn't bother to go into the kitchen and fix anything to eat. I knew without crawling out of bed that the refrigerator and the cabinets were empty. Even if there was something frozen beyond recognition in the freezer, Mama already said I couldn't go near the stove.

The walls cleaned themselves, because I did not do them. Let's just say that quickly I forgot. Mama wouldn't notice that the walls were not clean anyway. She'd only told me to clean the walls because she figured it would keep me busy and out of mishap all day. The drugs kept her brain blind to everything. As soon as she walked through the door, her arm would be lying across Uncle Nard's lap with the contents of a needle poisoning her veins, and eventually her brain.

As long as Mama was okay, I could have lived with the thought of her never coming home again. Uncle Nard, on the other hand, I did not want to live without, except when he agreed with Mama and her threats to beat me.

When Uncle Nard sided with Mama, all I could think about was Big-mama. Aside from Uncle Nard, Big-mama was the only other person who could save me.

Mama kept Big-mama away from the house, or at least she tried to. You can't keep your mother away from your house if you gave her a key. A key to the house meant come any time you want, and that's exactly what Big-mama did.

With spit running down the sides of my mouth, I crawled out of bed and found my way to Mama's room. A monster was inside of my stomach roaring, and there was nothing in the refrigerator to silence it.

Mama often kept snacks in her room, mainly Cheetos, lemon cookies, and sometimes turkey sandwiches that Uncle Nard would stop and get from 7-Eleven on his way to our apartment. The sandwiches were supposed to be refrigerated, but of course Mama didn't care. A turkey sandwich could sit in Mama's room for two or three days and she'd still eat it.

Now that I think about it, Mama keeping snacks in her room was probably one of the reasons why she didn't worry about shopping for food. As long as she had something to eat, she had no reason to worry about me eating. It was always all about Mama.

I expected Mama's bedroom door to be locked, because she normally locked it when she left me at home by myself. My eyes lit up as bright as the sun at the complete turn of the doorknob. Out of fear, I looked in back of me. I don't know exactly why. But I'm sure it was because I knew I wasn't supposed to be in Mama's room, especially when she was not there. All I needed was for her to appear behind me out of nowhere.

I crept into the room and closed the door behind me. In less than a second, I was all over the room searching for chips, candy, anything to stop my stomach from tormenting me.

Mama's room was trashed, as usual. I stepped over dirty underwear and extra small bras. I went around red and blue party cups; the kind of cups that Mama had at her late night parties.

I spotted a small, corner piece of a gold and black Magnum condom wrapper on the floor next to the bed, right beside a pair of oversized men's boxer briefs. The boxers belonged to Uncle Nard. I could tell by the size of them. Plus, Uncle Nard was the last man to be with Mama. Mama never left evidence of one man around for another man to see. Mama stayed high, but not stupid. Risk having her drugs cut off by one uncle after seeing the end results of Mama being with another uncle? Mama would never allow that to happen.

It's funny, because the drugs had Mama wrapped around the pipe when it came to being a mother to me. But even when she was high, she knew to hide all evidence of her whorish ways.

The bedroom reeked of body odors. Notice I said *odors* and not odor. As bad as it smelled, it couldn't have come from only one person. Mama was never alone, so I can't say that she made the smell by herself.

There was so much junk on the floor that I found myself hopping on one foot, like a kid during a game of hopscotch. The third or fourth jump left me crying out in pain.

"Awww, Big-mama," I cried after I crashed, left foot first, into a corner of the bed. My body collapsed to the floor. I wrapped my hands around my foot, toppled backward with my hand still cradling my foot, and rolled back-and-forth over Mama's trifling ways.

I cried for Big-mama to stop the pain. A kid my age would have normally screamed "Mama," but not me. I can't think of one time that Mama ran to my side and wiped away my tears. She was too busy causing them.

The plastic cups cracked beneath my back. I rolled over a pile of clothes and back over the cups again.

I continued to roll from left to right until my toes stopped aching. I then peeled my hand from around my foot and lay on my back with my arms and legs spread apart like an eagle.

My eyes inspected every corner of the ceiling until they found rest on a small, black spider. I watched the spider crawl back and forth over a web that wasn't visible to me, but that I knew was there. The spider had to be crawling on something.

The spider dropped from the invisible web, making a new web along the way. It crawled back up the new web and continued up and down its original path.

I was intrigued by the spider and how fast it spun its new web. It was as if it became bored or tired of its old home, and was in a hurry to build a new one. If only it were that easy for me to escape into a new life. I would have taken Big-mama with me and prayed daily for Mama's safety.

I could have lie there all day and watched the spider spin one new home after the next, but I didn't know what time Mama and Uncle Nard would be home, and I did not want to get caught in Mama's room.

I set my mind back on the task at hand, which was to find something—anything—to eat, and get out of Mama's room just as quickly as I had found my way in there.

I rolled onto my stomach and pressed the palms of my hands down on the floor. I was about to push myself up to my feet when I spotted Mama's photo album beneath the bed. The curious child in me wanted to see it for the hundredth time. I don't know if it was the excitement of seeing Mama and Big-mama getting along, even if it was only in a picture, or if the sorrow that loomed at the end of the album was calling out to me. Whatever the case might have been, I was determined to satisfy my curiosity.

When Mama was eleven, Big-mama bought her the photo album for Christmas. Baby pictures and pictures of Mama's birthday parties were placed against a thin, sticky board, and covered by a clear film. There were also pictures of happy times with the family; pictures of Mama, Big-mama, cousins, aunts, uncles, grandparents, and friends. Mama had even drawn pictures of flowers and happy faces on the cover.

Mama was clearly a happy kid. But at some point the album grew dark and angry. Whatever source was responsible for Mama's anger and sorrow, it followed her into adulthood and rained down on me with blows and insults.

Mama added pictures of her and her drunken friends to what should have been a memorabilia for me to share with my children's children. Pictures of sexual poses, middle fingers crossed in an X, and gang signs followed a picture of Mama blowing out sixteen candles. Across the middle of the cover were small, black, heart-shaped stickers that spelled out the words "I hate Mama." Mama was talking about my Big-mama. The once red, yellow, pink, and green flowers that decorated the cover were transformed into black roses. Mama took a permanent black marker and colored over the soft colors in each bud.

There was a picture of me and Big-mama taped to the cover. All I could see past the red bolts of lightning that Mama had scribbled over our faces and bodies was me sitting on Big-mama's left knee, like a man on a horse, with my back pressed against her breasts. I looked to be around two or three. I was wrapped in Big-mama's big arms, with a handsome smile on my face.

My smile had nothing on Big-mama's beautiful smile. Her teeth were as white as snow. They lined her gums with one tooth touching the next. I could not make out what we were wearing or how our hair was styled. It looked like Mama put a lot of time and work into trying to scratch me and Big-mama out of her life. Our heads matched the black roses.

The smiles on our faces were left untouched. Now that

I think about it, I wonder why Mama spared our smiles but tried her best to destroy our bodies. Only Mama knew the answer to that.

I scurried beneath the bed on my belly. For a minute, it seemed like I had crawled into another world it was so clean. Other than the photo album, two boxes of shoes, and a little dust, my new world was empty.

I pulled on one corner of the photo album, but it didn't budge. I pulled on it a second time. Again, it did not move. Mama had to have added more pictures to the album, because just a year before, I weighed less and could move it.

I pushed on the photo album until it slid out from the opposite side of the bed. I crawled backward and back into Mama's sex den, also known as her drug lab. I continued on all fours around the bed to the photo album.

Instead of trying to pick the photo album up onto my lap, I lay on my stomach in front of it. I flipped back the cover with quickness.

The first page was covered by four pictures that took up the entire page. In each picture, Mama appeared to be staring me in my eyes like she was silently scolding me for being in her room. Mama was probably around my age in the pictures, but that did not stop me from fearing the look in her eyes. You know that look your mother gives you when you are acting up? That is the look that seven-year-old Crystal was giving me in every picture.

I turned my attention to the pictures on the opposite side of the page. In one picture Mama was dressed in a checkered, navy blue and powdered blue school uniform with a white collar. I imagine she was in the first or second grade due to her missing front teeth and two ponytails that were separated by a part that zigzagged down the middle of her head. Mama's smile was as wide as the smile that I held on the cover of the photo album, only I had all of my teeth.

A second picture showed Mama blowing out four candles on a white cake with whole strawberry toppings. Mama was dressed in a pink and yellow shirt with pink shorts that stopped at her knees. The front of her hair was pulled up into a bun with a pink butterfly barrette on either side of it. The back hung loose with spiral curls sweeping across her shoulders. Mama was surrounded by Big-mama, Mama's cousins, aunts, uncles, and many of Mama's friends.

Two other pictures were of Mama and four kids at play. One of the pictures was taken in front of Big-mama's old house, while the second picture was taken at a park.

I turned the page, expecting to see baby pictures of Mama. Instead I was met by a blank page. Mama was probably caught in one of her moments of feeling sorry for herself, and with drunken tears running down her face, ripped picture after picture of herself from the photo album.

I can see Mama now, flipping through the photo album and reflecting on when she was sane and free of drugs. It should have hurt her heart to see who and what she had become over the years. Then again, she would have to possess emotions in order to feel sorrow or disappointment, and Mama was far from emotional.

The next two pages were blank, but I did not let a couple of blank pages stop me from continuing on in my state of curiosity.

I flipped the third page to the dark side of Mama. The very first picture left me slamming the album closed. Mama was seated on the couch with her back pressed against the back of the couch. Her feet were propped up on top of a wooden coffee table. The spaghetti strap sleeves of her red gown hung off her shoulders. Smoke spewed from her mouth and nose.

I pushed the album back beneath the bed and I shoved my back against a wall. I then scanned the room for something to get into. I was like a lonely dog in search of food, water, and maybe even a new master.

I stood and thumped the carpet with the heel of my left foot. I jerked my head from left to right while humming a song that Big-mama and I made up on our way to church one day. I looked from the dresser to a pile of shoes and boxes behind the bedroom door in hopes of finding something to hold my attention.

I looked to my left at Mama's nightstand. My eyes lit up at the sight of her mini drug lab. I always wanted to touch a needle and see how it felt. At that moment, I had my chance.

I dropped to my knees. I then walked on my knees to the nightstand.

The nightstand was covered with needles, three spoons, six very small bottles with a clear liquid inside, a rainbow of lighters, and rubber ties that I thought were big rubber bands.

I picked up one of the rubber ties and held it by both ends. I held my arms out as wide as they would go, stretching the rubber tie to see how long I could make it. I then looked it over. I spun it above my head like a cowboy does a rope as the cowboy prepares to catch a bull by its horns. My fingers moved along the rubber tie as visions of it cutting off the blood circulation in Mama's arms, and making her veins visible to the needle, flashed before my eyes.

I wanted to see what it felt like to have the rubber tie wrapped around my arm. Mama loved it every day of my life, so I was not worried about it hurting me.

Mama was very skilled with the rubber tie. One time I watched her wrap it around her arm, put one end between her teeth, and pull on the other end. The veins that were once hidden beneath her dark skin made themselves known.

I tied the rubber tie around my arm. I followed Mama's lead and put one end between my teeth while pulling on the other end. The needles then called my inquiring mind, and I was eager to answer them.

I picked a needle up from the nightstand and put the tip to my arm. Just as I was about to puncture my skin and test the poison that turned Mama into Satan himself, I heard Mama's dry giggles in the next room.

Chapter 11
Music to My Soul
Wednesday @ 2:00 p.m.

The needle went flying across the room as fast as I had picked it up. My heart jumped against my chest and my head felt light, like it was floating. I swear the bed was moving as I struggled to free my arm from the rubber tie.

I tossed the rubber tie back onto the nightstand and slid beneath the bed. I pushed myself over to Mama's side of the bed. My uncles' side of the bed was too close to the door, and I feared that Mama and Uncle Nard would see me as soon as they walked into the room.

My heart was beating for me to slide out from beneath the bed and run to my room. But no, I stayed right where I was. I was not about to risk getting caught by Mama's heavy hand and her manly voice.

I lay on my stomach listening and fearfully waiting for Mama and Uncle Nard to retreat to the bedroom. They could have easily walked into my room to check on me. And when they saw that I was not there, search the house until Uncle Nard managed to convince Mama to call 911. Why would Uncle Nard have to convince Mama to call 911? Just think about the abuse that I had sustained at the hands of the woman, who instead of protecting me, beat me. Do you really think she was worried about my safety? Then again, Mama peeking into my room to see if I was okay like a normal, loving mother was far from my reality. A loving mother would have never left me alone in the first place.

"Are you staying the night, Nard?" Mama's giggles made their way to her bedroom.

I watched her leap for the bed and then kick off her heels. I could tell by the position of her feet, as they hung off the edge of the bed that she was lying on her stomach. Her toes were pointed downward.

Uncle Nard wobbled into the room and dropped his pants down to his ankles. I guess he silently answered Mama's question about him staying the night.

Uncle Nard walked up to the bed and nudged Mama's legs apart with his knees. He stood between her legs and laid every bit of his three-hundred-pound frame on top of her. The bottom of the bed, my ceiling for the moment, came down on me. When the cracked, wooden frame touched the back of my head, I pressed the right side of my face against the floor. From the corners of my eyes, I then watched the wooden frame come down on me.

The bed came down on the left side of my face. Pain traveled from my jaw, through my face, and down my neck. The combination of both of their weight was slowly killing me, and there was no way for me to save myself.

"Hold on, Nard, let me go check on Michael." Mama's voice was strained and short of breath. "Nard, I can't breathe," she huffed. "Get up. I need to check on Michael."

I prayed for Uncle Nard to stay right where he was. Yes, I was in pain. Yes, Mama was having a difficult time breathing. No, I did not want her to die. I also did not want him to free her, which would have caused an all-out war once she discovered that I was not in my room.

To understand my thought process, one had to understand that I was very mature beyond my years. I was forced to grow up before my time, and I did not have a voice in it. Mama handed me my "man card" without instruction. Cooking, cleaning, and picking Mama up from the floor when the monkey knocked her down was my life. No one but my uncles, Mama, Big-mama, and I knew it. I had no idea what it was like to be a normal, happy-go-lucky kid. If I was caught making childish mistakes, I received teenage, and sometimes adult, penalties.

"He's okay. The boy been taking care of himself for the longest." Uncle Nard heaved. He was already out of breath, and their bodies had not yet united as one and created music together.

"Okay, Nard." Mama sighed with an attitude. "Can I take off my dress before you ruin it with all of your sweat?"

I was so relieved that Uncle Nard was able to talk Mama out of looking in on me that I almost cried. Tears of happiness beat tears of pain any day.

Mama's and Uncle Nard's weight shifted from the middle of the bed to Uncle Nard's side of the bed. My face was free of pain. I could now breathe easy, without flinching with their every movement.

Mama stood and slipped out of her dress. From where I was lying, all I could see was her panties and her dress sliding down to her ankles, and her stepping out of them.

Uncle Nard stood up from the bed and walked up to Mama. He left no room between them. I was blind to his next moves, but whatever they were doing had Mama singing to me through her moans.

Mama heaved a deep breath. I yawned. She sighed. I sighed beneath my breath. My eyes then fluttered as I fought to stay awake. The music was destined to put me to sleep, but I was not ready. I wanted to live in its melody and wrap myself in its warmth, yet my mind sought otherwise.

Instead of the music causing my heart to flutter like it normally did, it loosened every muscle in my body and weakened me. It caused my eyes to disobey my heart and grow heavy with sleep. Something was wrong. The music was not supposed to put me to sleep. I didn't want to go to sleep. I wanted to stay up and enjoy the oh so sweet melody that their bodies made against the stained sheets. I tried to shake the sleep off of me, but I was slowly losing the fight. Eventually I lost and found myself drifting off into a deep sleep.

I tried to assume my favorite sleeping position, with my knees tucked beneath me and my butt in the air, but the bed was too low. As many times as I had hidden beneath Mama's bed while listening to her and my uncles' lovemaking, I should have remembered how little room I had to get comfortable.

I dropped my legs with my toes pointed in opposite directions. I placed my right hand on top of my left hand and made a manmade pillow. The right side of my face massaged my pillow as it searched for comfort.

Several minutes passed since sleep had owned me. The longer I struggled to find comfort in my awkward position, the less my sleep controlled me.

The discomfort eventually shook sleep completely off of me and allowed me to stay up and continue to listen to my favorite music.

"Nard," Mama said in a soft whisper. She lay on her back, her legs spread apart. I could see one of her legs hanging off the side of the bed and her other leg hanging off the foot of the bed.

Uncle Nard's side of the bed dropped just inches from the floor. The downed mattress blocked my view of the door, but I was not mad. What I wanted did not require sight. All I had to do was to listen.

Mama's and Uncle Nard's moans grew louder and louder as their breaths grew shorter. The bed moved up and down, but very slowly. I closed my eyes and allowed their lust to take hold of me. Before I knew it, I was fast asleep.

Chapter 12
Starved
Thursday @ 4:00 a.m.

My eyes blinked open. I had no clue of the time, but believed that it was either around four in the morning, or close to it. It could have been after four, but I doubt it. I knew my body. I had never been late for Mama's prayer; early, but never late. And on the days that I did not make it to Mama's room, it was not because I had overslept. Someone was entertaining Mama, and I was not going to be staring down the barrel of unfamiliar eyes again.

I stretched out the kinks in my arms and legs as hunger bruised the walls of my stomach and caused my belly to speak to me. Growls and roars threatened to wake Mama and Uncle Nard. I pushed down on my stomach to muzzle the noise, but it refused to be silenced. Food was the only answer to my dilemma. Since there was no food in the house, I knew that I would be forced to listen to my nagging stomach until someone loved me enough to feed me.

I was starving, too hungry to think of a prayer for Mama. I needed something to eat, so saving Mama from her sins would have to wait.

Being careful not to make any noise, I slithered out from beneath the bed and stayed on my stomach until I made it to the door. The door was cracked, but not wide enough for me to slip out of the room without touching it. I rose to my feet. I placed my right hand on the doorknob and covered it with my left hand.

With my thoughts on opening the door without making the slightest sound, I glanced back over my left shoulder and cut my eyes through the darkness at the joined, naked figures that lie in bed.

Uncle Nard lay on his left side facing Mama. His left arm pinned Mama's arm down at her side, while his right arm was stretched out beneath her neck.

Mama was all over Uncle Nard. She appeared as a baby, fast asleep on her father's chest. She lay on her side with her left leg folded beneath her. Her right leg was at an angle over Uncle Nard's waist. I could not see her left arm, but her right arm was pinned down at her side. Her breasts were smashed against his chest. Mama and Uncle Nard appeared as the epitome of a loving husband and wife. A temporary married couple that would rip each other a new spirit had they been awake.

As I stood in front of the door watching them sleep, my thoughts drifted away from their nakedness and back to my throbbing stomach. The monster inside of my stomach was on the loose. His roars were much louder than before, and he twisted my stomach into knots to let me know that he was not going to leave peacefully until I answered to him.

I pulled open the door and ran on the tips of my toes down the hall to the kitchen. My toes met the floor with light thumps and came to a rest just over the kitchen's threshold. Although I knew it was probably useless to search for food, I had to at least let the monster in my belly know that I was putting forth an effort.

I did not bother to turn on the kitchen light. I gazed

through the darkness until my eyes adjusted to my surroundings. Between the bright, green light from the time on the microwave, and the light above the neighbor's back patio door that pierced our kitchen window and cast a streak of light on the kitchen floor, I could see everything inside of the kitchen just as clearly as I would have, had I turned on the light.

I stood in front of the refrigerator. I already knew what to expect before I opened the door. No milk for calcium, no fruit for healthy eating, and no eggs for protein; nothing to help me grow into a healthy adult, but everything to remind me of our dysfunctional household.

Whatever was inside of the refrigerator had been in there for weeks. And in the case of ketchup, mustard and mayonnaise, months.

I pulled open the refrigerator door and tightened my eyes at the extra bright refrigerator light.

When the refrigerator light blew out months earlier, instead of Mama replacing it with an appliance bulb that had a low wattage, she used a regular, one hundred watt light bulb, which was much brighter than an appliance bulb.

It took a few seconds for my eyes to adjust to the bright light. When they did, my heart jumped in happiness, while the monster in my stomach continued its rage. A silver, brown, and white bag sat on the top shelf. I recognized the bag as the bag that the Cheesecake Factory placed me and Big-mama's Styrofoam to-go container inside of. She and I had lunch there with some of the ushers of the church one Sunday.

When I grabbed the knot that held the bag closed, the bag rattled fear into my pulse. My hands trembled. I worried that the noise would wake Mama and that she'd catch me with my "hand in the cookie jar."

It's interesting. I was more worried about Mama catching

me with her food than I was her waking up to an empty container sitting on top of the full trashcan, or the beating that was promised to follow once she saw that I had eaten her food. I was hungry. At that moment, feeding the roaring monster inside of my stomach was the only thing on my mind.

Instead of carrying the noisy bag over to the table, I placed it on the floor at my feet. I crouched down in front of the bag and went straight for the knot that held the two handles together. I pulled and tugged at the knot like a cat going through trash. The rattling of the bag grew so loud that I threw my hands off of the bag, flopped down on my butt, and backed away from the bag.

It was a matter of time before Mama came storming into the kitchen with her hand fiending to slap me. Either that or a belt held back over her shoulder, just a swing away from cutting into my back, legs, or stomach.

A loud roll of thunder cut into my terrified heart. I snapped my neck around just in time to see a bolt of lightning streaking the skies outside of the kitchen window. Seconds later, I could hear rain meeting the ground like water in a shower.

The thunder and lightning scared me so bad that I contemplated running into Mama's bedroom and jumping into bed with her and Uncle Nard. Mama would not have wrapped her arms around me and accepted my fear. No, she probably would have been upset that it was not my fear of her that I was running from.

My eyes rested on the kitchen window as I nervously waited for the next bolt of lightning to compete with the light from the moon. It never came, and neither did Mama.

My heart slowed to its innocent beat. The fear that I was feeling escaped through my last, quick breath. My breathing returned to its normal pace, and it was now time to feed the fuming roars in my stomach.

I looked over the knot on the bag, longing for whatever was inside while knowing that there was no way I could loosen the knot without disturbing Mama's silent night.

I abandoned the idea of fighting with the knot and went with my only other option. I ripped open the bag with my teeth and pulled on it until the only thing that was standing between me and my missed breakfast, lunch, and dinner from the day before was the lid to the container.

I raised the lid and stared down at six cold cut sandwiches and a salad with a small, plastic container of Ranch salad dressing on the side. I turned my nose up at the salad and the spotted dressing. The dressing reminded me of an adult movie that I once watched as Mama sat across from me on the sofa, high off the prescription drug, Demerol.

Mama had inserted the devil's movie into the DVD player before washing down two Demerols with a mixture of Vodka and cranberry juice. I remember that day like the back of my hand. I walked around the house trying to find something to get into. I was around six at the time and had outgrown all of my baby toys years before that. Of course, Mama did not bother to buy me any new ones. Instead, she screamed for me to be quiet as I played with my imaginary friend, and forced me to stay inside of the house while all of the kids from the neighborhood were outside playing.

I trampled the floor from my room into the dining room, trying to get Mama to notice how sad I was. I was too scared to walk all the way into the living room. I didn't want to be too close to Mama just in case she decided to turn her house slipper into a boomerang, like she so often did when she was too lazy to stand and slap me.

Mama did not even look at me. She just sat there with her right arm propped up on the armrest with an empty pill bottle curled beneath her fingers. Her left arm lay across the pillow next to her with a small, empty, wine glass teetering between her fingers.

The television was on. I could hear a man talking as music played in the background. But from where I was standing, I could not see the television screen, not that I was interested. Mama and her deathly pose had my full attention.

I watched Mama's chest rise and fall. I stood as still as a statue, hoping for movement of her arms and legs. I must have stood there for a good five minutes waiting for Mama to do something, anything but just lie there.

When Mama's arms and legs failed to move with her rising chest, I crept into the living room and stood in front of her with my eyes glued to her eyes.

I watched Mama's eyes open and close. Right before her eyes closed, her pupils rolled back into her head. Mama appeared to be a blink away from death.

When Mama's eyes dropped for the last time, I leaned in closer to her. For the first time, I stood in her face without flinching. All of a sudden I heard music; the same music that kept me awake most nights.

The music sounded nothing like the music that Mama and my uncles made together. The woman behind the moans had a high-pitched voice like an opera singer. The man's voice was real deep. He sounded like one of Mama's favorite singers, Berry White. Both the man's and woman's voices were in harmony. This time I was granted the opportunity to see the vocalist behind the music.

My socks helped me to spin around to the act on the television. I won't describe what I witnessed in detail. However, I will say that a man's and a woman's bodies were confined to each other and twisted into a knot, maybe even a pretzel.

Without taking my eyes off the television, I held my left arm out at my side and walked to my left. My hand served as a guide stick as I made my way over to the loveseat.

I climbed onto the loveseat and watched the two lovers' performance with as much excitement in my heart as I had when I watched my favorite cartoons. I was in a zone. My emotions, not my eyes or my mind, were glued to the television. I was very calm. There wasn't an ounce of fear within me.

Mama could have awakened at that very moment and caught me watching her "soap opera," and I wouldn't have so much as flinched at the sight of her fist. Honestly, I don't think Mama would have done anything to me if she'd caught me. As unfit as she was, she probably would have sat there watching it with me.

I watched Mama's "soap opera" until the man relived himself on the woman. When the man rolled off of her, both the music on the television and the music in my head stopped. The man's yucky fluids—like Ranch dressing—turned my stomach and sent me running out of the living room to my bedroom.

My stomach now roaring brought my thoughts back to the present. I removed four of the six cold cut sandwiches from the container and closed the lid. I placed the sandwiches on top of the lid and ate all of them while wearing a smile on my face. I put the half-filled Styrofoam container back into the refrigerator and closed the door. I dropped my eyes to the bag, trying to figure out how I could pick it up without making any noise. The rattling of the bag was inevitable, but I could not leave it on the floor.

Holding my breath, I picked up the bag and rushed over to the trashcan. I shoved the bag down into one side of the trashcan and ran out of the kitchen to my room. I was full, sleepy, and anxious to crawl into bed and pull the blanket over my head. My body embraced my sheets. I took a deep breath. Thinking about how good the sandwiches were, I allowed my mind to drift off to sleep.

I went to bed with a smile on my face, but only God knew what I was going to wake up to.

Chapter 13
Mama's Wrath
Thursday @ 8:00 a.m.

"Who the hell told you to eat my damn food?" Mama screamed while torturing my unconscious body with three switches that she braided together into what felt like a knife. The switches ripped my skin apart and fully awakened me from my sleep.

I jumped up in bed with my blanket in hand. I backed against the wall and covered myself with the blanket from the neck down.

Mama was naked and full of rage. The whites of her eyes were as red as fire. The corners of her mouth were bound by crust. Her skin was an ash white, or maybe even gray, and her hair was all over the place.

Mama stumbled from left to right in a drunken state. Her body, from the waist up, moved in a circular motion.

"Awww!" I cried.

"Huh?" Mama continued to scream. "Did anybody tell you that food was for you?"

My cries prevented me from answering Mama.

"Did they?" Mama growled.

I still didn't answer her. I couldn't. My body was stinging so bad that I could not talk past my cries.

Mama waved the switches around like a teacher shaking a ruler at a disobedient student. I should have prayed for Mama that morning. The devil and the monkey were riding her back. While she was screaming and calling me a "little brat who thinks he can walk around here messing with stuff that don't belong to him," I prayed on the inside for the devil to turn Mama loose.

After years of abuse, I learned to deal with the wrath of the drugs, but the monkey and the devil riding Mama's spirit? I was in trouble. Mama looked so bad that I could easily compare her to death itself. All she was missing was the casket.

If it wasn't the devil, then who was it? God would never let Mama sit back and beat me with three switches over no food. He would have struck Mama down like lightening on a tree.

"Oh, you not gon' answer me?" Mama asked through gritted teeth.

The switches sliced my legs through the blanket. I was in so much pain that my tongue vibrated against my teeth. I couldn't answer Mama even if I did have an excuse for eating her food without asking first. My screams controlled my voice box, just like the switches controlled my pain.

The switches rained down on me with fury. Mama spared my face, but showed no mercy to my body when I failed to answer her.

I jumped around the bed, ducking and dodging the switches. Each time I jumped to avoid the lashes, the blanket flew off a different part of my body, inviting the switches to have their way with me.

There was no escaping the switches. All I could do was make sure that I didn't get hit in the same area twice, which was almost impossible to do. Mama was welding the switches like a mad woman. The expression on her face matched her angry actions.

"Now get in there and finish the rest of that food," she ordered. "Ate what you wanted to eat and left the scraps! We don't waste food around here." Mama's head snapped back and her hysterical laughs bounced off my bedroom walls.

All of a sudden she was laughing for no reason at all. Mama went from Mommy Dearest to a laughing hyena at the blink of an eye.

With my eyes on the sword in Mama's hand, I crawled, slid, and scooted to the foot of the bed. Mama smacked her lips and crossed her arms, aggravated by how slow I was going. She shifted from her right foot to her left foot while waving the switches like a hand fan.

"Hurry yo' tail up and get in there!" Mama was screaming and cussing so much that she was losing her voice. Her words faded in and out. "And I see you didn't—" The switches came down on my back and forced me out of bed and onto the floor. "—Clean," Mama said, pausing between each hit.

"Awww, Big-mama!" I cried.

Before I could stand, the switches penetrated my shoulder.

"My walls—" Mama puffed. It felt like the switches had engraved an X into my back. "—Like I told—" She grumbled through clenched teeth. My right foot caught the switches before I could fold my feet beneath me. "—You to," Mama said and held her breath. My right arm received five lashes in a row as Mama finished her rant.

"Why the hell didn't you clean my walls like I told you to?" Mama held the switches back over her shoulder. She went to bring them down on me, when I jumped to my feet and ran out of the room to the kitchen.

The first thing I noticed when I walked into the kitchen was the Styrofoam container that once held the cold-cuts.

It was sitting in the middle of the floor with the lid pulled completely back. A white, plastic fork was stuck inside of the salad that was now dressed in Ranch dressing. The other two cold-cuts that I left for Mama were gone.

"You gon' eat all of that," Mama said, appearing behind me. "You don't pick and choose around here."

The cold-cuts churned in my stomach. Bits and pieces of bologna, lettuce, bacon, cheese, and whatever else was on the cold-cuts, worked their way up my throat and stopped right before exiting my mouth.

The food lingered in my throat in the form of a knot and made it difficult for me to breathe. The sight of the Ranch dressing did not make it any better. I could not stand to look at it, and here Mama was forcing me to eat it.

My two index fingers pulled down on my bottom lip. My feet dragged along the kitchen floor to what I viewed as death waiting to happen. Yes, believing that I would die from indulging in Ranch dressing was a bit extreme, but the thoughts were still there.

"Get down there and eat it!" Mama ordered. She shoved me in my back and pushed me closer to what I just knew would kill me. Her nails gripped my right shoulder and forced me to the floor.

"Pick up the fork!" she commanded. "You gon' eat all of that dead salad!"

Dead, I thought. *How was salad dead?* I looked down at the salad, beyond the white fluid, at the leaves. The leaves were pink in some areas and a purplish-black in other areas. The corner of almost every leaf was broken, with small, black holes within them.

Mama noticed my hesitation. "If you don't pick that fork up and eat that salad, I'm going to beat you in the head with my fist," she threatened. Mama made good on her threats. "I see them switches ain't working, because you still ain't doing what you supposed to be doing."

Mama's fists were small, but they were big enough to spill my thoughts from my head onto the floor and knock me unconscious.

I reached down and picked up the fork. I shook three small pieces of salad from the fork and stared at the dressing that covered the tip of the fork.

"You supposed to eat." Mama's fist met the left side of my face, causing the right side of my head to crash to the floor with a loud thud. My body bounced off the floor. My left foot landed on top of the Styrofoam container, tossing the salad into the air.

"Look what you did!" Mama screamed.

"You made me do it," I whimpered.

"What you say?" Mama's left eye drew partially closed. I could immediately tell that I hit her last nerve with my accusation.

Why was my mother beating me? What mother could hate their child as much as my mother hated me? Why was I lying there beneath an umbrella of hate; Mama towering over me with her right foot raised to stomp my intestines out of me? She despised me past those cold-cuts. Eating her food had nothing to do with her knocking me in my head with her fist. Mama's anger ran deeper than a cold sandwich.

With all the beatings with the belt, the lashes with the switches, and the blows to the head, I should have been dead years ago. The sad part about it was that I prayed every night for God to spare Mama's soul, because I knew He had the power to free her lungs of air for all of the bad things that she had done to me.

"I made you do it?" Mama yelled. Her spit bathed my face. "Get up!" She grabbed me by the front of my shirt, twisted her hand within my shirt, and snatched me up to my feet. I blocked my face with my hands and looked between them and through my fingers at Mama. I just knew she was about to slap the taste out of my mouth.

"Go on the back porch and get the broom. Sweep this mess up. Then you gonna wash these walls like I told you to do yesterday!"

"Okay." I sobbed.

I turned away from Mama to walk to the back porch where the washer and dryer was, when I heard pounding on the front door. I glanced back over my shoulder at Mama, who was looking at me.

"Go get the broom," Mama said, storming out of the kitchen.

I walked to the back porch, wondering who was at the door. My uncles only showed up at night, and Big-mama had a key. It couldn't have been Uncle Nard, because he had spent the night. He was already here.

Whoever was at the door was not leaving until they entered our den of hell.

"Why Michael ain't been to school this week?" I heard my savior angrily ask Mama. My Big-mama showed up, and right on time.

"Because he's sick!" Once again, Mama lied. "He has the chickenpox." Mama's lies slid off her tongue like hot butter on bread. She was very skilled at lying, and Big-mama knew it. But lying about a kid having chickenpox? That's actually believable, and no one wants to be around a person with chickenpox.

Big-mama loved me too much to stay away, even if I was contagious. Thank God I wasn't. And when I was standing in the laundry room with my arms wrapped around the broomstick listening to Mama tell one lie after the other, I pleaded with God to send Big-mama to search for me.

"Big-mama, I'm in the kitchen," my heart cried out, but my voice remained silent.

"So why you didn't call the school and tell them he had chickenpox?" Big-mama questioned Mama. "They said they been calling and calling and you ain't answering the phone. You knew they was gon' call me if they couldn't get you. He done missed a lot of school work."

"Oh, please! Today is Thursday. He's only been out of school for three days. He went to school Monday. And they get out at twelve all week. He ain't missed no whole lot of work."

"Crystal, you should have gone down there to that boy's school and got some work for him to do at home. He's gon' miss his spelling test Frid—" Big-mama suddenly fell silent. Then she said, "Wait a minute. Didn't you and Nard just take him out yesterday?" Big-mama was no fool, and that was one of her best qualities.

"Uh . . ." Mama stuttered. She was probably thinking of another lie to feed Big-mama. I knew it wouldn't work, because once Big-mama catches someone in one lie, she does not believe anything else they tell her.

Big-mama made me promise never to lie to her, and I can honestly say that I always held up my part of the agreement.

"Yeah, we took him to get something to eat, but, uh, that was it. Came home, rubbed him down with Calamine lotion, and put him to bed."

"If that boy got chickenpox, like you say he do . . ." Big-mama's voice changed from a high pitch to a low, masculine tone when she dropped the "like you say he do." That was her way of telling Mama that she knew that she was lying. "Then you wouldn't have taken him out the house," Big-mama said.

"Look, don't come in my house questioning me about my

son, and you ain't paying no bill around here!" Mama yelled, cutting Big-mama off.

"Here's ten dollars on the light bill, now where is my grandson?" Big Mama scoffed. I don't know if Big-mama actually gave Mama ten dollars. But Big-mama's response was funny. She had jokes.

"Get out of my house!" Mama screamed. "Tired of you showing up any damn time you want."

"I was nice enough to knock on the door when I could have let my damn self in. You didn't have to answer the door."

"Yeah right," Mama scoffed. "And you would have let yourself right on in had I not answered the door. Just leave."

"I'll leave as soon as I check on my grandson." Big-mama's feet dug holes in the floor as she made her way through the house.

"No!" Mama growled.

I heard running. Then I heard Big-mama say, "Get out of my way, Crystal, before I knock you to the floor. You still my daughter and can be treated as such."

"I'm a grown woman and this is my house! You think I'm about to sit back and let you lay down your laws in my house? You crazy."

"What laws, Crystal?" Big-mama said, in the same tone as Mama. "I just want to see my grandson. You say he sick with chickenpox? Okay, I want to see for myself. I ain't seen him since this past Sunday. You kept him with you yesterday. Hell, if he was well enough to leave the house to go out with you and Nard, he was well enough to go to school. He *should* have been at Bible study."

I moved the broom from my left hand to my right hand, when its handle slipped out of my hand. The broom hit the floor like a light knock at a door.

"Who's in the kitchen?" Big-mama asked.

"Nobody," Mama said, smacking her lips. I could feel the attitude in her voice.

"Somebody in that kitchen," Big-mama said. There was a slight pause then Big-mama asked, "Where is Mic-"

"He's in his room, in bed sleep." Mama cut Big-mama off before she could finish her sentence. Her lies rested on the tip of her tongue, waiting to invade the thoughts of anyone who was willing to listen.

Mama couldn't tell the truth to save her soul. If there was room to lie—and in Mama's world there was plenty—then Mama was sure to lie before she even thought about telling the truth.

"It's Nard. We was just about to cook breakfast before you came."

"Crystal, I'm about to get out of here," I heard Uncle Nard say, as if he was being cued in to defame Mama's testimony.

"Thought you said he was in the kitchen," Big-mama said in her knowing voice. Big-mama had a habit of dropping her voice to a low, rough pitch when she was challenging Mama's lies.

"Mama, look, Michael is sick. He has chickenpox and I'm not sending him to school to infect those kids. The school is going to send him right back home anyway, so why take him out into the air?"

"According to you, he was out there in the air with you and Nard yesterday. Wasn't concerned about him *infecting*, as you put it, the people where y'all went to eat."

"We didn't take Michael with us yesterday." Uncle Nard, Mama's knight in shining armor, had just given her up. "He was here with a babysitter."

Now Uncle Nard was lying just like Mama did. I wonder if she was rubbing off on him.

Mama and Uncle Nard failed to rehearse their lies together.

Then again, in a normal life, they wouldn't have had to. In an honest life, either I would have really had chickenpox, or I would have been at school. In a normal life Mama would have called Big-mama at the first sign of a chickenpox, and she and Big-mama would have taken care of me, feeding me chicken noodle soup and sitting by my bedside until I was better. No way would I have left the house.

My life was far from normal. And as long as Mama was my mama, I knew that it would never be normal. I knew not to ever expect it to be.

"No, Nard, we took him out to eat with us, remember?" Mama said, trying to edge Uncle Nard away from his lie and into hers. Uncle Nard could have tried to change his story if he wanted to, but Big-mama would not have believed him. I could tell by Big-mama's line of questioning that she was on to Mama's lies.

Uncle Nard was Mama's lover, and Big-mama used to always say, "You can tell what type of person you're dealing with by the company they keep." So if Mama was lying, so was Uncle Nard.

"Michael!" Big-mama called out to me.

"I told you he's sleep!" Mama yelled. I heard a stomp and then a clap. I assumed it was Mama throwing a tantrum. "He's sleep." Mama clapped after speaking her last two words.

"He's in the kitchen," Big-mama snarled. Big-mama was tough, and that's what I've always loved about her. "Michael, come to Big-mama."

"Stop!" Mama yelled.

"I'm out of here," Uncle Nard said, removing himself from the situation.

"Just like a loser, leave when the heat is on his woman," Big-mama mumbled.

"Mama, don't start!"

"I'm not starting nothing. You knew what you was getting into when you chose to lay up with this pimp." Big-mama laughed under her breath. She was hitting way below the belt, and Mama wasn't having it. But what surprised me the most was that neither was Uncle Nard.

I never imagined Uncle Nard disrespecting Big-mama, but he did. That was my Big-mama, and if I was bigger, when he said, "Listen old woman, don't come in here to the house where I pay the bills and disrespect me. I'm far from a pimp. I'm a retired vet. I used to build weapons for the army. All my money is justified," I would have punched him in his belly and sent him crashing to the floor on his back. He would have been like a roach on his back, beating his arms and legs to get up.

"Ha!" Mama scoffed like she was big and bad since Uncle Nard was on her side. Now they were both bad-mouthing Big-mama.

Some daughter Mama was. No matter how much she disliked Big-mama, she should have never let Uncle Nard disrespect her mother. Then again, how could I have expected any different from Mama? The word respect was not exactly in her vocabulary.

Nard was no longer my temporary dad *or* my uncle. He was just Uncle Nard, and I hated him.

The thought of me, Mama, and Big-mama going to heaven together was the farthest from my thoughts. Ganging up on Big-mama was a definite no-no. If I had been in my teens, Mama and Uncle Nard would have been lying beneath the soil pushing up daisies.

Both Mama and Uncle Nard would have been close to losing their lives that day. I would have ran out of the kitchen swinging a butcher knife like a natural born killer, sliced Uncle Nard's ankles, and watched him crash to the floor. Then when

Mama came to his rescue, she would have given birth to the knife after I punctured her stomach and sliced through her intestines. Sorry to sound so angry, but Mama did this to me. Years of abuse and neglect; a person *never* forgets that type of pain.

I would have probably missed out on heaven, but I don't think I would have worried about my spirit dodging flames. Mama and Uncle Nard, on the other hand, were guaranteed a cell in hell after the way they disrespected Big-mama.

Mama got away with a lot with me being a child. But again, had I been in my teens—maybe fourteen or fifteen—I would have tried to kill Mama and Uncle Nard.

"You're going to stand there and let this man disrespect your mother?" Big-mama fussed.

"You started in on him first." Mama continued to laugh. Mama was laughing so hard that she started choking. I listened to her struggle for air, and within her laughs were coughs.

With my ears trained to the disrespect in the living room, I picked the broom up from the floor and flinched when it hit the floor a second time.

"I just came to check on my grandson," Big-mama mumbled. "Michael, get in here now!" she ordered. Big-mama was not leaving until she seen with her own two eyes that I was okay. I think I smiled through my hurt heart. I wanted to see Big-mama just as much as she wanted to see me.

"Stay there, Michael!" Mama yelled. I could tell by the tone of her voice that there was a smirk on her face. She had more power over me than Big-mama did, and knew it. If I had walked out of that kitchen against Mama's word, I would have been swallowing my teeth once Big-mama left the house.

No child should have been put in the position that I was put in; having to defy my grandmother to keep from being beat by my mother. Thank God Big-mama knew my heart.

She knew that I would never willingly defy her.

"Crystal, if you don't let me see my grandson, I'm going to call Children Protective Services like I *should* have done years ago. I will point them straight to your drug lab of a bedroom, tell them to pull Michael's school records, then tell them to check Michael out so you can explain that iron mark on his back and them cigarette burns on his chest.

"To this day, I don't know how you were able to convince that same social worker who showed up at the hospital both times Michael was getting his arm fixed that Michael broke his arms on his own. Child falls off his bike when he was three and breaks his left arm, and then a year later he falls off his bike and breaks his right arm? You lucky my grandbaby couldn't understand them police when they questioned him about his arms. You'd be in jail," Big-mama huffed. "And you know what? It might not be too late for that."

Oh, no, I thought. Mama was about to go to jail. But maybe that's exactly what it would take to be free from her.

Chapter 14
Failed System
Thursday @ 9:00 a.m.

Mama didn't go to jail the first time she broke my arm. As I sit here thinking back to that day, I can feel the excruciating pain all over again that traveled from my shoulder and down my arm when Mama tried to physically break me apart.

The combination of cocaine, Vicodin, and alcohol probably had Mama seeing three or more of everything at once. She was going on a crazy rampage the day she broke my arm the first time.

"Throw two of them damn cell phones out," she screamed to my former uncle, Bennie.

When Bennie failed to see the other two cell phones lying on the table next to his cell phone, Mama kicked him out of our apartment and threatened to cut off his private area.

"Yous bastard make me sick. If you ever come back here . . ." Mama slurred through a mouth full of spit. "Stay away from my house!" Mama slammed the door behind him and stammered to the bathroom.

I listened to the sound of glass breaking in the bathroom. I ran in the direction of the noise just like a curious child, only I did not go inside. The bathroom door was open and there was blood everywhere; blood on the sink, the mirror, the toilet, the floor, and all over Mama.

The glass toothbrush holder lay in pieces in the sink.

"Toothbrush, if you don't sit still," Mama screamed at the toothbrush in the sink. I couldn't see the toothbrush, but since she was screaming for it, I assumed it was in the sink.

Mama reached into the sink and clawed at the toothbrush like a cat clawing its way up a couch. The glass sliced her fingers, and I could see small pieces of glass lodged in her hand. Mama's hand resembled a cutting board, yet the look on her face was free of pain. It was the drugs. The drugs made Mama numb to pain and open to hallucination.

"Stop effin' moving," Mama hollered to the toothbrush. Her face was twisted to the left. Her bottom lip hung low and was coated with a white powder. Back then, I didn't know what the white powder was. But years later, when Mama pleaded for one of my uncles to hurry up and break the powder down to a liquid so that she could get high, I learned that the white powder was cocaine.

Mama's eyes were so red that she could have cried blood. I looked at her hair, wondering how she'd gotten carpet in it. The navy blue rug in her bedroom rose several inches from the floor, but it wasn't loose. Mama must have pulled the carpet out with her bare hands and tossed it in her matted fro for it to get into her hair.

Mama's body was brittle. Her spine manipulated her filthy, once white gown. Her fingers and toes were as skinny as sticks. Her cheekbones could have sat on the outside of her skin, they were so visible.

Mama was a dead woman walking, and she scared the heck out of me at every turn.

I was shaking in my pull-ups I was so scared. I stood there watching Mama for a good ten minutes before she noticed me.

"Three arms?" Mama said with fire in her eyes. "Boy, you got three arms? You got something evil in you, boy, come here." Mama took two, large steps toward me and reached for my shirt. I backed away from her before she could touch me.

Mama was the boogeyman with blood all over her, and there was no way that I was willingly going to walk into her arms.

"You don't snatch away from me. Get the hell over here," Mama ordered. She pointed at a spot on the floor directly in front of her.

I didn't move. I was covered in fear bumps. I just wanted to run back to the room and hide in the closet, or under the bed.

"Nooo," I cried.

Mama's face sort of softened into a smile. "Come, come to Mama," she stuttered. Mama dropped her voice to a sincere tone. I could feel love all in it, even if it was fake. Her crazed movements stopped. She bent forward and covered her bony knees with her bloody hands. "Michael, come to Mama." She reached for the air around me. I was standing less than two feet away from her and directly in front of her, yet she still missed me.

Mama reached over and around me, until she finally took hold of my left arm. She didn't waste time hurting me. Her long, dirty nails pressed against my skin felt like a throbbing pinch.

"No," I cried. I tried to twist my arm from her grasp, but every twist was met with more pressure. Mama was not about to let me go, and my little heart knew it, but that didn't stop me from fighting for my life.

"You gon' make it worse," Mama said, out of breath. "I'm trying to help you. You ain't supposed to have three arms."

Mama yanked my arm and slid her hand up my wrist to my shoulder. She locked her free hand around my elbow and squeezed it. She then raised both of my arms above my head, took me by both hands, and forced me to dance like a puppet.

I knew that I was one of God's sheep and that He was my Shepherd, but I had no idea that I was a puppet. That was new to me.

"I almost got it," Mama said through clenched teeth. Every last one of her black and beige teeth were showing. Her eyes were ready to pop out of her head they were so wide. "Let Mama take care of you." She took one long breath, releasing the horrid scent of beer and rotten teeth into the air.

Mama held her breath. "Here we go. Yes, I'm gon' rid you of this extra arm." She put her foot in my side. She then pulled on my wrist and snatched my arm right out of its socket at the shoulder.

My lifeless arm dangled within my skin. And if it wasn't for my skin, my arm would have been lying out on the floor.

I screamed a gut-wrenching scream and fell to the floor while holding my arm. I rolled onto my right side and looked up at Mama. She had returned to the sink and was back to yelling for the toothbrush to sit still.

My pain had no effect on her. Thinking back to that dreadful day, tears begin to flow down my face. I'm not even going to wipe them away. They are just going to fall all over again as I share with you the second time that Mama broke my arm.

Mama stood in the kitchen cooking. I can't remember exactly what she was making, but I do remember her standing in front of the stove stirring something in a pot while talking on the phone. It was one of those kitchen phones from back in the day; the kind with the cradle that was screwed into the wall with a real long, spiral cord running from the receiver to the cradle. The cord was so long that a person could walk out of the kitchen, around the dining room, and a few feet into the living room before the cord snapped them back into the kitchen. Okay, I'm exaggerating, but the cord was very long.

I had been in my bedroom playing with my imaginary friend, Jaylen. Jaylen was chasing me in circles around my room. I ran out of my room, through the living room, and into the dining room before dancing my way into the kitchen.

"Ha. Ha. Ha! You ain't right." Mama laughed into the phone receiver.

"You can't catch me." I giggled. Jaylen chased me into the laundry room and back into the kitchen. I dropped to my knees and crawled beneath the kitchen table. My knees slammed against the floor as Jaylen jumped on top of me and tickled my stomach. I crawled out from beneath the table and jumped to my feet, and right behind Mama.

"Go to your room," Mama said, never taking her eyes off of whatever she was cooking. Mama was real calm. Her attention was on her phone conversation and I was that fly buzzing around her ear.

Mama shooed me away, but I continued to run around her.

"Michael, I said go to your room," Mama said, still calm. She continued to stir the food on the stove while talking on the phone.

Mama's mind wasn't on me and I knew it. Her running her mouth to whomever she was talking to on the phone required thought. And I could tell by the way that she uttered, "Michael, I said go to your room," without looking at me, that her attention was not on me.

"Get away from me, Jaylen. You can't catch me." I ran to the living room and spun out of Jaylen's reach. I ran back into the kitchen, past Mama, and tried to cram my body into a corner.

"Oh no, no. No!" I yelled when Jaylen almost caught me. I ducked under his arm and ran out of the kitchen. I then ran back into the kitchen and around Mama.

"Hold on for a minute," Mama said to the person on the other end of the line. She pressed the receiver against her chest and turned her attention to me. "Go to your room, Michael."

I stopped running and gazed into Mama's eyes. I took small steps toward the doorway and her eyes remained on me the whole time. Mama didn't stop watching me until I was out of the kitchen and out of her sight.

"What you say?" I heard Mama say. I assumed she was back on the phone. "I told you to hold on. Michael running around here like he ain't got no sense."

I smiled at the sound of my name. For fifteen minutes, I was a bug on Mama's shoulder. Just like any other mother, she screamed for me to go somewhere. And just like any other child being a child, I ignored her. I was able to be a kid. For those few minutes, I didn't need to be perfect to avoid being beaten with a belt. Our house appeared as a normal house, with me playing with my friend while Mama was in the kitchen cooking.

Jaylen and I took off down the hall and switched the game up. We went from playing tag to hide-and-go-seek, with Jaylen hiding and me searching all over the house for him. Of course I would never find him. I could have spent seconds, hours, days, months, and years in search of Jaylen, when the only place that I would ever find him was in my head.

I was laughing and searching all over for Jaylen; my bedroom, under the dining room table, all closets, and under Mama's bed. Jaylen was doing a good job of hiding. Even in my mind I could not find him.

I ran to the kitchen where Mama was still on the phone. The phone cord was stretched from one side of the kitchen to the next, with the cord dragging along the floor. Her right shoulder held the phone to her ear, and she was standing in front of a counter chopping a bell pepper on top of the cutting board.

I stepped over the cord and opened the door to the closet where Mama kept the broom and mop. "Jaylen, you in there? I'm going to get you and you'll be it."

I could hear a child's voice in my head saying, "*You'll never find me.*"

I looked up at the ceiling and laughed at the voice. I then screamed, "Yes I will."

The voice in my head laughed and laughed. The giggles grew so loud that they made me deaf to Mama's screaming for me to get out of the kitchen. By the time Mama's anger finally caught my attention, my spine was pinned against a corner of a counter, and my right arm was broken at the elbow.

"Didn't I tell you—" Mama never finished her sentence. She dropped her shoulder that held the phone up to her ear, causing the phone to crash to the floor. She then attacked me. "I told you!" Mama yelled. She folded her lips over her teeth and pressed her lips together. Her top teeth then forced their way from behind her lip.

Mama dug her top teeth into her bottom lip, which was still covering her bottom teeth. And with hate written all over her face, pressed her hand against my chest, pinned my back against the counter, and bent my arm back.

"No . . . no! Stop-p-p-p-p! Big-mama!" I screamed. My cries could have awakened the dead and given them a second chance at life.

"Now take yo' ass to your room and take a nap."

"My arm," I cried. I held on to my left elbow. The pain was

ten times as shocking and memorable as the first time Mama broke my arm. My back, chest, and arm were throbbing. I was in shock, not just pain. A burning sensation sent me trembling to the floor. My arm was broken and Mama was screaming for me to go to my room.

I didn't move. Well, I couldn't move. My body wouldn't cooperate with my brain *or* my heart. Both were telling me to run before I got what I called a whipping, yet what Big-mama called a beating. I was frozen in hurt. Both my feelings and my body hurt, and all I could do was remain there on the floor looking up at Mama.

"Well lay there and cry then," Mama yelled. Her voice dropped to a mumble when she bent down to pick up the phone. "Shoot, stay there and cry yourself to sleep. I'm tired of talking to you." Mama put the phone back to her ear. "Hello," she said into the receiver. "PJ, you better come check this boy." Mama looked down at me and sucked her teeth. "I didn't do nothing to him. Been telling him to take his ass somewhere." Mama stepped around me and picked a can of beer up from the counter. She took the beer to her head and slammed the empty can down on the counter. "I ain't did nothing to his arm. I don't care what you heard. I'm telling you I ain't did a damn thing to him. He screaming about his arm like he screams about everything else. Yeah, and when you get here, you can beat his ass and tell him to start listening to me when I tell him to do something."

Uncle PJ came over to the house. He cringed when he found me on the floor. His face looked as if he was the one in pain as his shoulders stiffened. He scooped me up into his arms. He and Mama argued over taking me to the hospital. Mama was screaming about nothing being wrong with me as Uncle PJ followed up with threats to call the police. Mama cursed him to every bastard that she could think of, and furiously fought to pry me from his arms.

My eyes were closed, so I didn't see what was going on, but I did hear Uncle PJ calling her a whore and a slut.

Uncle PJ switched me from being cradled in his arms, to laying me upright on the left side of his chest, with my head resting on his shoulder. I felt him stoop down while asking Mama, "Where the hell is his medical card?"

"You all in my purse, keep looking," Mama sarcastically said.

The sound of papers rustling and coins clashing together was Uncle PJ going through Mama's purse.

"Found it," Uncle PJ finally said after spending a good five minutes going through Mama's purse.

Everything around me was moving in and out of silence. Mama and Uncle PJ's arguing was fading off into the distance. My vision became gray and slowly moved into darkness. As soon as everything around me faded to black, my hearing regained itself.

"This boy done passed out in pain," Uncle PJ said.

"Passed out?" Mama answered in disbelief. "You putting extras on it. Kids don't pass out? Hell, I'm a grown ass woman and I ain't never passed out."

"You stay passed out from them drugs," I heard Uncle PJ say.

"Yeah, and you stay lying there right next to me." Mama laughed.

"We're out of here," Uncle PJ declared.

I heard a door open and felt warm air sweep across my face. A breeze carried the scent of every flower in the yard pass my nose. Not trying to sound soft, but it was a pleasant smell. It smelled like freedom. It smelled like happiness. I had been outside many of times before. But on that day I felt safe and free of everything that Mama represented. At least

I did for a quick moment. Just when I thought I was free of Mama's wrath, Mama was locking the door behind us and headed to Uncle PJ's car.

Uncle PJ forced Mama to come to the hospital with us. It was either come with us, or risk losing me to a social worker that was sure to be called to the hospital after Uncle PJ made it clear he wasn't going to lie for her. He also made her call Big-mama to meet us at the hospital.

When Uncle PJ mentioned Big-mama's name, Mama went off. She screamed every word that flew out of her mouth until her voice lost its flavor and left her coughing to catch her breath.

"Call your mother," Uncle PJ demanded. "Or I'm going tell the hospital the truth. Once I tell 'em you broke this boy's arm, they gon' take him for sure."

Once Mama finally agreed to call Big-mama, Mama and Uncle PJ practiced their lies in the car on the way to the hospital. They wanted to make sure that their stories matched if they were separated and questioned at the hospital.

"I had just finished mopping the kitchen floor." Mama laughed while going over her script. "I was on my way out of the kitchen when Michael ran past me and into the kitchen so fast that he was already sliding across the floor before I could stop him. I ran into the kitchen behind him, almost sliding across the floor myself. When I finally got to Michael, his arm was folded under him some kind of way, and it looked to me like it was broken."

Mama's lie was incredible. I swear she didn't stutter or stop to think about anything. And the fact that I didn't dispute her lie only confirmed her lie. The doctors, Big-mama, and the same social worker that had been lingering around the hospital the first time Mama broke my arm, all looked at me through piercing eyes as they questioned me about my injury.

But I kept my mouth closed. Not one word escaped these lips. Mama would have surely killed me at the first opportunity had I told anyone what really happened.

I moaned in pain, even whimpered, but I didn't so much as whisper one word to anyone.

Big-mama stormed out of the examination room, furious beyond belief. She knew Mama was lying about my arm and was angry with herself for not being able to prove it.

After the doctor finished wrapping my arm in a cast and released me from the hospital, I was hoping to see Big-mama waiting out in the lobby for me. She wasn't, and it hurt me deeply.

Me, Mama, and Uncle PJ headed out of the hospital; Mama and Uncle PJ with a stroll, and me dragging my feet behind them.

Big-mama showed up at the house that night with her eyes ablaze and her breaths short and sharp. She was not in the mood for Mama's games and wanted to know the truth. "You broke my grandbaby's arm!" Big-mama screamed.

"That's all in your head." Mama chuckled. "Doctors say he fell."

"No, you and your Mr. Pete lied to them doctors and said he fell."

"Mr. Pete?" Mama screamed in laughter. "You are so funny. His name is PJ."

"I don't give a damn what that man's name is," Big-mama grumbled. "You did it. You did it. You did it." Big-mama was chanting so fast that a pastor would have sworn she was speaking in tongues.

My mother broke both of my arms in less than a two-year period of time, I was taken to the same hospital both times, and they let me stay with her. Should I have been angry with the doctors for not pulling me away from Mama the second time that it happened? Should I have hated Mama? I don't have an answer for either question. I doubt that any kid that age would have hated their mother. She was still my mother. I feared her. I hated the beatings. But at the end of the day, when the tears dried and Mama's screams and abuse were put to rest, for that second, minute, hour, or day, she was still be my mother.

Just like the first time Mama broke my arm and managed not to go to jail for it, she didn't go to jail the second time either. As I stood in the kitchen listening to Big-mama make the threat, I wasn't so sure I'd ever be free if it depended on Mama going to jail.

Chapter 15
Silenced
Thursday @ 9:15 a.m.

I pressed the broom against my chest and walked slowly toward the entrance of the kitchen. I listened to Big-mama insist on seeing me, and Mama's pleas for Big-mama to leave. The apple did not fall too far from the tree. Not that Big-mama once did drugs, but that both Mama and Big-mama were stubborn.

As long as Mama was alive with enough breath and strength to control me, even from a distance, I was damned. In Proverbs 13:24 it says, "He that spareth his rod hateth his son: but he that loveth him chasteneth him betimes," and I agree. Disciplining a child shows love, and that the parent only wants what is best for the child. I doubt God meant for a mother to beat her son to a pulp and leave him close to death.

"Would you please just leave?" Mama groaned.

"No! you gon' hear this, Crystal," Big-mama told her. "If my grandbaby would have known how to talk, like other kids his age, when you broke his arms, he would have been able to speak the truth and tell them folks you was beating him. You traumatized that boy to the point where all he could do was stutter when he should have been learning his alphabet. Then you managed to convince everybody that he was one of them special needs children. You used that reason for him not being able to talk right when the doctors and the police questioned him."

"I'm out!" Uncle Nard said laughing. "Now yo' mama is preaching."

I heard the living room door open and close. There was silence for maybe five seconds, and then Big-mama said, "Twice this system has failed my grandson. Then I failed him by not telling them folks what I see here in this house. I ain't never seen you hit him, but I'd bet my life before a judge that you've tried to kill him.

"It stops today, Crystal." Big-mama heaved. "You can be evil if you want to. Just know that evil dies. Evil dies to protect the innocent. I hate to say this about my own daughter, but you will die so that my grandson can live."

I gasped.

"Is that a threat?" Mama asked.

"No, I'm not gon' touch you." Big-mama puffed. "God is."

"Mama. Mama. Mama," Mama screamed. "Don't come in here with that BS. Your church is a cult, and the only reason I let Michael go is to shut you up. Your pastor is a devil walking amongst the living. I never liked him. You forced me to go to that church. You forced what you call 'the Word' on me. And it's because of you that I'm on drugs."

"Me?" Big-mama yelled. "How the hell are you going to blame me for that cocaine you running up your nose and veins?"

"You want to know?" Mama laughed.

"Didn't I just ask you?" Big-mama asked.

"You wouldn't be able to handle the truth to that question."

"Crystal, I ain't got time for your games."

"Bryan turned me on to cocaine," Mama said matter-offactly.

"What?" Big-mama yelled. "Girl, you crazy."

"No I'm not. Your old boyfriend Bryan? Every time you left to go to the store and left him there with me, he was feeding your thirteen-year-old daughter cocaine. Now how do you like that? You saw the change in me, but you thought I was just going through a phase. You convinced everybody that I was acting out because my period was about to start. No, I was high. And, well, look at me now." Mama's laughs were full of venom.

"Then you thought that you could take me to church and run what you called the devil out of me. I didn't take in none of it." Mama giggled. There was a short pause before Mama said, "I wasn't paying attention to all that, 'And the Lord said, na!" Mama said in her ministering voice as she mocked Pastor Kidd. "We have to stay away from sin, na. And if you don't walk with God, na, you might as well walk to hell, na.' Your pastor must have said 'na' a hundred times.

"It was funny to be honest." Mama laughed. "But what I did take in was how many times they passed that collection plate around the church. Let's see, there was the tithes, then the offerings, then the building fund. Let's not forget the benevolent fund for the people on the sick and shut-in list. Half of them people been on that list since I was a kid. When they died, their names were still on that list.

"All those churches are about money." Mama smacked her lips. "The Word comes last. And half them women in church is getting it in with Pastor Kidd."

"Shut your mouth before I knock your eyes out your head!" Big-mama screamed. I think she was talking with her teeth clenched, because there was strain in her voice. She sounded like Mama right before Mama pulled me by my ear or slapped me. "Bryan ain't did nothing to you. He wasn't on no drugs, so don't stand there and lie."

"That's exactly why I never told you." Mama sighed. "You not even with Bryan, but you taking up for him. Imagine what your reaction would have been back then. Just know that the man that you was lying up with turned your daughter on to drugs."

"Yeah, okay." Big-mama huffed.

"I knew you wouldn't believe me. And that's why your crooked pastor's prayers didn't work for me. He didn't know the root to my evil, and you don't believe it."

"I'm not gon' sit back and let you disrespect my pastor. He baptized you when you was two. He put food in our refrigerator when my body wouldn't let me work. He took up a collection to pay our bills when I had that heart bypass. That collection paid the rent, gas, lights, phone bill, put clothes on your back and shoes on your feet. For six months my heart wasn't working and the church shared theirs. You wouldn't know about sharing love from the heart, because your heart is black."

"Oh, and I'm the only one that's evil?" Mama asked.

"Is that a trick question?" Big-mama wanted to know.

"*You're* judging *me?*" Mama questioned. "Don't the Bible talk about judging folks? Huh? 'Do not judge, for ye too shall be judged. For what judgment you judge, you will be judged; and the measure you use shall be measured back to you?'"

I was shocked. Mama actually knew the Bible. Not word for word, but she knew the Word. Matthew 7:1-3 says, "Judge not, that ye be not judged. For with what judgment ye judge, ye shall be judged: and with what measure ye mete, it shall be measured to you again." Her quote was kind of off, but I got the message, and so did Big-mama I think. I hated to admit it, but as I was putting the broom away, I remember thinking to myself, *Mama is right. Big-mama not supposed to judge her.*

"I'm not judging you," Big-mama said.

"Yes you are," Mama yelled. "I don't have to deal with you. You pop up here every few days trying to run my house."

"Your apartment," Big-mama corrected Mama.

"House, apartment, whatever I choose to call it, it's mine, and I don't ask you for a nickel on it. Ugh! Mama, just go. Please go."

"Michael, come in here. Big-mama is about to go."

Without thinking about Mama or what she would do to me for disobeying her, I ran out of the kitchen, into the living room, and wrapped my arms around one of Big-mama's legs. I looked pleadingly into Big-mama's eyes. I wanted to tell her about Mama beating me, but did not want to tell her in front of Mama. If only my eyes could have spoken to Big-mama on my behalf. Since my mouth could not tell her about the hell that I had been through over the last few days, the tears in my eyes should have told her something. If my tears were not valid enough, the strength in my arms wrapped around her leg should have told her something.

"Michael, get up," Big-mama told me.

I shook my head wildly and pressed my face against her leg.

"Boy, get up. You gon' make me fall. What's wrong with you?"

I continued to shake my head.

"Let my mama go," Mama yelled.

Big-mama waved a finger at Mama. "Uhn, un, Crystal. Don't do that."

"Do what? I told him to let go of your old ass leg." Mama held a straight face as Big-mama reached down and took me by an arm. Big-mama pulled me up to my feet when she noticed bruises on me.

"What's all these bruises on your arms?" Big-mama

asked, as she took me by an arm and kind of slung me back away from her. She dropped my arm and grabbed my right hand. She twisted my wrist like she would a rag to free it of water. She then grabbed my shoulder and spun me around. I was getting dizzy from her spinning me this way and that way. A cool breeze from the open living room window bounced off my back after Big-mama raised my shirt to examine the marks on my back. Big-mama then looked at my face. She spun me around to Mama and pointed at whatever was on my face.

Mama must have left a bruise on my face when she punched me.

Big-mama gasped at the sight of my face. "You beat this boy!" Big-mama screamed. "He ain't had no chickenpox. You kept his tail at home so them teachers at his school don't see what his whore of a mother did to him."

Mama didn't say anything. She didn't deny Big-mama's truths, and she didn't admit to them either. She didn't even try to defend herself against being called a whore.

No, I didn't know what whore meant, but I could tell by the way that Big-mama said it that it wasn't a God-given name. Then I remembered Uncle PJ calling Mama a whore when she broke my arm. Both Big-mama and Uncle PJ calling Mama a whore left me curious and wanting to know the meaning.

Eventually I looked up the word *whore* in my dictionary. It took me some time to find it since I didn't know how to spell it. After around twenty minutes of searching through the W's and H's after sounding the word out a million times, I finally found it. There was a verb and a noun definition of it, and I could see Mama's face and her actions in the very first definition.

I skipped the second definition because it defined a male whore. My uncles might have fit that description, but it was the definition for Mama that I was looking for.

I went from the first definition, straight to the third one.
Whore (noun)
> 1. *"Woman who engages in sexual acts for money: Prostitute; also: a promiscuous or immoral woman."*
> 3. *"A venal or unscrupulous person."*

I had to think on number three. I didn't know what venal or unscrupulous meant. Pastor preached on promiscuous and immoral women, which helped me to understand the first definition.

I went on to read the verb version of a whore.
> 1. *"To have unlawful sexual intercourse with a whore."*

I had to think on that one too. Once again, it sounded like it was talking about my uncles. And my mother was the whore.

The second definition of the verb description of whore totally lost me. It said that *whore* meant "To pursue faithless, unworthy, or idolatrous desire." There was more, but I stopped there.

Faithless. Mama was faithless. She always had negative things to say about God and questioned everything about the church. She didn't believe that Jesus healed the sick and raised people from the dead.

Mama mocked the woman who was healed after touching Jesus' robe. That woman had faith. The Bible said that before she touched His robe, she said to herself, "If I may but touch his garment, I shall be whole." Mama swears there wasn't anything wrong with that woman in the first place. Mama claimed the woman was crazy.

"I didn't touch him," Mama lied. "He fell off that cheap bike you bought him and scraped up his body."

Big-mama snapped her head to the right and looked at

Mama out of the corner of her eyes. "Is there anything you *don't* lie about? Do you even think to tell the truth? You don't let him outside. Too afraid of what the neighbors will say about his clothes. You know you not doing right by him, so you try to hide him. You even tried to convince me one time that the kids in the building and on the streets were bullying him so you could keep him in the house. If bullying him is talking about his clothes, then yes, he's being bullied. You made it seem like they were fighting him.

"I'm calling 9-1-1." Big-mama pulled her cell phone from her purse. She pressed down on the nine. Before her finger could find its way to the one, she was reaching for her cell phone as it flew from her hands.

Mama slapped Big-mama's cell phone out of her hand.

"Mama!" I screamed.

Big-mama peered at Mama with scorn on her face. "Are you crazy?" she screamed. Big-mama drew her flat hand back and used every muscle in her arm to slap Mama to the floor.

"Big-mama, No," I cried.

I dropped to my knees next to Mama's bruised face. Mama's hand was pressed against her face where Big-mama had taken her back to her disobedient teenage years.

I covered Mama's hand with both of my hands and leaned down to kiss her hair when her elbow pushed two of my front teeth all the way up into my gums. She pushed them so far up, they were almost no longer visible.

"Owwwweeee!" I screamed out in pain.

Blood spewed from my gums and polished the wooden floor. The sight of the blood scared me to uncontrollable tears. I pressed my lips together, which temporarily stopped the blood from spilling from my mouth. My groans cut through Mama and Big-mama's arguing.

My tongue was submerged in a pool of blood. Unable to

hold back the blood any longer, my lips slowly moved apart, with blood pouring from my mouth and adding a second coat to the floor.

With her eyes glued to Mama, who was still on the floor looking pitiful, Big-mama rushed over to me. "Let Big-mama see." Big-mama pulled my hands away from my mouth.

I moved my hands away from my mouth and looked past Big-mama at Mama. Mama's hand hadn't moved away from her face. Her body grazed the floor as if she was dying. Mama was clearly in pain, her own pain, and not the pain that she should have felt for knocking my baby teeth up into my gums with my permanent teeth.

I lay on my back and collapsed my arms and legs. Big-mama delicately pulled my lips apart to inspect my mouth.

"Where your teeth?" Big-mama asked me. She took me by an arm and pulled me up in a seated position. "You swallowed your teeth?"

"No," I whined. I put a finger to the gashes in my gums, where my teeth should have been, and balled like the baby that I was. "They up there," I whimpered.

Big-mama forced my head back. Forgetting all about her pain, she slipped her thumb between my top lip and my gums and pressed down on my gums.

I flinched in pain.

"You done knocked this boy's teeth all the way up his gums." Big-mama was shocked.

"He will be okay," Mama casually said. "Same thing happened to Cousin Shirley when she hit her mouth on the monkey bars when we was kids. Dentist pulled them right out and stitched her gums up."

"Let me get this boy dressed and take him to the dentist," Big-mama said. Her forehead was drenched in sweat and her eyes held pain for her grandson.

Mama jumped to her feet and hurried over to me. "He ain't going to no dentist or anywhere else with you!" She reached down to take my arm, but was met by Big-mama's knee to her left arm.

"You—" Mama said, raising a hand to strike Big-mama.

"You lay one hand on me, and I will shoot for full custody of him. Now try me!" Big-mama placed her hands on her hips and stared Mama straight in her eyes. In their exchange of angry stares, I could see Big-mama daring Mama to hit her.

It was hard to believe that Mama was once baptized in the name of the Father, the Son, and the Holy Spirit. I thought the anointing oil purified a person and made them holy for the rest of their lives. Notice that I said, I thought. It wasn't something that someone told me, but more so what I believed. The people who attended Big-mama's church every Sunday seemed full of the spirit every single Sunday, so I assumed the spirit lasted a lifetime.

Mama dropped her arms loosely at her sides. She ran her fingers through her hair and held on to the back of her neck. Her head jerked from left to right as rage controlled her. Mama looked like she was ready to explode, and me and Big-mama were sure to be her victims.

"You can't take my son away from me!" Mama yelled.

"Well let's try it," Big-mama said with a jerk of her head. She crossed her arms over her breasts and sucked her teeth. "I'm going to call the police right now, and we'll see whose roof he'll be sleeping under tonight."

Big-mama walked slowly over to the entertainment center. She first looked down at her cell phone and then back to the phone, which lay next to it. Shaking her head, she reached down and picked up both pieces. She then went on to put her phone back together.

Mama's eyes ripped Big-mama apart. If her eyes held

bullets, Big-mama would have been lying out cold in a puddle of her own blood.

Big-mama strolled over to me and helped me to my feet.

"Go take a shower and get dressed so Big-mama can take you to the dentist," Big-mama said to me. "Roll some tissue in your hand and put it in your mouth to stop the blood. Bite down on the tissue, you hear me?" Big-mama looked between me and Mama as she spoke.

Mama didn't object to Big-mama's instructions. I think Big-mama scared some sense into her. Mama wasn't trying to go to jail. But if the police did show up to the house and arrest Mama for beating me, I doubt that Mama would have missed me. If anything, she would have missed her drugs and maybe even the sex.

"My mouth hurt," I moaned.

"Big-mama knows." Big-mama's voice was filled with sympathy. "We gon' get your mouth fixed all up, then Big-mama gonna take you to get some sweets." Her words were convincing, but her face held an uncertain expression. "Press your tongue against your gums to stop the blood."

I pressed my tongue against my gums.

"Now go on in there and get dressed. Forget that shower. Wash your face, throw on something clean, and try not to get blood on your clean clothes."

I held my head back and strained my eyes to see what was in my path as I made my way to the bathroom.

Once I was out of Mama and Big-mama's sight, tempers flared, with Mama sounding like she was on the verge of crying, or even losing her mind.

I followed Big-Mama's orders to wash my face and put on something clean while I listened to the two of them argue over me.

"What you going to tell the dentist when they ask you

what happened to his mouth?" I heard Mama ask Big-mama. I sensed the word "lie" buried in Mama's question. She was the cause of my teeth being hidden within my gums. She beat, slapped, and tortured me, showing no remorse or mercy, and there she was indirectly asking Big-mama to lie for her.

"I'm gon' tell them the truth," Big-mama answered. "What else am I gon' tell them?"

"That he fell on his face," Mama said in a childish voice. "He tripped over his remote control car and fell on his face."

"But that ain't the truth," Big-mama angrily said.

"I know it ain't!" Mama grimaced. "I'm asking you to tell them that."

"No," Big-mama said in disgust. "I'm not going to lie for you. I'm not lying for nobody. And I can't believe that you would ask me, of all people, to lie for you. And even if you *could* get me to sin with you, they would still find out the truth. Michael ain't like he was when you broke both of his arms. He can talk now. I can go in there and lie for you, but they gon' talk to him. Right before they get ready to put him to sleep to fix his mouth, they're going to drop their voices to meet his voice." Big-mama sounded like she was trying to scare Mama. "And they're going to say, 'You fell over your remote control car and hurt yourself?' And Michael, he's going to fight through the pain to tell them that his no good, selfish and destructive mother drove his teeth into his gums with her elbow."

"Mama, I can't go to jail!"

"Glad you know that's where you're going after the dentist sees his mouth."

"Please, Mama, just this once," Mama pleaded.

"Michael, come on. Let's go," Big-mama yelled out to me. Mama's pleas went in one of Big-mama's ears and out of the other.

I ran into the living room with blood flying from my mouth and spotting my clean shirt. I was still in pain, but it wasn't as bad as it was when Mama first struck me.

"Mama," Mama said, dropping her shoulders.

"Michael, you're getting blood all over your clothes," Big-mama said, still ignoring Mama.

"Please, Mama." Mama sighed.

"Michael, hold your head back and go over there and sit on the couch while Big-mama clean this blood up off the floor," Big-mama told me, as I went and did just what she'd ordered me to do.

"I got it!" Mama yelled. "I got it." Tears watered her eyes. "If you tell them the truth, they'll lock me up."

Big-mama walked over to me and took my hand. "Let's go," she said.

"Mama, did you hear me?" Mama cried. "They'll lock me up. I can't go to jail."

"And whose fault is that, Crystal?" Big-mama said, pulling me up from the couch. "Is your life more valuable than his?" She looked down at me and nodded her head. She then looked back up at Mama. "Do you think you deserve to walk away without suffering some kind of consequences, when you hurt my grandson every day? If anything, you should rot in someone's jail so that my grandson don't have to worry about waking up to another one of your beatings."

"I-don't-beat-my-son." Mama said, holding her breath. "He's a kid. He runs around here playing all day and getting hurt like any other child." She rolled her eyes at the sarcastic look that Big-mama was giving her. "You don't have to believe me," Mama said. "But don't be walking out of here lying to folks and telling them that I beat my son. It ain't like you seen me do it."

Big-mama led me to the front door and opened it. She

then pressed a hand against my back and gently pushed me out of the house.

I stood on the porch, looking back at Big-mama. I then followed her gaze to Mama. Big-mama was staring at Mama with an intense look on her face.

"I don't be here to see you lay hands on Michael, but I see the aftermath," Big-mama said in something like a haunting voice.

Big-mama was very relaxed, like the argument never took place. She was too relaxed, like Mama had never knocked her cell phone from her hands and raised her blood pressure.

"But I just watched you tear his gums open with no remorse on your face," Big-mama said through a frown. "You didn't even run to his side to see if he was okay. All that blood. It did nothing to you. Well, it made me feel like I've been failing him all this time. I know what he's going through here in this house, yet I ain't done nothing to save him from you." Big-mama reached for the doorknob, but Mama got to it first.

Mama concealed the doorknob with both of her hands. She swung the door and pushed it back with such force that the doorknob on the opposite side of the door slammed into the wall. She stood in Big-mama's face, forcing Big-mama to step out onto the porch, where she accidentally bumped me in my face with her butt.

I raised the bottom of my shirt and pulled it up to my mouth. I pressed it against my gums and walked down the stairs. I stopped in front of the last step and continued to listen to Big-mama give Mama a piece of her mind.

"I'll bring him back tomorrow," Big-mama said while turning her back to Mama.

"Hell no! You bringing my son home as soon as y'all leave the dentist."

Big-mama looked back over her right shoulder. "I am?" She huffed.

"Yes you are, or I'm calling the cops," Mama threatened.

Big-mama spun on the heels of her Dr. Scholl's tennis shoes and peered into Mama's eyes. "And tell them what? 'My mama kidnapped my son after I elbowed him in his mouth and sent his teeth through his gums?'" Big-mama was sending Mama a clear message. And I could tell by Mama's raised left eyebrow, her hands on her hips, and the way she ran her tongue along her top teeth, that she got the message.

"Bring my son back first thing in the morning." Mama stomped. She slammed the door, and I could hear her feet driving prints into the floor.

Big-mama took me by a hand after watching the door slam in her face. I was scared and worried about what would happen to me the next morning when Big-mama dropped me off to Mama.

Big-mama and I stood there in silence. I don't know what she was waiting for, but my ears were tuned to Mama yelling at the top of her black lungs about hating Big-mama.

"I hate that woman!" Mama screamed. "I hate you. I hate you. I hate you."

Big-mama looked down at me as I was looking up at her. I'm sure the sadness in my eyes was obvious to her. If it wasn't, my pulse had to have aroused her attention as it thumped her hand through mines.

Big-mama squeezed my hand and smiled. Her smile looked like it was forced. It wasn't genuine, but there wasn't a hint of anger in it either.

Big-mama was smiling to make me feel better. She was smiling to hide the pain from hearing that her only child hated the ground she walked on.

Big-mama told me never to use the word hate, because of

its strength. She compared the word hate to the strength that it takes to stab someone in the heart. I guess Mama missed that message. Because if Big-mama told me never to use the word hate, I know she told Mama.

"Let's go get your teeth fixed up," Big-mama said. She led me to the car and unlocked the doors with her keyless remote. She opened the back passenger door for me and helped me into the car. She then walked around the back of the car to the driver's door and opened it. Big-mama slid into the car and lowered her head.

My eyes wandered around the car before finding rest on the rearview mirror. Big-mama's eyes looked closed, but I knew that they weren't. Through my side-eye, I could see her going through her purse.

Big-mama pulled her MAC compact from her purse. She lowered the sun visor, and then looked at herself in the mirror. She turned her head from left to right. She lowered her head, rolled her eyes upward, and then raised her eyebrows.

Big-mama admired herself in the mirror like a model preparing for the runway. I don't know why Big-mama wore makeup; she was naturally dark and lovely.

Big-mama opened the compact and removed a sponge. She blotted the sponge with the powder, which was a little darker than she was, and ran the sponge over her face in a circular motion. She then flipped the sponge over and ran it through the powder a second time in order to cover the sweat on her nose and the bags beneath her eyes. Her face was no longer shiny with sweat from her argument with Mama. It was as smooth and beautiful as her soul.

Big-mama noticed my watchful eyes through the rearview mirror. She turned at an angle and blew me a kiss. Big-mama didn't use her hands to blow me a kiss; she just kissed at the air.

"Love you, Michael," Big-mama said, smiling.

"Love you, Big-mama," I said through my temporary snaggled teeth.

Chapter 16
My Savior
Thursday @ 2:00 p.m.

The dentist asked Big-mama a million questions. "How did this happen? How fast was he going on his bike? Where are his teeth? Do you want us to pull them out since they're his baby teeth?"

Big-mama gave him short, straight answers. Without going into details, let's just say that she lied without even blinking. The lies rolled off her tongue just as smooth as Mama's did. I'm not saying that Big-mama was a professional liar, because she's wasn't. I think Big-mama was showing a little compassion for Mama, despite Mama's evil ways.

I never knew Big-mama to lie, but I understood why she did it. If Big-mama had told the dentist the truth, Mama would have been thrown in the backseat of a police car and hauled off to jail. They would have then taken me to a home, and there is no telling how long it would have taken Big-mama to get custody of me. I know Big-mama's heart, and I also know that she was not about to let the system keep me away from her for a long time.

My gums swelled up so big that it hurt to even move my lips. This saved me from having to share in Big-mama's lies and disappoint God.

When I sat in that dentist chair, the first words out of the dentist's mouth were, "What happened to you, young man?"

I mumbled. I whined. I drooled spit mixed with blood all over the paper the dentist fastened around my neck.

Big-mama stood behind the dentist with a finger pressed against her closed lips. It was a silent message for me to remain quiet.

Big-mama went on to relay Mama's lie to the dentist. I don't remember too much of what happened after that. An Anesthesiologist gave me some type of oral medicine that made me real drowsy. I vaguely remember her putting a needle in my arm, but I did not feel any pain, I was so out of it. Seconds after whatever was inside of the needle filled my veins, I was overcome by a deep sleep.

I woke up two hours later to a heavy lip and absolutely no feeling in my top gums. My battered teeth were yanked completely out of my mouth. I was drowsy, falling in and out of sleep. I remember crying, but not because I was in pain. I was scared. Not being able to feel my lips and tongue frightened me and had me looking around the dentist office in a complete panic.

Big-mama took me straight to her house and tucked me into my bed where I went right to sleep. I had my own room at Big-mama's house. That was one of the advantages to being the only grandchild. There were toys all over the place. Well not all over the room. I just had a lot of toys at Big-mama's. Big-mama kept them stacked neatly in three corners of the room. I had so many toys that instead of calling it a bedroom, I called it my playroom.

The scent of food cooking in the kitchen aroused my senses and pulled me from my sleep. The first thing that I noticed when I woke up was that the feeling had returned to my lips and tongue. I could feel them, which meant that I could eat whatever it was that Big-mama was brewing in the kitchen. It smelled like spaghetti and meatballs. As I sat up in bed with a huge smile on my face, I just knew that there was a big bowl of spaghetti and meatballs waiting for me on the kitchen table.

I threw back the blanket and crawled out of bed. I started to run when I noticed that I was dressed in my Clifford the Red Dog pajamas. I must have been knocked completely out, because I do not remember Big-mama taking off my clothes and helping me into my pajamas.

I ran to the kitchen and stopped at Big-mama's side. She was standing in front of the stove stirring the spaghetti with a big, wooden spoon. I got my wish.

"How do you feel?" she asked in her sweet voice.

"Fine," I answered. And I really was fine. I was with my Big-mama, the love of my life. I was in the midst of my physical and spiritual savior.

"Do you feel good enough to eat some of Big-mama's spaghetti?" She grinned. Big-mama was playing with me. She knew how much I lived for her spaghetti, and just wanted to hear me say it. "You love Big-mama's spaghetti?"

"Yes. Yes. Yes," I babbled.

I hurried over to the table to get the stool that Big-mama always sat in when she pressed her hair at the stove. I pulled the stool up to the side of the stove, making sure I did not get too close, yet close enough. Big-mama warned me time and time again about what could happen if I got too close to the stove while the burners were going. Afraid of getting burned, I always kept a nice space between me and the stove while Big-mama was cooking.

"Don't get too close," Big-mama warned.

"I'm not." I chuckled.

"Okay, baby," Big-mama said. Her soft hand massaged my

chin. Her kiss wasn't too wet, yet it moistened my cheek.

Big-mama placed a hand on her hip. She leaned her head to one side. While stirring the spaghetti, she sang "His Eye Is on the Sparrow."

"Why should I feel discouraged?" Big-mama sang.

"When Jesus is my portion," I uttered.

Big-mama looked at me with a pleased expression on her face. She turned off the flames beneath the pot and walked over to me.

She continued to sing while pointing directly at me. Me and Big-mama then went on to sing the rest of the song together.

Big-mama placed a hand above my heart. She sang over my soft voice. It was like she wanted me to really hear particular verses of the song.

With her voice still on the sparrow, Big-mama helped me down from the stool. She moved the stool to the side and pointed to one of the chairs at the kitchen table.

I pulled out the chair that Big-mama had pointed to and sat down. My eyes followed Big-mama to the cabinets, the refrigerator, the pantry, and the drawer of silverware. It was time to eat. Our souls were full from God's words, and now it was time to fill our stomachs.

Big-mama sang as she placed a plate on the table in front of me, continuing to feed our spirits. This is when I joined Big-mama in the closing of the song.

By the time our duet ended, our plates were filled with spaghetti and topped with parmesan cheese.

"You ready to eat?" Big-mama asked, while covering her hands with a pair of floral mittens.

"I been ready for a long time, Big-mama, but we was singing," I told her through a huge smile on my face.

Big-mama lowered the oven door and removed a cookie

sheet that held two slices of garlic-cheese toast from the oven. She placed the cookie sheet on the stove and slipped out of the mittens. She then pressed down on one of the garlic-cheese toast.

"Them toast is hot." She stuck her thumb in her mouth. She looked at her thumb and rubbed it on her apron.

Big-mama picked a piece of toast up by a corner. The heat from the toast caused her to drop it back onto the cookie sheet. She tried picking up the same piece of toast a second time, but again, she dropped it onto the cookie sheet.

"We gon' have to wait for them to cool off," Big-mama said through a slight grin. "You okay with that?" Her oval-shaped, beautiful face was within inches of my face. "Give Big-mama a kiss."

I chuckled and covered my mouth with my hands. My face tightened with a beautiful joy that slowly traveled to every limb of my body. With Big-mama, I was covered in childhood; away from the adult that I was forced to be when I was with Mama. If only I could have stayed in that moment forever. If only Mama would have taken after her mother.

I poked my lips out to Big-mama's love, and laughed.

"Muahhh." Big-mama hummed through the kiss. "Does your mouth feel good enough for you to eat?"

"I'm ready, Big-mama." I smiled. Since the dentist ended up pulling my mangled, two front teeth, I was forced to use the teeth on the side of my mouth to bite into the food, and all of my other teeth to break it down.

Big-mama laughed so hard. "Just making sure my grandbaby is okay," Big-mama said.

She picked the bread up from the cookie sheet and placed one on her plate and the second one on my plate. She pulled out the chair closest to me and sat down. My left hand became lost in her strong hold when she took my hand in prayer.

"Thank you, Father, for blessing me and my grandbaby with this food that we are about to receive. I pray for your continued blessings, and I pray for those that are in need and have not turned to you, everyone's Father, with their troubles. In Jesus' name, Amen."

"Amen," I said as I watched Big-mama open her eyes and smile into mines.

I picked up my fork and dug right into the spaghetti. I wasn't just hungry, I was starving.

"Big-mama?" I said, looking up from my plate.

"Yeah, baby?" Big-mama answered thorough the spaghetti in her mouth.

"I don't want to go home," I told her.

"You not going home tonight. You're staying with me." She switched her fork from her right hand to her left hand and rubbed my shoulder.

"I don't ever want to go back. I can see Mama sometimes like I see you."

Big-mama just looked at me. Her eyes became glassy with tears. "It's going to be okay, I promise."

I believed Big-mama. If Big-mama said something was going to be okay, then it was going to be okay. She never lied to me. She may have lied to the dentist, but she had never lied to me.

"Love you, Big-mama." I smiled.

"Love you too, baby."

***

You Can't Die on Me
Friday @ 8 a.m.

I dreaded going back to Mama's house. When Big-mama

woke me up that morning, I pleaded with her to let me stay as she helped me into my clothes.

"I don't wanna go home."

"Come on, lift your arms up," Big-mama told me.

I jumped down from the edge of my bed and raised my arms high above my head. Big-mama held on to the bottom of my pajama shirt and pulled it over my head.

"I told yo' Mama I'd bring you home this morning. Big-mama has to keep her word."

"No, Big-mama," I whimpered. "Don't keep your word."

"Take them bottoms off," she instructed.

I slid my pajama pants down my legs and stepped out of them. "I don't want to go home."

"You're going to see Big-mama on Sunday." Big-mama smiled that famous, beautiful smile that made me all warm inside.

I could tell she didn't want me to leave just as much as I didn't want to go. Her eyes spoke to me. There was sadness and worry surrounding her pupils. Big-mama was giving me the same look that she always gave me when it was time to drop me off to Mama.

I stuck out my lip. My attitude was in full swing. I called myself being mad at Big-mama.

Big-mama kneeled down in front of me. She held my pants open for me to slip one leg in at a time. I raised my right leg and purposely brought my foot down on the back of the pants. I watched the pants slip out of Big-mama's hands before I backed into a wall.

"You better come on here and put these pants on," Big-mama said in a threatening voice. Her face didn't match her voice. There was love in her face, but anger in her voice. And if I had to choose, of course I would have chosen her face.

Big-mama pulled me close to her, wrapped her soft arms

around me, and gave me a big hug. I wrapped my small arms around her neck and hugged her back.

Love was always in the air at Big-mama's house. Whether it was a family member there, a friend, or a foe that Big-mama could never hate because of her spiritual beliefs, love was all that the walls in Big-mama's house had ever known.

"You love Big-mama, but you won't put these pants on?" Big-mama asked through laughs.

With my arms still wrapped around her neck, Big-mama picked the pants up from the floor. I pressed the right side of my face against her left shoulder. I closed my eyes and left it up to Big-mama to dress me.

Big-mama took me by my left ankle and slipped my leg into the left pants leg. She then put my right leg into my pants. I giggled as she fastened my pants and zipped them up.

Big-mama pulled my arms from around her neck and stood. "Let's go."

"Okay." I smiled. Just that quickly, I had forgotten all about not wanting to go home to the apartment that misery built.

After I was dressed, Big-mama and I ate breakfast, then we got in the car. The ride home was the same as always. Big-mama and I played a game. She started off singing a gospel song, and when she stopped, I picked up where she left off. Sometimes she would recite a scripture from the Bible and ask me where the scripture was found. As hard as it might be to believe, I knew exactly where the scriptures were in the Bible. I was young, but I knew my Bible. Big-mama made sure of that.

Big-mama pulled up to Mama's apartment, turned off the engine, and sat staring straight ahead out of the front window. She was focused on something up the street. She stared off for a good five minutes without batting an eye. I didn't say a word. The longer I got to sit there with Big-mama, the better. Maybe she was even contemplating on letting me stay with her forever after all.

Big-mama rolled down the passenger window and switched her unblinking gaze to our apartment. My eyes followed hers.

The living room curtains were pulled back, which was odd, considering the fact that Mama never liked for people to be able to see inside of our apartment. Mama's bedroom and the living room stayed dark. It could be a nice, sunny day outside with the sun beating against the blinds and curtains for someone to let them in, yet our apartment remained dark.

"Wonder why your mama got them curtains wide open," Big-mama said. I could see the wonder all in her face. Her forehead was covered in wrinkles. Her eyebrows were drawn a few inches apart.

I shook my head real slow.

"Come on, let's go on in there." Big-mama grunted. "I have to see Dr. Johnson this morning." She leaned to her right and held on to the driver's door handle. She opened the door and mumbled her way out of the car.

"See what this child I created is up to," Big-mama said, and closed the door.

It took Big-mama forever to walk around the back of the car. Her steps were short, and I could hear her every breath with each step.

Big-mama fumbled with the handle outside of my door. She swayed from side-to-side like she was off-balance, and her eyes rolled around in her head like she was out of tune with her surroundings.

I gazed into Big-mama's eyes. Her pupils were red and dilated, and her left eye was filled with tears. The tears crept down the right corner of her eye and sent mascara running down her face and down the side of her nose. Beads of sweat covered her forehead. Something was definitely wrong with Big-mama.

Minutes passed before Big-mama finally opened my door. She stumbled backward with her mouth opening and closing, yet no words were ever spoken.

"What's wrong, Big-mama?"

Big-mama stared at me for a good ten seconds before saying, "Big-mama not feeling too good." A flurry of coughs rocked her body. Her Adams apple rattled her neck. Sweat ran down the side of her face onto her earlobe. It lingered on her earlobe before spotting her shirt.

"Big-mama!" I screamed at the sight of her eyes rolling back into her head. "Big-mama, you're scaring me." I pushed open the door and swung my legs out of the car. I went to jump out of my seat when the seatbelt stopped me.

Keeping my eyes on Big-mama, I struggled to free myself from the seatbelt. There was a broken sewer cover in back of Big-mama, and the heel of her left foot was headed straight for it.

"Big-mama, you gonna fall," I cried, but she continued to take short, off-balanced steps backward. Whatever was wrong with her made her deaf to my voice.

The left corner of her mouth moved down into a frown. The fingers on her left hand curled into claws before forming into a deformed fist.

"Big-mama," I continued to yell. "Big-mama, don't fall."

I freed myself from the seatbelt and jumped out of the car. I ran for Big-mama and grabbed for her hand to keep her from falling, when her foot got caught in the sewer and sent her crashing to the ground.

Big-mama's head bounced off the pavement. The impact knocked her out like a broken lightbulb.

"Big-mama's dead!"

Chapter 17
Pray for Big-mama
Friday @ 8:20 a.m.

I ran to Big-mama's side and dropped to my knees. "Wake up," I cried. I shook her arm. "Big-mama, wake up! Don't die!"

"What the hell y'all doing out here?" Mama's voice appeared out of nowhere. I looked toward the house where she was standing in the doorway half-dressed. Her left pant leg was ripped across the thigh, close to her private area. The bra or bikini top that she was wearing did a bad job of covering her breasts. Her right nipple looked sliced in half, with half of it tucked inside of her bra and the other half exposed.

Mama flew off the porch and ran over to me and Big-mama.

"Mama, Big-mama sick," I cried. Both my body and my lips trembled.

While glancing between Mama and Big-mama, I noticed that Mama appeared to have been beaten. Black thread spotted with dried blood ran from the left corner of her top lip, to the left corner of her bottom lip. Her right earlobe was split in two, with her fake, diamond-stud earring missing.

I leaned to the right to see if Mama's left ear was as mangled as her right. It wasn't. The earring Uncle Nard gave her for her twenty-seventh birthday last year was still there, and her ear was free of bruises.

While Mama was screaming, "Go into the house and get my cell phone," my eyes remained on her scars. Mama pulled on my shirt and screamed, "Go in the house and get my damn cell phone," but I couldn't move. My mind was on the thread that kept the corner of her mouth together.

"Michael?" Mama ended my name with a rough slap across my face.

"No," I screamed. My tears watered Big-mama's arm. My face tingled with pain. And even after the slap, I could still feel the roughness of Mama's hand.

"Snap the hell out of it," Mama ordered. "Go in my room and get my cell phone. It's on the dresser. You sitting here crying like a little stupid bastard, and my mama about to die."

Big-mama die? Oh no, I thought. Big-mama couldn't die before me and Mama. We were all supposed to go to heaven together. I know that's not realistic, but to a child it made sense. I believed we could all go home to God together.

In the book *A Mansion in the Hills of Heaven,* I read about children flying around heaven and going camping in the Spiritual Garden and Elijah's Cave. I wanted to go there, and I wanted Big-mama and Mama to go with me. God would make them a Sister like the women in the book who cared for the mansion.

I struggled to get to my feet. I stumbled from my left knee to my right knee. I was trying to get up so fast that I fell. I reached in back of me, thinking I was about to fall backward, when I fell onto my right side.

"Get your clumsy ass up and go get the phone," Mama said. She rose up on her knees and reached over Big-mama with her fingers formed like she was going to grab me. They were curled up. She went for my shirt. I backed away from her. Terror ran from my heart, down to my legs, and ended at my feet. The terror then turned to strength.

I ran up the walkway into the house. I stepped over a dirty mattress on the living room floor and took a quick glance down at a hammer that was sticking out from between a blanket and sheet on the mattress.

I got to the entrance of Mama's bedroom and was about to cross over from hell into the flamed pit, when the scent of death greeted me at the door and cleared my sinuses. I covered my nose and backed away from the room. The stench, my God, it smelled like raw meat that had been left out overnight. Or maybe even days or weeks. I wanted to turn on my heels and run back outside. The thought of Big-mama dying and Mama's voice screaming out in my conscious, threatening to beat me with a belt, pushed me in my back and forced me into the room. I was afraid of Mama's beatings, but the fear of the belt was not really what gave me that extra nudge. The thought of Big-mama dying was all of the strength that I needed.

I pulled my shirt up to my nose, held my right hand out in front of me, and walked into the room.

Get back, the smell insisted.

"I can't let Big-mama die," I told myself.

The room was as dirty as it normally was plus some. A plate with half a sandwich in the center of it sat on the dresser that Mama used as her drug lab. One of those rainbow-colored tall cups that you get from either Magic Mountain or a circus was next to the plate with a blue straw in it. Mama emptied cans of beer into the cup. Why, I don't know. To me it was the same as drinking out of the can.

I looked at the bed, expecting to see one of my uncles sprawled out sleep with dried spit tucked in the corners of his mouth. He would have been half-naked, if not naked, but there was no one wrapped in the dirty, sex-stained blanket or the sheet.

I walked over to the drug lab and searched for Mama's cell phone. Seemed like the closer I got to the dresser, the stronger the stench got. I pulled my shirt up over my nose and stood over the dresser like a rat over cheese as I searched for Mama's cell phone.

"Yuk," I mumbled after the deathly scent in the air forced its way past my shirt, up my nose, and down my throat. It was the sandwich; a tuna sandwich gone bad. The aroma from the beer in the cup only added to the nausea that I was feeling at that point.

I searched unmercifully for Mama's cell phone. I needed to hurry out of that room. The dresser was cluttered with orange and white medicine bottles, spoons with black rings in the center of them, lighters, rubber ties, needles, and whatever else Mama used to poison her soul.

Mama's entire setup was there, but her cell phone was nowhere to be found.

I panicked. All of a sudden I was scared. I spun in circles searching for Mama's cell phone until my eyes landed on the big dresser.

I ran over to the big dresser and searched frantically for the cell phone.

"Michael," Mama called out to me. "Michael, come into the living room. Mama is okay."

Hearing that Big-mama was okay was like music to my ears. I dismissed the thought of ever finding Mama's cell phone and ran out of the room and to the living room. I stopped next to the TV and watched Mama help Big-mama into the house. Big-mama's left arm was around Mama's neck, and all of Big-mama's weight was weighing Mama's frail body down.

Mama walked Big-mama over to the couch. Big-mama flopped down with her head resting on her left shoulder. Her right arm lay across her lap, wrapped in the strap of her purse. Her left hand was on the cushion next to her.

Big-mama's eyes were puffy and red. Her tongue fluttered within her open mouth.

"My insulin." Big-mama heaved.

I ran to her purse.

"Get away from her. Can't you see she's sick?" Mama yelled.

I stopped running and peered between Mama and Big-mama. "Big-mama's insulin." My heart raced for Big-mama. I was anxious to be next to her, to give her, her insulin shot.

"It's okay, Crystal," Big-mama said and gasped. "He knows how to give me my insulin shot."

Mama looked at me like she despised the day I was born. "Go 'head," she said with an attitude.

I jumped onto the couch next to Big-mama and took her purse from her lap.

"Slow down, Michael," Big-mama whispered.

"Big-mama can't die," I said, while searching through her purse for the small, black makeup bag that she used to keep her medicine in.

Big-mama raised her head and gazed into my eyes. "Die?" she questioned. "Big-mama ain't going nowhere no time soon. God ain't finished using me." She forced a smile. I could tell by the way the corner of her mouth trembled, and by the twitch beneath her right eye that her smile was more of an effort than it was natural.

"You find it, baby?" Big-mama asked me.

"No," I whimpered.

"Take your time. Big-mama is okay," she tried to assure me.

"Hurry up and find that insulin before my mama dies," Mama hissed.

"Don't say that, Crystal," Big-mama said in a rasped voice. "You're scaring him."

"I got it, Big-mama." My heart slowed to its regular beat. Big-mama wasn't going to die. And in the world that Big-mama and I lived in, we would live happily ever after. Me and Mama's world, on the other hand, was a totally different story. We would never be happy, not then, not after.

I pulled the makeup bag turned medicine bag from Big-mama's purse. I happened to look up at Mama as I was pulling back the zipper. Mama rolled her eyes at me and walked off toward the kitchen, with her feet abusing the floor. She stomped like a child during a tantrum.

"Come on, baby, hurry up. Big-mama's eyes have a mind of their own. Can't keep them open too long," Big-mama told me. Her weariness caused her voice to rise and fall. She sounded as if her mind was drifting in and out of consciousness.

I took a small bottle of insulin, two small alcohol packets, and a needle from the bag. I placed everything on my lap and sat the bag and the purse on the cushion next to me. I picked up the bottle of insulin and rolled it between my hands. I screwed off the top, ripped open one of the alcohol packets with my teeth, and pulled the alcohol wipe from the packet. I then ran the alcohol wipe across the top of the insulin bottle.

"Keep that bottle upright until you ready to fill that needle," Big-mama reminded me.

I steadied the bottle between my thighs, being careful not to let it fall over. I removed the cap from the syringe without touching the needle. I made sure that I did not touch the needle because I didn't want to contaminate it, per Big-mama's repeated instructions when she first showed me how to give her the insulin shot. I then ripped open the second alcohol wipe and lay Big-mama's arm across my lap.

It took me a few minutes to look beyond Big-mama's chocolate complexion for a vein. After vaguely spotting a small, green lump beneath her skin, I cleaned the area above it with the alcohol wipe and dropped the wipe onto my lap.

I pulled the plunger on the syringe back and drew air into the needle. I took the bottle of insulin from between my thighs and inserted the needle into the rubber stopper. I then pushed the plunger to inject the air into the bottle. With the needle still inside of the bottle, I turned the bottle upside down, pulled back the plunger, and filled the needle with insulin.

"Check the needle for air bubbles." An almost inaudible tone escaped Big-mama's lips.

Wearing a serious look on my face, I looked at Big-mama and said, "I know." I didn't play when it came to giving Big-mama her medicine. She had explained what could happen at the slightest mistake. I wasn't about to be the cause of Big-mama suffering a diabetic coma.

My mind was in a zone each time I prepared Big-mama's insulin shot. I loved Big-mama to death. I would never do anything to hurt her.

I removed the needle from the bottle and put the bottle on top of Big-mama's purse. I had just put the tip of the needle to Big-mama's arm when Mama's deathly figure appeared in the living room, nearly distracting me.

Mama walked over and stood in front of me and Big-mama with ice cradled in a stained, white rag. "Here, Mama, hold this against the back of your head," I heard Mama say as my eyes remained on Big-mama's arm.

I didn't look up from the needle. My ears were turned to Mama, but my mind remained with my eyes, which moved from Big-mama's arm to the needle.

"What's that, Crystal?" Big-mama asked Mama.

"It's ice," Mama replied. "There's a knot on the back of your head."

"It is? I don't feel anything." Big-mama reached in back of her and rubbed her head.

"Big-mama," I said. "Don't move." I had the tip of the needle pressed against Big-mama's arm.

Big-mama leaned her head back and smiled at me. "Big-mama sorry." She turned her attention to Mama. "Crystal, ain't that rag dirty?"

I glanced at Mama. I then looked at the rag before continuing on to nurse Big-mama back to health.

I punctured Big-mama's skin with the needle, pressed down on the plunger, and watched the insulin empty out into Big-mama's vein.

"This rag ain't that dirty." Mama tried to force Big-mama to take the rag of ice. The corner of Mama's top lip was turned up, and her forehead was tight with wrinkles. "I used it to take a pot out the oven. Hell, the ice ain't going in your mouth, and the rag ain't for your face."

"Finished," I said, removing the wrapper from the alcohol wipes, and the empty insulin bottle from my lap.

"Crystal, get that dirty rag out of my face." Big-mama scowled. "You need to put it on your own face. Ice them bruises and cuts. Who done beat you?"

"None of your damn business," Mama shot back.

Big-mama rolled her eyes away from Mama and looked at me. "Thank you, baby." She grinned. "Give me the needle." I handed Big-mama the needle. "Now pass me my purse and make sure my medicine bag is in there."

I stuffed the medicine bag into Big-mama's purse and placed her purse on her lap. Big-mama's head was turned facing me, yet her eyes followed Mama into the kitchen.

Big-mama sat up straight. She took me by my right arm and pulled me close to her. I pressed my head against her breasts. She slipped her left arm between my back and the back of the couch. She brought her hand around to my lap. She then laid her right arm across my thighs.

Me and Big-mama sat cuddled on the couch, watching Mama. We listened to her talk to herself. I thought it was kind of funny, but I could tell by the puffs and the angry changes in Big-mama's facial expressions that she did not find any humor in Mama's actions. Big-mama probably thought it was sad.

Mama pulled the hammer from beneath the sheet and blanket and dropped it onto the floor next to the mattress. She walked on top of the mattress and kicked the sheet and blanket off onto the floor. She then raised one end of the mattress and stood it up on its side.

"John could have at least put the damn mattress back in the room before he left," Mama mumbled. "If I couldn't bring the heavy shit out here, what makes him think I can put it back? That's why I had him tote the damn thing out here."

Mama glanced at me out of the corners of her eyes. Her hands moved along the edges of the mattress as she struggled to grip it with her small, bony fingers.

"Is that who beat your face?" Big-mama questioned. "John, one of Michael's *uncles*?"

Mama placed a balled fist on her hip while balancing the mattress with one hand. "Why don't you take your crippled self home?" She stared Big-mama down from head to toe before turning to me. "Michael, come help me with this mattress."

I pulled myself up to help Mama, when Big-mama snatched me back down.

"He's too small. That thing will fall all over him," Big-mama told her.

"It's not going to fall on him!" Mama's nostrils were flared open. I think her eyes turned red right before our eyes. "Michael, grab that end of the mattress." She jerked her head toward the opposite end of the mattress.

"Call up John, the woman beater." Big-mama paused and turned her head away from Mama. She rolled her eyes to the left and looked Mama up and down.

"Mama, don't start!" Mama screamed.

"You the one with the many brothers," Big-mama replied. "That I don't know nothing about birthing."

Big-mama's hot breath smothered my face and ears. I could tell she was mad.

"Got these uncles, men I ain't birthed, lying up with you like this some kind of motel," Big-mama said and shook her head. "Michael in the next room listening to his Mama and all his uncles having sex."

"I should have left you out there to die!" Mama shouted. She threw her hands back and watched the mattress crash down on top of the coffee table.

The coffee table grazed the floor and pounced Big-mama's knee, pinning her leg against the couch.

"Awww, God," Big-mama screamed. Big-mama's knee swelled almost instantly.

Big-mama rocked back and forth like a child at play in his grandfather's rocking chair. Her cries sent my pulse into an uproar and my body flying up from the couch. I stood in Big-mama's face and watched sweat trickle from her hair down to her forehead, and then down the sides of her face. Her tears ran free and added to her already disrupted makeup. Her left hand covered her heart.

My Big-mama was in pain. Instead of Mama checking

to see if Big-mama's brittle bones were broken, she stood laughing as loud as ten drunks in a room full of alcohol.

I tried to slip between Big-mama's knee and the coffee table, but the mattress weighed down the coffee table, making it as heavy as the couch.

I moved hysterically from the coffee table to the mattress, checking on Big-mama. I probably looked like a rooster running in circles with its head cut off. My eyes slid from the tears in Big-mama's eyes to the smirk on Mama's face. Mama took great pleasure in Big-mama's pain. Since Mama was obviously not going to help me save my Big-mama, it was up to me to be the savior of the day.

"Ha! Ha! Ha!" Mama's dry laughs blanketed Big-mama's cries.

I held my breath and put all of my strength into forcing the coffee table back away from Big-mama. I managed to move the coffee table a few inches away from Big-mama's leg, which was nothing short of a struggle. The coffee table insisted on fighting me. The more strength I put into holding it back, the more pressure it put on my stomach and threatened to pin me against Big-mama's knee, and pin Big-mama's leg back against the couch.

My mind raced a mile a minute. Between Mama's laughs and Big-mama's cries, I felt helpless.

"Michael?" Big-mama whimpered. "Baby, move that mattress. Try to move that mattress off the table."

"Okay, Big-mama." I ran out from around the table, when the table suddenly sprung back and pinned Big-mama's hands against her knees.

"M-i-c-h-a-e-l!" Big-mama's cries sliced through my helpless heart, and all I could do was start bawling like a baby.

"Ha-a-a, this is too funny!" Mama screamed in laughter.

"Big-mama!" I yelled. "Sorry. Sorry." I held my breath a

second time and put all of my strength into saving Big-mama. I shoved the coffee table; the bed forced it against my waist. I grabbed my waist in pain, but refused to give up.

With growls rattling my vocal cords, I shoved the coffee table and dragged it across the floor until it was nowhere near Big-mama. The mattress fell back and crashed against the entertainment center, sending the television, picture frames, and four cheap candles crashing to the floor.

"Oh, hell no!" Mama screamed. "Look what you did? I'm gon' beat yo' ass, Michael."

I ran to Big-mama, glanced at her closed eyes, and buried my face in her chest. "Big-mama?" I wept.

"Get over here." Mama grabbed one of my legs and tried to drag me off the couch. I held on to Big-mama while staring her in the face. Something was wrong. She was there in the physical, but mentally somewhere else. Her back was pressed against the back of the couch. Her hands clawed at the cushions on either side of her. The right side of her face rested against the back of the couch and her eyes remained closed.

It looked like Big-mama had passed out. I began to whimper and beg. "Please, Big-mama, wake up." I looked back at Mama just as she was releasing my leg.

Mama stood in bitter happiness with a smile that could have competed with the bright sun. Once again, she was enjoying what looked to be Big-mama's demise.

Mama was no longer screaming about her television or her cheap picture frames. No, she was openly praying for Big-mama's death to come. It was written all over her face.

Mama's black feet scratched the floor on her way to her bedroom. She slammed the door and screamed, "Die, with your broken ass."

I heard a loud bang like Mama was punching the bedroom

door. Every time one of my uncles made Mama mad, she punched walls, doors, and one time she even punched the toaster and knocked it to the floor. I imagined she would have been in pain after punching the toaster, but Mama walked out of the kitchen like nothing had ever happened.

It was one of many of Mama's drug-ravaged days. Mama had cooked pork bacon, forgetting that the uncle that had spent the night that night hated pork.

"You know damn well I can't stand the smell of pork, and I sho' don't eat that crap." The uncle was fuming at the mouth while shielding his nose with a dingy shirt. "What the hell is it doing in this house anyway? Smells like a pen of dirty pigs. Is that what you spend my money on? Do I need to start doing the grocery shopping myself?"

I was standing in the doorway of the kitchen, hoping that Mama would let me have the bacon. The scent of the burnt bacon had my stomach growling mixed and intertwined. I wouldn't have been surprised if Mama and my uncle could hear the growls they were so loud.

I took baby steps into the kitchen and stood in front of the stove. I watched the once pink bacon turn a delicious dark and crispy. I was hoping Mama was watching me and would let me have the bacon.

I thought my wish was about to come true when Mama wrapped a kitchen towel around the handle of the skillet that held the bacon and smiled at me.

"You want this bacon, Michael?" Mama sounded so loving that it brought a smile to my face.

"Yes," I mumbled. My lips were spread into a heartwarming smile. You know the kind of smile where all the child's baby teeth are showing, and the tip of their tongue rest between their teeth? That was me. That is until my real mother surfaced.

"Hell no, you can't have nothing!" Spit flew from Mama's

lips and added to the dirty pig grease in the skillet. "Fix some cereal."

My smile quickly turned into a frown. "No milk," I whispered.

"Use water." Mama yelled at me like I was her biggest enemy instead of one of the only people who loved her. My uncles didn't love her. And if they did, their love was not greater than my love for her, abuse and all.

"Michael?" Big-mama gasped, pulling me out of my thoughts from the past.

I hugged Big-mama for dear life. I climbed onto my knees and kissed her cheek. I wiped tears from her eyes like she so often did mines.

Big-mama's eyes crept slowly open. Her body sat frozen as she sized up her surroundings. Our eyes smiled at each other. Her hands soothed my back and arms. God showed up and showed out. He brought my Big-mama back to me.

"I'm okay, baby. Big Mama is okay." She looked around. "Where your mama go?"

"She in the room," I replied.

Big-mama and I sat there with our ears glued to the sound of Mama destroying her bedroom. I was so scared that my heart felt like it was going to do somersaults out of my chest. I feared Mama would bolt out of the bedroom and come after me.

"Big-mama, can I go back home with you?" My voice quivered in fear. If that wasn't enough to show her that I was afraid to stay with Mama, my pleading eyes were sure to tell her something.

"Big-mama going to see the doctor," she told me. "Have him look at this knee. Got to make sure it's not broke." She rubbed my chin and kissed my forehead.

I dropped my head and slowly opened and closed my

eyes. Mama was on a warpath, either hurting for drugs, or the drugs were hurting her. Big-mama could clearly see it. Yet once again, she was leaving me with Mama. I would be Mama's punching bag until Big-mama came to my rescue.

"Don't leave me, Big-mama," I pleaded.

"I'm coming right back," Big-mama said. "You can't be in the room while Dr. Johnson is examining me, and I sho' ain't leaving you in the waiting room by yourself."

"I'm a big boy. I'm not scared." My arms formed an X over my chest. I lowered my head and drew my eyebrows together. I looked at Big-mama from the top of my eyes.

"I know you a big boy, but I'm still not leaving you in the waiting room by yourself." Big-mama chuckled. She wrapped her arms around me and squeezed me real tight. "Big-mama will be back faster than you can blink," which was enough time for Mama to tear me a new layer of skin.

I playfully caused my eyelashes to flutter and laughed at Big-mama's beautiful smile.

"Boy, boy, boy, what am I going to do with you?" Big-mama laughed so hard her breasts bounced up and down.

"Take me with you," I answered in a squeaky voice. I nodded my head with my chin touching my chest.

Big-mama dug her fists into the cushions on each side of her. She rocked back and forth and said, "Yo' head gon' come clean off yo' neck you keep nodding like that." Her voice was filled with strain as she struggled to push herself up from the couch. "Help Big-mama up," she said and held a hand out to me. "But watch out for my knee."

"Oh it's okay for him to break his back trying to pull them big bones of yours up, but he can't help me with that mattress?" Mama walked out of the dining room and into the living room. She stopped in front of me and Big-mama and placed her thin fingers on her shapeless hips. Her hands slipped right down her sides and rested on her thighs. White powder lined Mama's nostrils and covered her nose hairs.

"I hope you plan to buy me a new TV since yo' nappy headed grandson broke it trying to help you."

I was shaking beyond belief. Mama was high and Big-mama was leaving me.

I looked frantically from Mama to Big-mama, just as Big-mama was snatching away from me. Big-mama took me by the arm and forced me down onto the couch. She then pressed down on the cushions and stood bent at the waist.

Big-mama straightened her back and looked Mama dead in her eyes. "You got the devil on yo' nose," she told her. Big-mama shook her head and looked down on me. "Michael, let's go. Big-mama wants you to come to the doctor with her after all."

"No!" Mama yelled. "He just got home. He needs to spend some time with his mama."

"No he don't." Big-mama grimaced. "His mama ain't in her right mind to care for a cat, let alone a child. Drugs ain't kicked in yet, but they will. Then you gon' be walking around here kicking over furniture and yelling and screaming at Michael for only God knows what. But I'm sure it will be nothing that *Michael* did. Think I'm gon' leave him here for another episode of your wrath, when I *know* you ten minutes away from being high?" She dropped her eyes and met my gaze. "Come on, Michael, let's get out of here."

"Mama, you come here damn near every day trying to take my son away from me." Mama's drug-induced tears were pitiful. "You trying to turn my son against me?" Her voice suddenly became deep and strong. Had I not been in the same room as Mama and Big-mama, witnessing their conversation, I would have sworn that Big-mama was talking to a man.

"I come here to check on my grandson," Big-mama

retorted. "And as far as turning him against you, looks to me like you doing a good job of that yourself. You don't cook. You don't clean. Every time I look up you got a different man up in here. My grandson goes to school looking like some homeless child. Only time he looks decent is when he's leaving for school from my house." Big-mama grabbed me by my wrist and pulled me up from the couch. "Bruises all over his body, it don't make sense," she said on our way to the door. "You not going to be satisfied until I take Michael away from you for good." Big-mama opened the door. "Michael, go on to the car."

I walked out of the house and off the porch. I didn't go to the car, but instead stood waiting for Big-mama.

"One day, Crystal, one day. You gon' look up and me and my grandson gon' jump in that car." Big-mama pointed to her car. "And never look back." Big-mama and I headed for the car.

"You make me hate the day that little bastard was born," Mama screamed. "If he wasn't here, I wouldn't have to deal with you."

On the verge of crying, I took short breaths and set my eyes on Big-mama. Every night I prayed to God never to take Mama away from me and Big-mama. I pleaded with Him to spare Mama's soul, when I knew that there was a one-way ticket to hell waiting for her. I fought the devil through prayer for Mama's life, and there she was dreading the day that I was born. No, it was nothing new. But keep in mind, children never stayed angry with their parents for long. Mama could curse me one minute and abuse me the next. And five minutes later, once the tears cleared, I' forget all about it. Then when a new form of abuse would arise, the pain was fresh all over again.

"Give him to me," Big-mama said with her back still to

Mama.

Me go to live with Big-mama? I was more than ready.

"You'd love that wouldn't you?" Mama chuckled. "You can't have nothing." She slammed the door, cutting off the light in my spirit.

Chapter 18
Please Don't Leave Me
Friday @ 10:00 a.m.

Big-mama gasped when she noticed how crowded Kaiser Permanente's waiting room was. There wasn't an empty chair in sight.

"Looks like we gon' have to stand," Big-mama said. She took me by a hand and led me to a desk with the words "Check In" inscribed in black lettering along the front side of the desk.

As soon as the receptionist at the desk noticed Big-mama heading her way, her pleasant smile turned into a look of concern. Her left brow was raised and her mouth hung slightly open. She held a finger up to Big-mama, stood up from her desk, and started to walk away when Big-mama stopped her.

"Ma'am, I have an appointment with Dr. Johnson." Big-mama's words were slurred, causing me to stare into her face.

Frightened by the monstrous look that had replaced Big-mama's beautiful smile, I urinated on myself. I was too young to be embarrassed. The eyes that watched me were the furthest from my mind. The nurse that rushed over to me and moved me out of the path of the urine that streaked the floor was there, yet she wasn't. I could feel her delicate hand around my wrist, yet all I saw was Big-mama.

Big-mama's left eye was closed. Her bottom lip was twisted to the left, while her top lip was normal. A fine line ran from the left corner of her mouth down to her chin. Something was very wrong with Big-mama. And for the first time ever, I was afraid to be near her.

"Big-mama, what's wrong?" I hesitantly reached for her left hand, which was cold to the touch.

"Stay right there," the receptionist told Big-mama. "I'll be right back."

Big-mama looked down at me and said, "Ain't nothing wrong with Big-mama. Big-mama is fine. When we leave here, I'm going to take you up to your school to get all the assignments you missed this week. Then we're going to go to downtown Long Beach to the Aquarium and look at all the big beautiful fish. Would you like that?"

Even when the custodian appeared with a mop bucket and two yellow "caution wet floor" signs, all I could feel was my love for Big-mama. My mind and ears were deaf to everything around me. All I could think about was Big-mama.

I wanted to smile at Big Mama's offer to go to Long Beach, but at the same time, I was scared. Big-mama had no idea that something was wrong with her, despite her tongue not forming her words correctly. She obviously couldn't hear herself as she spoke from the corner of her mouth, because she sounded just like Mama in Mama's everyday life of being high.

As I glanced around the lobby, I noticed that all eyes were on Big-mama.

"Excuse me, please move to the side," I heard a woman say. I looked in back of me to see the receptionist that had paused Big-mama in her steps when we first arrived at the hospital. The receptionist was now rushing toward us with a wheelchair.

Patients, families, and friends parted ways like the Red Sea to make room for the receptionist. She stopped in front of me and Big-mama and gently removed Big-mama's hand from my hand. She helped Big-mama into the wheelchair and stood in back of it.

I looked frantically around us. One, two, three ... female nurses dressed in all white nursing uniforms hurried over to Big-mama's side. One of the nurses replaced the receptionist behind the wheelchair, while a second nurse stood to the right of the wheelchair. The third nurse positioned herself in front of the wheelchair.

I ran around to the front of the wheelchair and gazed into Big-mama's face. Her eyes were closed and her chin rested on her chest. Just that quickly, Big-mama was out of it. I didn't know if she was dead or alive, but feared that she was dead. One minute she was talking to me, trying to convince me that she was okay, and the next minute she was sitting motionless in a wheelchair, unresponsive to her surroundings.

"Move to the side, baby. She's okay," the nurse that stood in front of the wheelchair told me.

I spun back around to Big-mama and trained my eyes on her left shoulder. Big-mama's left shoulder was lower than her right shoulder, and her fingers were curled into a claw.

A man in a white medical coat ran out from behind a corner and approached the nurse that was pushing the wheelchair. I moved from left to right, like an inexperienced boxer in a ring, while listening to the nurse explain Big-mama's condition to the doctor.

"Dr. Johnson, it appears she's suffered a stroke," the nurse that was behind the wheelchair said.

My thoughts traveled back to Big-mama and I sitting in the living room two hours earlier, and her mentioning a Dr. Johnson.

"Check her into the hospital immediately," Dr. Johnson told the nurse. He turned on the heels of his shiny, black dress shoes, nearly bumping into me. "Wo-o-o, go on to your mother, son." He placed a hand on my back and nudged me to the side to clear a path for Big-mama's wheelchair.

"Big-mama." I reached for Big-mama's curled fingers.

"Oh . . . um." Doctor Johnson shared a glance between me and Big-mama. "We're going to have to call someone to pick you up. Your grandmother has to stay here."

"I want to go with Big-mama," I cried.

Dr. Johnson ignored me and turned to a receptionist at the desk. "Go through Miss Love's files and see if you can find a number for her daughter."

"No-o-o, I don't want to go home. I'm scared." I backed into a wall and balled each hand into a fist. I pressed my fist against my closed eyes and wept. "I don't want Mama. I want Big-mama."

A large grin made up most of Dr. Johnson's face. He knelt down in front of me and rubbed my head. "Your Big-mama will be home before you know it." He continued to smile. "She is going to stay here overnight so that our wonderful doctors and nurses can watch her and make sure that she is okay. Tomorrow . . . tomorrow is a new day, and I am going to do everything that I can to make sure that your Big-mama comes home to you. Okay?"

No, it was not okay. My savior was just taken away from me and they were calling the devil to pick me up. How was that okay? My life wasn't okay. But how was the doctor supposed to know what I was going through at home? How was anybody supposed to know? The abuse was a secret; a secret kept between Big-mama, Mama, and me.

At that very moment I wanted to cry my heart out to the doctor and tell him that my mother was hurting me. What stopped me? Mama's groggy voice started playing in my head. I could picture her standing in front of me with a hand on her hip as she shook a finger in my face and said, "If you ever tell anybody about the scars on you, I'm going to jail and they are going to put you in a dirty, dingy foster home with a bunch of bad ass kids."

Mama spoke fear into me, and her words scared me every time. The part about living in a dirty, dingy home was not what scared me. Our apartment was always dirty and dingy, so making myself comfortable would not have been a problem. The thought of never seeing Big-mama again was what worried me. Mama could go to jail, but as long as she was alive, I didn't care about being taken away from her. But Big-mama, she was my life-line, and I was not about to tell on Mama and risk not seeing Big-mama again.

"What is your mother's name?" Dr. Johnson asked me.

"Crystal," I uttered.

"I know Crystal." The smile on Dr. Johnson's face was so big that all of his teeth were showing. He said Mama's name like Big-mama was walking around giving Mama praise. "The receptionist is calling your mother now. She should be here in no time."

Dr. Johnson sounded all excited. He had no idea that the Crystal that he was gloating over was the devil that walked the Earth in the book of Job.

***

The devil in disguise
An hour later
Friday @ 11:30 a.m.

"No time" was more like an hour or longer. I literally sat there watching patients walk into the hospital sick, and walk out feeling better. That's how long it took Mama to pick me up. And when Mama finally decided to walk through the sliding double doors, she was absolutely unrecognizable.

Mama looked simply beautiful. A teal green scarf covered her hair. I could tell by the way the scarf was tied around her head that her hair was pulled up into a ponytail. The scarf resembled a beehive.

Her shirt was the same color as the scarf, and the material was a cross between satin and silk. It was as shiny as satin, yet as smooth as silk. Bronze buttons lined one above the other ran down the center of her shirt. Above the top button were two drawstrings that were tied into a bow. The shirt hung off both shoulders, exposing Mama's beautiful complexion.

Mama's ankle-length, brown skirt matched perfectly with the bronze buttons on her shirt. The bottom of the skirt was trimmed in lace and covered the top of her sandals.

Mama's open-toe sandals had to have been new, because I'd never seen them before. I wouldn't be surprised if she'd stopped at the mall and shopped before picking me up. Of course, it would have been my uncle's money putting shoes on her feet. Mama would have walked barefoot on top of water with Jesus before she spent her own money on a need rather than a want. Seeing Mama behind Him, Jesus probably would have told Mama to look behind her so that she could fall into the water like Peter did when he doubted Jesus' Word.

The part of the sandals that covered the top of her feet were shaped like diamonds. They were made up of green, tan, yellow, orange, baby blue, and lavender small triangles. Mama's toes were not done, but they did not look bad either. They were free of nail polish and filed down to a straight tip.

My eyes moved from her toes to the balls of her feet. Her feet were actually clean. There were no cracks with streaks of dirt running through them, and her ankles were free of ash.

Mama's perfume filled my nostrils. I do not know what kind of perfume she was wearing, but whatever it was cleared the stuffy waiting room.

Mama glanced at me with a smile on her face before approaching the receptionist desk. "I'm Miss Love's daughter, Crystal, and I'm here to pick up my son." Mama turned at an angle and smiled at me.

The receptionist stood and looked past Mama at me. "He's over there," she said, and pointed at me.

"Thank you," Mama said in a soft voice. She walked over to me with the same beautiful smile that she had shared with the receptionist.

Mama hovered over me with love, protection, and sincerity written all over her face. "You ready to go?" she asked all jolly and full of life. I'm sure she had drugs running from her veins to her heart.

Mama looked like she could have been the most beautiful angel in heaven. An angel, who as soon as we made it home, would be cast to hell and became known as the devil.

Chapter 19
A Father's Love
Friday @ 12:00 p.m.

Mama slung me into the house and slammed the door. My real Mama had finally shown herself. You know the angel I spoke of that was kicked out of heaven down to hell and received a new title? I knew she would show up once we were out of the public's eye. Mama was overly loving in the hospital and held me close to her in the cab, neither of which was normal.

The taxi cab was not your regular taxi with the light on top and writing on the outside of both the passenger's and driver's door. Taxi cabs in poverty-stricken areas were old Cadillacs, owned and operated by alcoholics who lingered around liquor stores preying on money. Every mother and grandmother in the neighborhood had the Cadillac's number on speed dial.

Mike the wino had pulled up in front of the hospital and waved at me. I waved back and waited for Mama to open the door for me to climb inside. I climbed into the musty nineteen seventy-five Cadillac Eldorado and watched Mama slide in next to me. Once inside, Mama placed an arm around my shoulder, pulled me close to her, and kissed my cheek.

For the first time since learning right from wrong, I actually felt loved. Every bad thing that Mama had ever done to me was pushed to the back of my mind. When I stared into her eyes, I did not see her beating me with a belt. I saw love. Her eyes weren't red from drugs or anger, only love. Her kiss kissed away all of her heart-pounding screams, the thoughts of her rubbing lettuce in my face, and the terrible names she called me. When Mama kissed me, I felt love.

When we got home, Mama pulled a wrinkled five dollar bill from her bra and passed it between the driver's and passenger's seat to Mike. I pushed open the back door and ran out of the car, with Mama walking graciously behind me. I stood off to the side of the front door, free of worries. Mama had just shown me a lot of love, and I was happy.

Mama pushed the front door open. I started inside of the house when she grabbed me by the arm and flung me inside.

"What happened to my mama?" Mama yelled. She was screaming like she cared. Mama came at me like I had hurt Big-mama, and if I didn't answer her right away, she was going to hurt me. "Answer me!" Mama yelled. "What the hell happened?"

Before my lips could utter the words, "I don't know," Mama shoved me in my chest and forced me back against an end-table. My back bounced off the corner of the table. Pain sent me to the floor on my knees. I opened my mouth to answer Mama as fast as I could, when her screams were met with a breathtaking wail.

"I don't know!" I cried. "I want Big-mama."

"Shut up!" Mama rushed over to me with her hand raised to slap me. "Shut yo' damn mouth. Mad 'cause you had to bring yo' tail home. Get in yo' room and don't come out until I say so!"

"I'm hungry," I sobbed.

"What?" Mama leaned in closer to me.

"I'm hungry." I continued to cry.

"Mama ain't feed you?" Mama rose up out of my face and put her weight on her left sandal.

"Stop screaming at that boy." A man walked into the living room dressed like a deacon of the church. He looked nothing like my uncles. He was dressed in a navy blue suit, a white shirt, and a navy blue and white striped tie. His handkerchief matched his tie. His hair was cut into a fade with waves running through it. The studs in his ears were as shiny as the diamonds on the Kay's Jewelry commercial. I believe the diamonds were real; not like those fake diamonds with dirt rings around them that my uncles wore.

The man was of a light complexion, and there were no signs of drugs on his lips. His lips were pink, while Mama and my uncles' lips were black from either getting burnt by the pipe that held their cocaine, or from the cigar wrapper that they used to smoke their weed in. The man looked like he'd never touched drugs a day of his life. So why was he in our house, also known as the devil's den? And how had he gotten inside? Mama must have left the door unlocked rushing out to pick me up.

"Tyson, what . . . what are you doing here?" Mama covered her mouth with both hands. She took small steps toward, who I believed, was my new uncle. Her tears watered his shirt and tie. His blazer muzzled her cries.

"I'm sorry?" Tyson slid the scarf off Mama's head. He ran his hands through her hair and showered her with kisses. "You look so beautiful."

I stood there watching Tyson and Mama hold each other. Mama's back was to me while Tyson faced me. Tyson stared at me with a sense of peace on his face. I can't explain it, but he didn't look at me like someone that was seeing me for the first time.

Normally, Mama's men friends would say, "Oh, is that your son?" or something to that effect. Tyson stared at me like he knew me. He smiled at me like a proud father would a son after his son hit a homerun.

"Why did you leave me?" Mama cried. "You left me alone to take care of Michael by myself."

"I know, and I'm sorry." Tyson held Mama's face in his hands and gazed into her teary eyes. "I'm sorry. I'm here now, and I promise I will never leave you again."

"I waited for you for five years." Mama wept. "Did the best I could to make sure that *your son* was well taken care of." She pulled away from Tyson and pointed at the front door. "I've moved on."

His son? My father? My real father? Not my uncle or a play Dad, but my real father?

I wanted to leap into his arms and stare into his eyes then hug his neck as he rubbed my head while saying, "I'm your father, and I promise you I will never leave you again."

I pictured him holding me like the fathers did their sons or daughters in the 80s or 90s family television shows. In those shows, if the TV dad's son or daughter was hurt or did something to make him proud, he held them in his arms, hugged them as if his heart depended on it, and told them how much he loved them. My father not being there during some crucial years of my life meant nothing to me. At seven, I was not going to hold it over his head. I was ready to start my new life with my father . . . my real father.

"Tyson, you're my father?" I asked with a look of peace on my face. My eyes were smiling. My heart was racing. Out of all of the men that walked in and out of our apartment like a revolving door, this was the first time that Mama had ever mentioned any of them being my father. There must have been some truth in it.

"Yes, I am, son," Tyson said sadly. If I didn't know any better, I would say that his eyes were turned down into a frown.

"Yay, I have a real father now!" I cheered. "Tyson, do you want to go outside and play football?" I was ready to get started on some father and son stuff.

Tyson wore a weary expression on his face as he looked from me to Mama. "He's calling me Tyson." His teeth were hidden behind his lips. He looked up at the ceiling and shook his head.

"What do you expect?" Mama said. "He don't know you. He don't even know *of* you."

Tyson lowered himself to my level. He stood on his knees, held on to my shoulders, and stared into my eyes. "You feel like calling me Daddy?" he asked through a slight smile.

"Let's not talk about this in front of Michael." Dad took Mama by her wrist and pulled her close to him. He dropped her arm, wrapped her in his love, and rubbed her back. "I'm going to order pizza and see what kind of movies you got here." He strolled over to the entertainment center and scanned our age-old movies.

I looked at the television, wondering who placed it back on the entertainment center. It had been on the floor when Big-mama dragged me out of the house. The television and everything that the mattress forced off of the entertainment center were now back in place.

"That's *if* it works. This disobedient child you walked out on knocked it off the stand." Mama rolled her eyes at me.

Dad looked at me and smiled. "Don't talk about my son like that. He's just a kid."

Wow. Someone other than Big-mama was there to protect me and defend me against Mama's verbal abuse. I was loving every moment that my father was there, and did not want it to end.

"I'm sure it works." Dad went on to look through the movies. "Girl, when was the last time you bought some movies?" He laughed. Mama giggled and I joined in on the laughs.

Dad turned and looked at me. He walked over to me and crouched down in front of me. "That's funny, huh?" He tickled my stomach and sent me falling all over him in laughter. For the few seconds that I was able to look up from my laughs, I caught Mama pointing at us laughing.

Dad watched Mama laugh at us. "Oh, you think it's funny too?" he asked her. He held me by my waist and reached for Mama with his free hand. Mama tried to back away from him, when he caught her by her skirt. Dad pulled Mama down to the floor and pretended to bite her ear.

"Stop!" Mama laughed. "Tyson, stop."

"Nope, you want to laugh, I'll give you something to laugh about," he joked. He released Mama and me, and he and Mama rose to their feet. He picked Mama up into his arms like a mother would a baby, and then kissed her all over her face.

"Put me down!" Mama laughed so hard she was crying. She kicked her feet and pulled on Dad's shirt. "If you drop me?"

"You gon' do what?" Dad chuckled.

"You better not drop me!" Mama's laughs subsided into giggles.

"And if I do, what are you going to do?" Dad lowered Mama to the floor and held her waist firmly. He set his eyes on me and said, "Come here, Michael." I ran to him and wrapped my arms around his thigh. He reached down and rubbed my back and head.

I looked up at Mama and at the tears in her eyes. She was smiling and crying at the same time. Tears of joy is what she was shedding, and seeing her happy made me happy. No more uncles or aunts. Just me, Mama, Big-mama, and my father.

Chapter 20
Family Time
Friday @ 9:00 p.m.

Me, Mama, and Dad sat huddled together on the floor eating pizza and watching *Transformers the Movie*. Mama wanted to watch *Love Jones*, but Dad said I was too young to watch stuff like that. He told Mama to choose between *Toy Story* and *Transformers the Movie*. Mama was in such a good mood that she let me choose the movie.

For hours, we laughed and shared jokes about how strong one of Mama's favorite TV characters, Pippi Longstocking, was. All of a sudden Mama started scratching. Her nails left small scratches on her arms. Her hands then moved down to her thighs, where she scratched herself through her skirt.

To Dad, it might have appeared as if Mama was relieving an itch, but I knew better. Mama's scratching ran deeper than an itch. The monkey was on her and would eventually reveal itself through anger.

"You okay?" Dad asked Mama.

"Yes," Mama answered. "Feels like something is crawling on me, that's all."

"Oh." Dad looked suspiciously at Mama.

"So, Tyson. I appreciate you popping up, the pizza, the movie and all, but why did you leave me?" Mama blurted out.

"Why did you leave us?" I don't know if Mama was trying to put the attention somewhere else besides the monkey creeping up on her, or if she really wanted answers.

Dad picked a napkin up from the floor and wiped grease from the pizza from his lips. He rolled the napkin into a ball and placed it on the floor next to him, while staring into Mama's eyes.

Dad looked at me. "Michael, go to your room."

I looked between Mama and Dad, wondering why he was sending me to my room. I was forced to indulge in adult conversations when it was just me, Mama, and one of my uncles, so I couldn't understand why Dad was sending me to my room.

"No, he can stay right here," Mama told him.

Dad rubbed Mama's hand. "He shouldn't hear this. He's a child." Dad helped me to my feet. "Go to your room for a minute."

"I said no. I want him to hear this. He needs to hear why his dad up and left him. Better he hear your version of it, because mines is nothing nice."

Dad took a deep breath. "You know when you and I first met we were both doing drugs. We shared needles. I would hit the pipe and then pass it to you. Neither one of us was strong. Neither one of us could uplift the other. We were both weak, giving into our flesh. Keep in mind that I was doing drugs long before I met you. I had been chasing the monkey since I was sixteen. The last day you saw me, I didn't plan for that to happen. I didn't plan for that to be the last time I saw you. I had every intention of returning. That morning I left you, I told you I was going to see Curtis for drugs, and then from there going to the store to buy Michael some pampers and milk."

"But you never came back." Mama was still scratching,

but not as much as before.

"No, I didn't come back," Dad replied. "When I got to the stash house, Curtis was sitting at a table with different color bottles of pills in front of him. I didn't know what was inside of the bottles. You know that at the time, all I was doing was weed and cocaine. I gave him a hundred for the cocaine and got up to leave. But before I could even straighten my back, he had his hand out to me with six pills resting in the palm of his hand. I told him no, because I didn't have the money to pay for them. I still had to buy Michael's milk and pampers. Curtis said, 'Take them. They're on the house.' So I did."

"What kind of pills were they?" Mama wanted to know.

"Blue pills with letters on them," Dad said.

"Ecstasy pills?" Mama asked.

"Well yes, I know that now, but I didn't know what they were back then." Dad looked at me and shook his head. "I really don't want to talk about this in front of him."

"He not even paying attention to us, he's watching the movie," Mama replied, without even looking at me.

"I swallowed the pills," Dad continued.

"You swallowed all of them?" Mama asked through wide-eyes

"Yes," Dad answered.

"I'm surprised they didn't kill you." Mama huffed.

"They almost did." Dad sighed. "I popped all of them into my mouth and sat there with Curtis, making small talk. Before I knew it, I was sweating. My heart pounded against my chest. I got real dizzy. I fell out of the chair and it was all that I could do to crawl over to a blowup mattress that Curtis had pushed against a wall. I couldn't breathe. I struggled for every breath taken until I passed out.

"I woke up hours later," Dad continued. "I'm not sure of the time, but I know that it was late. The whole house was dark. I mean I couldn't see my hands in front of my face, and Curtis was nowhere to be found. He left me in that stash house and took off.

"I struggled to get to my feet. I ran my hands along the walls and stumbled into the kitchen. I made my way over to the sink and turned on the cold water. I then held my mouth beneath the running water. Before I could enjoy the water flowing down my dry throat, I started throwing up blood and could not stop.

"I was standing there, throwing up my insides, when the front door came crashing open. I don't know who called them, but I found myself staring into the eyes of maybe six police officers and two Emergency Medical Technicians. I was happy to see them. Curtis must have at least had the decency to call them and not leave me for dead. Then I thought, *Wait a minute, I'm in a drug house. I'm going to jail.* I tried to figure out the fastest way to get out of that house. I think God heard my cries, because I don't remember what happened after that."

"Huh?" Mama said, confused.

"I blacked out," Dad said." I probably passed out. I woke up in the hospital with a tube running down my throat and Jesus hovering over me."

"What in the world?" Mama giggled. "Jesus?" She unmercifully scratched one area of her arm. She hugged herself and rocked from side to side. I could tell she was trying her best to control her hunger for drugs, and Dade talking about getting high wasn't helping the situation at all.

"Yes, Jesus." Dad laughed. The smile on Dad's face vanished into thin air. His laughs dropped to a serious whisper. He lowered his head. He trained his eyes on Mama.

Mama's smile disappeared right behind his. Me and Mama both watched Dad, with our facial expression being just as serious as his.

"Something was going on with my heart." Dad looked away from Mama and cast his eyes on the TV. "My heart felt like it was slowing down. Then it would sort of flutter. And every time it lost its rhythm, I would take short breaths until my heart claimed its beat again. Flutter, normal, flutter, normal. It would not stop. Then I saw Jesus. Well I didn't actually see His face, but I know it was Him."

"You didn't see Jesus' face, but you know it was Him?" Mama asked. I could tell by the rolling of her eyes, and how she smacked her teeth, that she did not believe him.

"Just hear me out." Dad held a hand out to Mama to silence her. "Before I saw Jesus, the lights above my head were blinding me. My eyes were sensitive to the lights. For some reason, it was difficult for me to keep my eyes open." His eyes pierced Mama's eyes. "Crystal, I thought I was close to death. I didn't feel right.

"The lights are blinding me, right?" Dad continued. "I said to myself, 'I'm going to sleep this off, walk the hell out of here as soon as I wake up, and never touch drugs again in my life.'"

"Did me and Michael ever cross your mind? Did you ever think to call me?" Mama cut in.

"Of course, the whole time I was in there. But I didn't know if I was going to live or die, and did not want you to see me lying up there like that."

"What if you would have died?" Mama leaned her head to one side and tightened her eyes.

"Probably would have been the best thing for me at the time."

"Don't say that." Mama shook her head slowly.

"It's true. I was killing myself with drugs anyway." Dad closed his eyes and inhaled deeply. "I started to close my eyes, to sleep off whatever was going on with me, when Jesus pulled me away from the thought of sleep."

Mama covered her mouth and laughed.

"Why are you laughing?" Dad wanted to know.

"You and all of this talk about Jesus," Mama replied through laughs. She was laughing so hard that tears filled her eyes.

"Oh," Dad said, wearing a straight face. "And it wasn't that funny."

"Yes it was." Mama giggled.

Dad cut his eyes at Mama. "I started to close my eyes when Jesus stopped me. He hovered above me with His arms kind of out at His sides. He was dressed in a white robe with a brown rope-like belt tied around His waist. He wasn't wearing any shoes or Jesus slippers, as people call them. His hair was brownish-red and touched his shoulders."

"His hair was dyed?" Mama asked with a serious face. I knew she was being funny, but I don't know if Daddy was aware of it.

"It might have been," Dad replied, wearing the same serious expression as Mama. My guess is that he did not know that Mama was being funny. "I pressed my body against the bed and my head against the pillow in an attempt to get away from Him. I know it was Jesus."

Dad ran a hand over his head. "When you think of Jesus, you think of heaven. But with all of the bad stuff that I had done in my life, I was afraid that Jesus was there to take me to hell." He rubbed his chin. His eyes moved from left to right like he was searching his brain for what to say next. "I tried to back away from Him. I couldn't get too far, being that I was confined to the bed. I pressed my body against the bed, as if I could slip through the mattress and hide beneath it. A sharp pain shot through my left arm, traveled to my chest, and rested in my heart. My body froze. My eyes shot wide open. It was death calling out to me."

Mama crossed her right leg over her left leg, placed the palms of her hands on the floor in back of her, and leaned back. She studied Dad like a scientist does a rat in a maze.

"I fought to hold my eyes open," Dad said. "Death was winning the fight. Then—" He looked up at Mama with fear in his eyes. "Jesus reached down and placed a hand over the left side of my chest." Dad's gaze met Mama's piercing eyes. He then trained his eyes on me. "The throbbing pain in my chest and arm stopped. My body fell limp and relaxed. I could breathe easy. My heart beat with great fear of Jesus, yet I was not afraid." He locked eyes with Mama. "Does that make sense?"

"No," Mama answered dryly and in disbelief.

"I feared Jesus, my Lord and Savior, but . . . but not like a person would fear someone who was trying to hurt them," Dad explained. "I feared Him like I would my father. Before he passed, my father loved me unconditionally and would do anything for me. When I was wrong, he would let me know that I was wrong. Sometimes he would correct me, and other times he would let me find out the hard way."

"You know you sound like a preacher right about now?" Mama chuckled. "You a saint now?"

"Yes I am," Dad replied earnestly.

"What?" Mama smiled.

"I said yes." Dad repeated himself. "Two days after seeing Jesus, I checked out of the hospital and into a rehab center. Curtis had cleaned all of the drugs out of the drug house, so I didn't go to jail. I spent twelve months in rehab, sweating all the drugs that I had taken out of my system and learning about God. From the rehab, I moved into an all men's facility. I did odd jobs around the facility as payment for me staying there. I worked for them during the day and was enrolled in Manuel Arts High School at night, working toward my diploma. Once I got my diploma, I got a job working at Walmart." He sighed. "I checked into West Los Angeles College, majoring in engineering. I then transferred to UCLA and got my Masters in Engineering."

"Wow!" Mama said. "Look at you."

"Yes, and after I graduated from UCLA, I started working as an engineer with General Motors." Dad lowered his head and smiled. He then looked from me to Mama. "I have a house."

"A house? Really?" Mama asked shocked. She was so used to everyone she knew living in ghetto apartments that hearing that someone had freed themselves from the chains of poverty was shocking.

"I have a two-story, four bedrooms, three car garage house in Palos Verdes, overlooking the beach. I am also very active in my church. I'm happy." Dad smiled. "Very happy. I'm good, but I could be great."

"Could be?" Mama questioned. "What do you mean? Sounds to me like you are doing beyond great." She scratched her neck and arms. "You are set for life."

"No." Dad shook his head. "There's two people missing in my life."

Mama's eyes filled with tears. Her lips trembled and so did her hands when she brought them to her face and dabbed tears from the corners of her eyes. "Why didn't you call me?" she cried. "You think you can just walk in here and expect everything to be okay? I'm supposed to take you back just like that? You want me to forgive you for abandoning me and Michael and forcing me to turn to the streets for help?"

"I'm sorry," Dad apologized. "That's why I'm back, to right my wrong. I want God's best for me, and that day I went to the store, I left my best behind. I realize that now and that's why I'm here. I want us to be a family."

"Just like that, huh?" Mama threw her hands up into the air and slammed them down on her lap.

"I stayed away to make a life for us." Dad stood and looked down on me and Mama. "Once Jesus healed me, I swore I would not go back to that life again. I didn't even want to be tempted. Had I come back to you with you still being on drugs, I would have been tempted. I had to make sure that the drugs were completely out of my system, my heart, and my mind."

"You could have taken me with you." Mama wept. "We could have gotten clean together."

"I didn't think about that," Dad admitted. His cheeks filled with air. Shaking his head, he allowed the air to seep from his joined lips. "I can't change the past. It's done. I came back for you and Michael." He glanced around the living room at the tattered furniture, the dirt-stained walls, and me and Mama's dirty shoes by the front door. "Leave all this junk here, clothes and everything, and come with me."

Dad loved Mama unconditionally. His love for Mama brought him back to us, when he could have easily gone out there and made any woman he wanted his wife. But God and Dad's new, clean life led him back to whom he believed was his missing rib.

Dad coming back for Mama reminded me of one of me and Big-mama's Bible study lessons. Pastor Kidd had covered several chapters in the book of Hosea, beginning at the first chapter.

In the Book of Hosea, God told Hosea to take unto him a whore and to bare children with the whore. Following God's instructions, Hosea took unto him Gomer, to which they conceived children. After Gomer threatened to go after her lovers that supplied her with her luxuries, God vowed to strip

Gomer of everything within reach that contributed to her whorish ways if she did not change, in addition to all that He had given her.

In my eyes, Dad was like Hosea. He was a good man, a holy man, and I looked forward to all of us being a family.

"But I'm not clean." Mama pushed the sleeves of her shirt back to her elbows. She held her arms out in front of her and looked from her arms to Dad.

"Wow." Dad reached down and rubbed Mama's arms. He pulled her to her feet and hugged her so tight that her bones could have pierced through her fragile skin. "I'm going to get you clean." He held on to both sides of her face and stared into her eyes. "We're going to get you clean. First thing in the morning, we're going to see about getting you checked into rehab."

"What about Michael?" Mama ran her nails up and down her arms. She rubbed her shoulders before hugging herself. She scratched the monkey on her back. She then dropped her arms and went back to running her nails up and down her arms. It seemed like every time Mama's hands met a certain part of her body, she scratched that area.

Mama's veins were in need of their medicine. I don't know if she was high when she picked me up from the hospital. I do know that she was very calm, which was unusual, being that she stayed high. There was evidence of her dirty deeds on her nose when Big-mama and I left for the hospital. That could have been the last time that she did drugs that day. Mama needed to be fed her medicine, or her skin would suffer terribly.

Mama's nails would draw blood from her chest, thighs, legs, and back. The drugs had an intimate relationship with anger and used Mama to inflict it upon others, mainly me.

"Michael, go on to your room and get ready for bed," Dad

told me. "You full?"

With my eyes on Mama, I nodded my head. "Yes."

"Good. Go on to your room and get ready for bed," Dad instructed.

Mama's nails started moving faster and faster across her arms. They moved as fast as the hands of a person cleaning sticky food from the bottom of a pot with a scouring pad.

Dad held Mama by the wrist and pinned her arms down at her sides. He held his body straight to control Mama's body, which was shaking uncontrollably. He then scooped Mama into his arms and continued to hold her arms down close to her sides.

I moved from sitting Indian style to sitting up on my knees. I climbed to my feet, my eyes refusing to leave Mama, and dragged my feet to my room.

"Crystal. Crystal." Hold on, I got you," I heard Dad tell Mama.

"I, I need my medicine." Mama's voice quivered.

"Where is it?" Dad grunted.

"It's in my room." Mama heaved.

"Come on, let's go get your medicine," Dad said. I think he thought that Mama was talking about prescription medication, because a saved man would not feed her drugs no matter how bad she claimed to need them.

"Put me down!" Mama screamed.

"No," Dad objected. "If I put you down, you're going to hurt yourself. I'm taking you to your room so you can get your medicine."

"I can get my medicine myself. Put me down." Mama grimaced. It sounded like they were right outside of my bedroom door they were so loud.

"Let me take care of you, Crystal."

"No, I can take care of myself," Mama groaned. "I've

been doing it."

I heard Mama's bedroom door open and close. The springs on her bed squeaked loudly. I think I heard Mama moaning, but it was not the kind of moans that I heard when she was entertaining my uncles. They were moans of pain; the sound of someone grieving over the loss of a loved one. A sound that hurt both my ears and my heart. And if Dad didn't hurry up and feed Mama her medicine, I was going to barge into Mama's room and stop the monkey myself.

"What are you doing?" Mama yelled.

"Throwing the devil out of this house," Dad said. "I'm not about to inject demons into your body."

"No, I need it! Give it here," Mama yelled. I heard a lot of sounds that included fumbling and feet pounding the floor.

"Get off me, Crystal," Dad yelled through grunts. There were more sounds.

"Stop! Don't flush . . . give it back!" Mama yelled.

Dad must have rushed into the bathroom and locked the door behind him.

"Open the door!" Mama screamed at the top of her lungs.

The heavy footsteps started up again. From a distance, I could hear them headed my way. As they grew closer and closer, Mama's screams grew louder. "Ha! You can have that little bit," Mama said. "There's way more where that came from."

I heard a door slam. The springs on Mama's bed started playing like a violin out of tune. I could hear thumps against the wall that separated Mama's bedroom from my bedroom. I then heard a flurry of stomps before the entire house fell silent.

"Crystal," Dad called out to Mama. "What are you doing in there?" The sound of taps swept across the floor. I believe it was Dad's shoes, but wasn't sure until he started kicking

Mama's bedroom door.

"Open the door, Crystal!" Dad kicked and banged on the door. There was complete silence. Then Dad yelled, "Crystal, I don't have time for this. Open the door or I'm out of here. Came here trying to be a family again and this is what I go through? You know what, stay in there. I'm out."

"Wait," Mama shouted from behind the door. "Okay." I heard Mama unlocking her bedroom door. Then I heard light thumps as if someone was running on the tips of their toes. I believe it was Mama since Dad still had on his dress shoes.

"No, them drugs are more important to you than having a family," Dad said. "Keep letting that monkey swing from your soul."

"Tyson, I'm sorry," Mama whined.

Oh, now she was sorry.

"Here take it. That's the last of it. I'm done. I want to be a family," Mama pleaded.

"You got more drugs where that came from, I'm sure."

"I swear this is it," Mama vowed. "Take it. Look, I'll flush it down the toilet myself."

I heard the light running again. Since I only heard it after Mama cried out to Daddy for a chance, I will say that it was Mama running.

"How much did you take?" Dad questioned.

"None," Mama said, but I'm sure she'd lied.

"Crystal, how much did you take, and what did you take?" Apparently Dad thought she was lying as well.

"Tyson, I didn't take no drugs. You flushed it all down the toilet."

"Yes, but you said there was more where that came from. And why are you so calm all of a sudden? You haven't dug your nails into your skin not once since you ran out from behind that locked door.

"Let's go to bed," Mama pleaded.

"I'm checking you into a rehab first thing in the morning," Dad told her.

"Okay. Okay, I'll go. Let's just go to bed."

Figures. The bed was where Mama was most comfortable with men.

"Don't play with me, Crystal. First thing in the morning I'm packing you and Michael in my car and we are out of here. All this junk in this apartment stays here, clothes and all."

"What about my mother?" Mama asked. I was surprised. Since when did Mama care about Big-mama? "She's in the hospital. I don't know when she's being released, but we can't leave without her."

Was Mama serious? Any other time she was running Big-mama out of her house. The evil, malicious things that Mama had done to Big-mama, I'm surprised she didn't wish death on her. Wait, Mama did that earlier that day when she slammed her bedroom door and screamed for Big-mama to die.

"We can take her with us," Dad replied. "She can live in my guest house. She can help with Michael while you are in the rehab and I'm at work."

"Okay," Mama said. "Can we please go to bed now?"

"Not in your room," Dad replied. "It's filthy and it stinks."

The house grew silent, dead silent. I placed my ear against my bedroom door. My eyes wandered around in my head as I waited to hear Mama and Dad's movements.

I started for my bed when my bedroom door swung open and Mama and Dad went flying into my bedroom. Dad wrapped his arms around my waist, picked me up into his arms, and dived onto the bed.

"Awww!" I laughed. I was happy to see that neither of them wore angry faces.

"Get him, Tysoin." Mama giggled. "Tickle him."

"No. No," I shrieked. "I gotta pee. I'm going to pee on myself."

"Go ahead. Your mother will change the sheets." Dad laughed

"Mama!" I laughed so hard my stomach hurt. "No, D-a-d. Let me go."

"Okay." Dad laughed. He moved me to the middle of the bed. He then sat on the edge of the bed and removed his shoes. "We are going to smash Michael between us like the cream in an Oreo cookie."

"No." I laughed.

"Yep," Mama said. She walked around to the side of the bed nearest the wall. She lay on her side next to me and stretched her arm across my stomach. She then looked past me at Dad.

Dad covered the doorknob with his blazer, shirt, and tie. He slipped out of his slacks and laid them neatly across my toy chest.

Mama rose up on her elbow and watched Dad with a smirk on her face. "Are your boxers tight enough for you?" She giggled.

"What?" Dad laughed and looked down at his black Calvin Klein boxer briefs. "They are not tight, they are just not baggy."

"They are tight," Mama corrected him.

"Good night." Dad brushed Mama off and climbed into bed next to me. He stretched his left arm above our heads and ran his fingers through Mama's hair. He placed his free hand on top of Mama's hand that covered my chest.

Other than Mama's performance when Dad flushed her drugs down the toilet, Mama was on her best behavior. And while my uncles brought out the anger in Mama, Dad brought out the Mama that I'd wished for.

Mama, Dad and I lay as a family huddled in a group hug. I smiled at Mama's closed eyelids. I then turned over to Dad staring at me. A smile raised the corners of my mouth when I realized that I was looking into eyes like mine.

Chapter 21

Give up the Ghost
Friday @ 11:00 p.m.

Dad bumped my arm as he jumped up in bed. I opened my eyes just in time to see him rush out of the bedroom. I assumed he was hurrying to the bathroom until I heard a heavy hand bounce off the front door.

I pushed Mama's arm off of me and scrambled out of bed. I tiptoed to the bedroom door, being careful not to wake Mama. I then glanced back over my shoulder to make sure that she was still asleep. And just that quick, Mama owned my entire bed. She was lying in the middle of the bed on her back with her legs spread apart.

My right foot crossed the threshold. Before my body could join it, I heard Dad ask someone, "Who are you and what do you want with Crystal?"

"Who are you and what are you doing at my woman's house?" a man's voice asked. I recognized the voice as Uncle Robert.

I crept through the dining room and stood by a wall out of sight of the front door. I lowered myself to my knees and peered out from around the wall at Uncle Robert and Dad. Uncle Robert was standing on the porch looking as sloppy as always. His pants were pulled up over his big stomach. His size thirty-four double B breasts were hidden beneath a dingy, sleeveless, white shirt with gray and black spots covering it. His salt and pepper hair was smoothed down beneath a beige baseball hat.

As usual, Uncle Robert did not come empty handed. He held a brown paper bag down at his side with Mama's medicine in it. I did not need to see inside of the bag to know that it was the devil's work. All of my uncles seemed to show up with brown paper bags.

"I'm Michael's father." Dad's head bounced to each word.

"Michael, go to your room," Mama said. Her voice scared me. She forced her fingers into the back collar of my shirt and pulled me away from the wall. She spun me around and pushed me in my back.

The classical music stopped. Mama, Dad and I were no longer floating on cloud nine together. All of my joy was pulled from the clouds. Mama, Uncle Robert and I were in our devil's den, and Dad was nothing more than a visitor.

My feelings were hurt, but I didn't cry. I didn't go to my room either. I walked slowly toward my bedroom until I felt Mama was no longer watching me. I turned on my bare feet and stared at Mama's and Dad's backs. I crept like a prowler to the same wall that I had been hiding behind, and watched the drama unfold.

"Crystal, this man tells me he's Michael's father." Uncle Robert coughed a fake cough. The devious smile on his face held secrets that only he, Mama and I knew about.

"Yes, I'm his father, and I have his birth certificate to prove it."

"Crystal, does that mean that you don't need me to pay these bills around here no more?" He gazed into Dad's eyes and smiled. "I don't mind, I'll just sex the hell out of you."

Dad lunged at Uncle Robert. Mama jumped between

them. Mama's eyes moved from Dad to Uncle Robert. "Uh, yes, Robert, he is Michael's father," Mama stuttered. "He came by to see him."

"Oh is that it?" Dad asked through a raised brow. "I'm just here to see my son and not you?"

Uncle Robert extended a hand out to Dad. "I don't mind you coming here to see your son. Just don't be trying to spend no nights. Crystal is my woman now, and I'm greedy."

Dad dropped his eyes to Uncle Robert's hand. He scoffed and shook his head. "I don't need your approval to see my son, *or* Crystal. As a matter of fact, you can take whatever it is that you have in that bag and get to stepping."

From where I was standing, I could not see Mama's facial expression, but I'm sure she was fuming. Uncle Robert was giving Mama up in front of Dad.

Dad stared at Mama with angry eyes I'm sure. His mouth hung open and his shoulders were heaving up and down from the deep, short breaths he was taking. I bet there was pain in Dad's eyes while he looked at Mama.

"What?" Mama said as if she didn't know why Dad was staring at her with questionable eyes. Mama turned, diverting her eyes away from the sorrow in Dad's eyes. She happened to lock eyes with me. To my surprise, Mama did not yell for me to go to my room. She just stared at me.

The look in my eyes probably matched the look in Dad's eyes. I was sad and disappointed. Mama was giving up our family for the monkey, and here Uncle Robert was egging her on.

"Crystal, don't play dumb with me." Dad pointed a finger at Mama. "You got drugs being sent to you special delivery." He looked slowly at Uncle Robert. "Creep making house calls?"

Mama exercised her right to remain silent. I don't know if

anything that she said could have been used against her. But from the look on Dad's face, not saying anything made her look guilty.

"Take your drugs, Crystal." Dad backed away from the door. He peered over Mama's head at Uncle Robert. "Come on in, I was just leaving."

"No!" Mama reached for Dad's hands but caught the wind. Dad raised his hands in defeat and continued to back away from her.

"Come on in, Robert." Dad turned his back to the front door and headed my way.

I ran to my room and stood in the doorway. I first thought Dad was going to Mama's room, but instead, he brushed past me and snatched his slacks off my toy chest. He slipped into his slacks and stepped into his shoes. He then took his blazer, shirt, and tie off the doorknob and started out of the bedroom until our eyes met.

"Don't leave me," I whimpered.

"Tyson, wait!" Mama cried. She interrupted my pleas for the only man who could save me from her abuse and promise us a life outside of drugs, alcohol, and anger to stay.

Mama reached for Dad's chest but was met by his hand. Dad knocked her hand away from him on his way out of the bedroom.

I ran on my toes in back of Mama and Dad. As soon as we got to the living room, I slipped between a wall and the entertainment center.

Mama ran ahead of Dad and stopped short of the closed front door. She turned around to face him. That's when she and Dad both spotted the unwanted visitor sitting on the couch with a huge smile on his face.

"Robert, I thought I told you to leave," Mama screamed. She stomped over to the couch. "Get . . ." Her eyes silenced her thoughts. One minute she was smiling and the next minute she held a straight face. Then the smile would try to creep up again. Mama struggled to conceal her excitement. It was Christmas in January, and Uncle Robert was Santa Clause.

Uncle Robert had emptied the brown bag of Mama's medicine out onto the coffee table. He placed the medicine side by side with at least seven to ten needles lying at one end.

Dad walked over to Mama and peered down at Uncle Robert's gifts. He trained his eyes on Mama, who appeared to be shocked and speechless, but in a good way.

Dad leaned in close to Mama's ear. "Happy now? He replaced all the drugs we flushed down the toilet, plus some."

Dad strolled over to the front door, and this time he was alone. Me, Mama, and Uncle Robert watched him wrap his hand around the doorknob and crack the door open. Dad looked back at me. He curled his lips over his teeth and shook his head. He then looked sadly at Mama.

Mama's eyes moved from her medicine to Uncle Robert, to Dad. I think she was trying to decide what should go and what should stay, and who should go and who should stay.

"Dad, don't leave me." I ran to Dad and clung to his legs.

"Boy, get over here and leave that man alone." Uncle Robert laughed.

Dad stared at Uncle Robert with contempt. He breathed heavy breaths. His hands formed into fists. I could see his chest rising and falling. Dad's spirit was on fire, and Uncle Robert was pushing him to lose his religion.

Dad closed the door without leaving. He took in a deep breath. He took light sniffs at the air like a child with a cold. He then glanced down at me. "I won't leave you again." Dad pulled my arms from around his legs and pressed a hand against my chest. He pulled me in back of him and out of the path of the destruction that was about to take place between him, Uncle Robert, and Mama.

Dad dropped his blazer, shirt, and tie to the floor. He kicked the table back and stood between Mama and Uncle Robert's gaze.

Needles and brown medicine bottles filled with weed, ecstasy, speed, liquid cocaine, and heroine rolled along the table in different directions, with many of them falling off the table onto the floor.

"Tyson!" Mama yelled and ran after the drugs like a dog after his bone. She crawled around the floor, scooping needles and drugs into her hands and placing them back onto the table.

Dad eyed Mama in disgust. "Crystal, you not ready. You—"

"Michael, go to your room," Uncle Robert told me.

It was perfectly clear that Uncle Robert did not respect the fact that my father was in the house. Uncle Robert spoke to me like he had more authority over me than my own father did. Regardless of if Dad had been there for me or not, he was not about to allow another man, a drug dealer, to challenge his manhood and chastise his son in front of him.

"Don't talk to my son like that." Dad's words were heated and filled with threats.

"What was that?" Uncle Robert asked Dad.

Honestly, I wanted Dad to repeat himself too. I heard what he said, then again, I didn't. I mean I did, but I guess I wanted to hear it again.

"I said don't talk to my son like that," Dad repeated.

Uncle Robert turned to Mama while pointing a thumb back at Dad. "Who is this joker?"

Dad licked his lips. "Like I told you, I'm Michael's father. That's who I am." He pointed a finger at his own chest. "And that Jezebel down there could have been my wife." He pointed to Mama, who was still on her knees collecting the drugs.

Mama used the edge of the table as a crutch to pull herself up to her feet. "Yeah, and you left this Jezebel broke, hungry, and alone with *your* son," Mama shot back.

I looked anxiously from Mama to Dad. "Tyson is my daddy," I said.

"Yes I am, Michael, and I'll never leave you again. I promise." Dad turned his attention to Mama. "Yes, Crystal, I left you, and I explained why."

"You told me you saw Jesus," Mama sarcastically said.

Dad lowered his head and looked from left to right. "You know what, Crystal? I no longer regret leaving you. You had a chance to change just like I did. Me being here with you is not going to change you. Look at how fast you ran after those drugs." He pointed to the drugs on the table. "Like they were going to grow legs and walk out of this drug house that you've lived in your entire life. I didn't know what condition you would be in. I didn't know if you would still be here. I was prepared for the worse, because when I left here, we were both at our worse. Michael was two when I left and—"

"Exactly, when you left us." Mama grimaced.

"It's been five years, yet you're still in this"—He looked over the living room–"Run-down apartment."

"Yeah, well. I thought about moving, but the little money I get from the county to take care of your son is only enough to move me into another run-down apartment. Leave your social security number. You got that high-paying job. Once they get finished docking your checks for the child support you ain't paid all these years, maybe I can move into a mansion."

Dad glanced around the living room. He then picked his clothes up from the floor. He kneeled before me and swept a hand back over my head. "Michael, I'm sorry for not being there for you, but I'm going to make it up to you." He gathered me in his arms and rose to his feet. His eyes remained on Mama as his right hand moved down my back and caressed the doorknob.

Mama and Uncle Robert spoke to each other through their eyes. Uncle Robert jerked his head in Dad's direction and mouthed something to Mama. Mama then glanced at Dad and laughed.

"Put my son down and get out of my house." Mama sucked her teeth. "Go play Captain save-a-Jezebel to someone else. Don't worry about us, we will be okay."

I lay my head on Dad's shoulder and clung to his neck. I wanted Dad to worry about me. Since Big-mama was in the hospital, I needed someone to worry about me. Uncle Robert had brought Mama enough drugs to last her for at least two weeks, which meant more hell on earth for me had Dad left me.

"Don't worry, son, I got you," Dad whispered in my ear and opened the front door. He walked out of the house with Mama rushing up behind him.

"What are you doing? You not taking my son out of here." Mama placed her hands on her hips and tossed her head back.

"Watch me." Dad hurried off the porch with me bouncing up and down in his arms.

"Give me back my son!" Mama yelled. She trampled the ground in back of us. She reached over Dad's shoulder and pulled on my wrist.

"No!" I yelled and snatched my wrist out of her grasp. I tucked my hands between my stomach and Dad's chest. I buried my head in Dad's shoulder to avoid making eye contact with Mama.

I peeked out from my savior's chest just in time to see Mama clawing at Dad's arms and back trying to get to me. I looked up to see Mama in tears, like she suddenly cared about losing me. Most of my beatings placed me a breath away from death. So no, Mama's tears had nothing to do with love. She was probably crying because she was being robbed of her punching bag.

Mama just wanted me there because she owned me by birth and was not about to allow the man, whom she now hated, to care for me regardless of his paternity. I didn't want to stay with Mama. Like any child, I could never stop loving my mother. I was fed up with the abuse, and finally being blessed with a way out of it, I was ready to love her from a distance.

I was young, so I wasn't thinking that I would never see Mama again. My eyes saw Mama and Dad fighting and Dad taking me with him, that's it.

Dad struggled to fight Mama off of us, while reaching in his pocket for his car keys. Mama snatched his blazer, shirt, and tie off his shoulder and tossed them on the grass. I ducked to avoid being a victim of Mama's fist as she punched Dad in the side of his head. When Mama's nails found their way to the left side of his chest, I moved to the right side of his chest, seconds before they found their host. Mama's nails left four blood-stained lines on Dad's chest.

"Awww!" Dad growled. He stopped and lunged at Mama. "Go on in the house and get high with your junkie. I'm taking my son with me."

Mama tugged on my leg. "Give me back my son," she ordered.

Dad lunged at Mama with a fist in the air. He held back right before his fist met her left temple. "Woman, you better fall back," he warned.

"Girl, let that man have his son," Uncle Robert yelled from the porch.

Mama's and Dad's necks snapped around toward Uncle

Robert.

"Mind your own business and take your fat mouth in the house," Mama screamed.

"See, even your junkie agrees that you ain't nothing but a self-righteous drug addict with a ticket to hell." Dad hissed.

I don't know how Dad got all of that out of Uncle Robert telling Mama to let me go with him, but Dad's words were nothing far from the truth.

Dad hurried to a candy apple red Jaguar XJ. He opened the back passenger door and shoved me inside. He slammed the door and told me, "Put your seatbelt on."

"You not taking my son," Mama yelled. She reached for the door handle at the same time that I was reaching for my seatbelt. I whimpered while clicking my seatbelt securely around me. I feared Mama would pull me out of the car and beat me all the way into the house.

Dad had just made it to the driver's door when Mama opened my door. I leaned to the left away from Mama and watched in fear as Dad ran around the back of the car and took Mama by an arm. He shoved her back away from his car and locked and slammed the door.

Mama stumbled backward, nearly falling over her own feet. Dad jogged around the back of the car, snatched open the driver's door, and jumped inside. He locked the door and looked through the rearview mirror at me.

"We'll be back to see your mother tomorrow."

"I—"

"Michael!" Mama yelled. Her heavy hand against the window cut off my thoughts. "Open the door, Michael."

With my eyes on Mama I continued to cry. "I don't want to come back to Mama, she hurt me."

Everything in me knew that if I went back into that house, not only would Mama hurt me, but this time she would probably kill me.

Chapter 22
My Father, My Hero
Saturday @ 9:30 a.m.

Dad shook me awake at around 9:30 that Saturday morning. By the time we made it to his house the night before, I was passed out sleep in the backseat of his car. I don't remember him carrying me inside of the house or putting me to bed. So when he shook me awake that morning, I had no idea where I was.

I rose from a deep sleep and twisted my fists over my closed eyes. I raised my arms above my head and yawned.

"Michael." Dad laughed. "Are you awake?"

My eyes blinked back sleep. I looked into Dad's eyes. I then peered around the room. I was surrounded by Spiderman, and it was not a dream.

The bedroom was the size of a master bedroom. The Spiderman twin bed sat in the middle of the hardwood floor. Its oval-shaped headboard held a picture of Spiderman clinging to the wall of what appeared to be an office building. The footboard was navy blue with a small picture of Spiderman in the upper right-hand corner of it. The navy blue Spiderman comforter and matching pillow held the same design as the Spiderman painted closet that sat in front of the ceiling to floor, checkered glass window. Every Spiderman design in the room held a city with cars parked along the streets and Spiderman flying through the air.

A navy blue and red, three drawer nightstand sat to right of the headboard. There was a Spiderman beanbag to the left of the nightstand and a Spiderman backpack on the floor next to the beanbag. A Spiderman toy chest, shaped like a football, rested in front of the beanbag.

A brown, wooden bookshelf, made of the same color as the floor, was pushed against a wall next to the door. The top of the bookshelf held both a red sliding door and a blue sliding door. Both doors shared the same picture of Spiderman flying through a city.

A shelf beneath and to the left of the sliding doors was filled with books that stood side by side. To the right of the bookshelf was a desktop computer with a plastic Spiderman cover over its screen.

A four drawer, red and blue dresser sat between the bookshelf and a ceiling to floor red and blue cabinet. The cabinet was composed of three shelves and two drawers. And to the left of the cabinet was a Spiderman punching bag.

I stood on my knees on the bed and glanced around the room. Of the four walls that made up the room, two walls were made of ceiling to floor, tiled glass windows.

"Is this my room?" I crawled out of bed and ran straight for the toy chest. I reached for a toy when I suddenly noticed that my clothes were changed. I was dressed in Spiderman pajamas. Both the shirt and pajama pants were covered in small pictures of Spiderman positioned in different poses.

"Wow! Spiderman." I gleamed. I pulled down on my long-sleeved shirt and looked from one Spiderman to the next. I then went on to pull a toy from the toy chest.

"Come here, son." Dad sat on the edge of the bed.

I dropped the toy back into the toy chest and walked over

to him. I stood in front of Dad and placed my hands on his knees.

"This is your new room?" Dad said. "I've been preparing it for you. Do you want to live with me?" He ran a hand over my hair before holding my chin with the same hand.

"Yes," I said, while nodding at the same time.

"You can stay here on one condition," he told me. I didn't know what condition meant, but was willing to go along with it; anything, not to go back home to Mama. "You have to keep this room clean and make your bed as soon as you get up."

I smiled a billion smiles. This time I had my real father, and he was never going to leave me again. "Okay," I said, still smiling.

"I'm your father, and for now on it's just you and me," Dad told me.

I was happy, very happy. Then out of nowhere, my smile turned into a frown. "Big-mama?" I pouted.

"Big-mama?" Dad questioned. "Mrs. Love?"

"Yes," I uttered.

"Where is she?"

"She's sick," I answered.

"What's wrong with her?" Dad wore a sympathetic look on his face.

"I don't know," I said, near tears.

"Do you know your Big-mama's number?"

"Yes. She's not home," I wept. "She's at the hospital."

"Let's try her phone number," Dad said with a weary smile. "And if she's not home, we will drive to every hospital all over this earth until we find her."

"Okay." I laughed, wiping tears away.

"First let's get you dressed, and then we will call your grandmother."

"Okay."

"Let me run you some bath water." Dad headed out of the room.

"I can run my own bath water." I ran ahead of him, but stopped when I got to the middle of the hall. For a minute, I forgot I was not at Mama's house. "Where is the bathroom?"

"Keep going," Dad said and laughed.

"I started down the hall, skipping, running, and chanting. "I love you, Daddy. I love you, Daddy. I love you, Daddy."

***

A Father's Love, a Son's Hero
Saturday @ 12:00 p.m.

Me and Dad shared the long mirror that hung on back of his bedroom door. Dad brushed waves into his hair, while I ran a hand over the Iron Man reflector design on the front of my shirt.

My closet was filled with new clothes. Sweat suits, jeans, sweaters, jackets, shirts, suits, and a hanger full of ties made up my entire closet. Many of the clothes were too big, while some were too small. Then there were the clothes that fit perfectly. I'm guessing that since Dad had not seen me in years and didn't know my exact size, he bought little boy clothes of every size to make sure that I had something nice to wear when he came for me.

The closet floor was lined with nothing but Nike tennis shoes and dress shoes. Excited, I tried on one shoe after the next, finding those that fit perfectly. Dad had wanted me to dress like him in a black and white Adidas suit. But once I spotted the gray Iron Man shirt, I started jumping up and down while screaming, "Iron Man!"

"You ready to call your grandmother?" Dad asked, walking away from the mirror. He took his cell phone off the dresser and sat on the edge of his bed. "Come here, Michael. What is your grandmother's number?"

I walked over to my father and took the phone from him. I knew Big-mama's number, but not without looking at the buttons on the phone. "Um . . . 323-555-7096." I called out each number as I pressed the keys. I put the phone to my ear, eager to hear Big-mama's voice. The thought of her being in the hospital completely slipped my mind. Big-mama was home, and was going to answer my call, or at least that is what I believed.

"Hello?" Big-mama answered

"Big-mama," I said through a huge grin. She could probably hear my smile I was smiling so hard. I was so surprised that she'd actually answered the phone. My Big-Mama was home!

"Michael, baby, where are you? Where is Tyson?" Big-mama sounded happy and worried at the same time.

"He here," I said, and looked into my dad's eyes.

"Let me speak to him, and then Big-mama will talk to her grandbaby."

"Okay." I held the phone out to Dad.

He put the phone on speaker and held it near his lips. "Hello, Miss Love."

"Tyson, what the hell you doing kidnapping my grandson?"

"Miss Love, I did not kidnap *my* son." Dad cleared his throat. He stared into my eyes with an uneasy look on his face.

"Why did you snatch him from his mother's arms and throw him in your car?" Big-mama asked. "Crystal told the police everything."

"The police?" Dad jumped up from the bed. He looked at me. He then took the phone off of speaker and turned his back to me. "She called the police? I did not snatch Michael from her. I went to see her and my son when some drug dealer showed up at the house, *after* she ran in her room and got high. That drug dealer brought her a whole bag of drugs. I took my son and got out of there." He ran a hand down his face. "Police? My goodness." He sat back down on the bed, took me by the arm, and pulled me close to him.

"I should have known Crystal was lying," Big-mama said. She was no longer on speaker phone, but I could still hear what she was saying due to how loud her voice was. "Now she got the police looking for you."

"I'm . . . I'm," Dad stuttered. I think he was trying to figure out what he was going to do. "I'm going to turn myself in, but not just yet. I want to spend time with my son."

"Tyson, no, bring Michael to me," Big-mama yelled into the phone. "You haven't been around in years. Last time I checked, you were just as high as Crystal."

"Miss Love, I have been clean for five years now. Last night your grandson slept in a four bedroom, three bath home in Palos Verdes, overlooking the ocean. He slept in *his* bedroom. I am an engineer, and most importantly, a man of God. I've been away all these years getting myself together and building a life for my son and your daughter. Crystal showed me last night that she is not ready to change. From my experience, a drug addict does not change unless they are ready to change. Right now, it's about what is best for Michael." Dad took a deep breath. "Give me your address. I will drop him off by eight and turn myself in."

"Promise you won't hurt my grandson," Big-mama said. "His mother done tormented him enough. My grandbaby can't take too much more."

"Miss Love, you have my word."

"Okay, take down my address," Big-mama told him.

"Hold on just a minute." Dad took the phone away from his ear. He leaned back on the bed and took a small notepad and pen from the nightstand. He strained to push himself up from the bed. "Hello," he said, putting the phone back to his ear. What is it?"

Big-mama gave Dad her address and phone number. After making Dad promise at least four more times that he would drop me off to her by eight, Big-mama ended the call.

Dad slipped the phone into his jacket pocket. "Your mama is something else."

"That's what Big-mama says," I said innocently.

Dad laughed and covered my head with his hand. "Let's get out of here. I have to get you back to your Big-mama by eight." With his hand still covering my head, he steered me out of his room and down the hall.

"Your house is real big," I said as we made our way down the stairs that led to the first level of the house.

"*Our* house is big." Dad smiled.

"*Our* house is big," I repeated and smiled as well.

Like father like son.

Chapter 23
Memories
Saturday @ 1:00 p.m.

The ride to LEGOLAND was just as fun and exciting as I was hoping LEGOLAND itself would be. Dad made a lot of promises. For the third or fourth time, he promised not to leave me again. He vowed to take me to Disney World in Florida during the summer. We would fish off the coast of Catalina Island, camp at Big Bear Lake, drive to Las Vegas Nevada to Circus Circus, and spend the rest of the summer visiting his side of the family in Texas and New York. I was excited and sad at the same time. I was excited at the thought of having so much fun, but sad because I worried Mama was going to step in and kill my joy.

As a child, the only thing that I had to look forward to was hanging out with Uncle Nard or going to Big-mama's house to get away from Mama's abuse. And when I was with Big-mama, all we ever did was hang out at her house or go to McDonalds or Burger King to eat. I had never been to Knotts Berry Farm, Sea World, or any of the other amusement parks. So when Dad named all of the places that he would take me over the summer, I began to wish that I had already done those things, rather than knowing that I would do those things. Does that make sense?

"We're here." Dad pulled into the parking lot of LEGOLAND. He parked and looked in the back seat at me. I could not believe my eyes. The ticket booth, walls, rides . . . everything was made of Legos.

I tried to get out of my seatbelt so fast that it took me longer than it would have had I taken my time. I pushed down on the orange button to release the seatbelt. I guess I did not push down hard enough, because I was still trapped in the seatbelt.

"Calm down," Dad said and laughed. "At the rate that you are going, you will never get out of that seatbelt."

It took me five minutes to free myself from the seatbelt. Excited to finally be free, I tugged on the door handle.

"Wait, do not open that door." Dad climbed out of the car. "You gonna run out there and get hit by a car," he said, and slammed his door.

I watched Dad walk around the back of the car to my door. He opened my door and helped me out of the car.

He locked the car with the keyless remote. He looked down at my eager face and smiled. "Let's go." He laughed

I walked ahead of Dad like a puppy pulling its master along during a walk. I did not stop until we made it to the ticket booth.

The line was so long that it seemed like it was taking forever for us to get to the ticket booth. But once inside of LEGOLAND, I was as happy as a kid on Christmas, not that I ever had a Christmas to look forward to.

I got on most of the rides at LEGOLAND. I was the captain of a boat that circled a Lego depiction of the White House where the United States President and the first family lives. Dad and I shared a Lego bumper car. With Dad helping me to steer the car and yelling, "Press on the gas," we sent every car in our path crashing into a wall.

An Engine number *LEGOLAND* fire truck took us on a tour of LEGOLAND and dropped me and Dad off in front of a wall made of Legos. There were people standing in front of the wall looking up at their friends and family members that scaled the wall. The people on the wall were strapped into a climbing harness with a rope attached to the harness and the top of the wall.

"You want to climb up there?" Dad pointed to the very top of the wall.

"No-o-o, not me," I said, shaking my head.

"I won't let you fall." Dad scooped me up into his arms and gave me a big hug.

I loved my dad so much. I had only spent a few hours with him that day, but loved him just as much as a child would a father who had been around since birth.

***

A Father's Rib Stolen
Saturday @ 4:00 p.m.

I stood at the entrance of Rain Forrest Café with my mouth hanging open and my eyes as big as the moon. It looked like something out of a Disney film, and Dad and I were the characters.

"Wow, that's a big fish tank," I said in awe. The entrance to the café resembled a huge fish tank with a doorway cut into the center of it.

The thick wall was made of fiberglass and filled with water and live fish. Trees, castles, strings of plants, and colorful rocks decorated the bottom of the tank as a beautiful waterfall spilled from the top of the tank, down inside of the tank

"It is, isn't it?" Dad said. "Are you hungry?"

With my eyes set to the fish within the glass walls of the café, I answered. "Yes."

"Come on, let's go inside," Dad said. He placed a hand on my shoulder and led me into the café.

The ceiling was covered in vines and gold Christmas lights. Tall trees with long limbs made up every corner of the café. None of the walls were made the same. One wall held sculptures of animal faces made of rocks. A second wall was made of an aquarium filled with fish, castles, rocks, and bushes.

"Good evening, how many are there in your party?" A hostess dressed in a white shirt and black slacks approached us with a menu pressed against her chest. Her blond hair was pulled up into a bun and her face was free of makeup. She reminded me of a Barbie doll. The only thing missing was her Ken.

Dad held up two fingers. "Two, thank you."

"Right this way." She walked ahead of us and looked back over her shoulder every few seconds with a smile on her face. "You may choose any of these seats." She pointed to two round tables in the middle of the floor. She then pointed behind Dad at a row of empty tables that lined a wooden wall, with vines and animal heads dressing the wall.

"Where do you want to sit?" Dad asked me.

"Right there." I pointed to one of the round tables in the middle of the floor. The animals above the row of tables looked vicious and real, and I did not want to be anywhere near them.

"We're going to sit right here," Dad informed the hostess.

I immediately climbed onto a chair facing the forest above the row of tables. I was fascinated, yet scared of the animal heads. Reminded me of a kid who would watch a clown from a distance, but would run screaming and crying for his mother if the clown was next to him. That was me at that very moment.

I watched Dad sit across from me. I then watched the hostess place a menu in front of him before setting an A-Z mini animal children's placemat with three crayons next to it in front of me. There was also pictures of kid's meals.

"Thank you," Dad said into the eyes of the hostess.

"A waiter will be here shortly to take your order." The hostess gazed between me and Dad.

"That's fine," Dad replied. He watched the hostess walk away and fade off into the distance. He then opened the menu and looked at me. "I'm starving. Are you starving?"

"Yep," I said. My fingers toyed with the crayons as I scanned the café.

Every wall in the dining area was adorned with vines, leaves, and flowers. A zebra's head rested in the center of a wall with a Rhinoceros head to the left of it and a dinosaur head to the right of it. A cheetah appeared fast asleep on a wall of rocks above the dinosaur's head. I held my head back and almost leaped out of my seat and across the table to Dad's lap after spotting a snake above our heads.

A yellow snake with red spots outlined in black was coiled around a tree limb above my head. Its head hung from the limb like the snake was freeing itself from the tree and would come down on top of us at any moment.

"Michael?" Dad called out to me. He followed my eyes to the snake." It's not real. It's a toy." He chuckled.

Never taking my eyes off the snake, I eased back in my chair. I guess Dad read the fear on my face, because he tried his best to convince me that the snake was not real.

"It's not real." Dad continued to laugh. His eyes moved around the café like a sightseer peering through binoculars. "None of these animals are real."

"Hello and welcome to Rainforest Café." A bubbly waitress, who bore a striking resemblance to the hostess, stood beside Dad with a black notepad in hand.

"We um, haven't looked over the menu, but . . ." Dad closed the menu and placed it on the table. "I would like a cheeseburger, fries, and strawberry lemonade for my son, and chicken fettuccini and raspberry lemonade for myself. "His eyes moved from the waitress to me. "Is that okay, Michael?"

"Yes." My smile took up my entire face I was so excited.

"Your order should be ready in a few minutes," the waitress said.

Dad thanked the waitress and handed her his menu before she walked away.

"Did you have fun at LEGOLAND?" Dad placed his arms on the table with his elbows hanging off the edge of the table. He then joined his hands together into a fist.

"Yes, can we go back again?" I was hoping he would say the next day. But even if he did, Big-mama was not having it. Rain, hail, snow or sleet, I was going to church with Big-mama, and right into the choir stand.

"No, not tomorrow, but we are definitely going back," Dad promised me. The smile on his face was quickly replaced by a serious look. He took a deep breath and stared into my eyes. "Your grandmother mentioned something about your mother tormenting or hurting you. Can you tell me about that?"

"Mama, she broke my arm," I blurted out without hesitation.

"She did what!" Dad's anger traveled around the café and sent all eyes our way.

"She broke my arm. She threw salad in my face with that nasty Ranch dressing on it. Mama said I took her cigarettes. She hit me in my head and beat me with my uncle's belt. Umm

". . . Mama slapped Big-mama in the face. Mama hit me in my mouth. She pushed my teeth up my gums." I raised my top lip and leaned forward for Dad to see my gums. "The dentist took my teeth out of my gums and threw them in the trash."

"Your mother did all of that to you?" Dad was pissed. His teeth were showing and deep lines creased his forehead.

"And Mama leaves me home by myself a lot." I was running off at the mouth. Mama's threats of me being sent to juvenile hall and shoved into a room with a big bully didn't cross my mind once. Dad said I had a house. I could go there instead of juvenile hall. "Mama says, 'Don't answer that door while I'm gone. Stay your tail out the window. Stay in your room. Don't leave this room unless you got to use the bathroom.' Mama would tell me the same stuff every time she left me home by myself."

"And what happens if you don't listen?" Dad rubbed his closed eyes. He pressed his back against the chair and placed his hands on his lap.

"Mama would take the belt and beat all over me. My arms, legs, back, stomach . . ." I pointed to every area of my body that had met my uncles' belt.

"Oh my God." Dad rolled his silverware out of the cloth napkin. He hugged the napkin in his fist. I could hear wheezing within his short breaths. I tried to look at his eyes, but he looked away from me and lowered his head.

"Cheeseburger, French fries and raspberry lemonade for the little guy." The waitress returned with our food. She held a big tray in one hand and a collapsible stand in the other hand. She shook open the collapsible stand and placed the tray on top of it. She then set my plate and drink on the table in front of me. "Chicken fettuccini and raspberry lemonade for you, Sir." As the waitress was placing Dad's food in front of him, she glanced into his face. "Are you okay, Sir?"

"Yes, yes, I'm fine," Dad said in a hushed tone. His eyes were still on his lap. "Thank you. That will be all." Dad was sending the waitress on her way when she hadn't yet placed his food in front of him.

The waitress hurried to give Dad his food. The plate that held the garlic bread rattled against the table. I guess the garlic bread was a part of the meal, because Dad did not request it with his order. The waitress calmed her nerves long enough to place the plate of chicken fettuccini and the glass of raspberry lemonade on the table. She picked up the tray from the collapsible stand and tucked it beneath her arm. She then folded down the collapsible stand and headed for the kitchen.

"Daddy, are you crying?" I hovered over my plate, trying to see his face.

Dad cleared his throat. "No, I'm okay." He ran the napkin over his eyes. He then placed his napkin across his lap. "I'm okay." He finally looked up at me through red eyes. "Got your food, huh?" he said.

I picked up my burger and bit into it. I dropped the rest onto the plate and stuffed a handful of fries into my mouth. The food was so good that I bounced up and down in my chair.

"My burger is good," I said. "My fries are good too."

I watched Dad spin fettuccini onto his fork. He stuck his fork into two strips of chicken and slipped the fork in and out of his mouth, like Big-mama did when she was sampling her special spaghetti sauce. Dad's eyes were closed when he removed the fork from his mouth. He wore a smile on his face as he was chewing his food.

"Mmmm," he moaned. "My food is good too."

The café suddenly grew dark. "Daddy," I yelled.

"It's okay, son," Dad said and laughed.

"No, Daddy." I reached over the table for him to save me.

"Michael, just watch and see what happens." He tried to calm me down.

"No!" I jumped out of the chair and ran around the table to my dad. I forced myself between him and the table.

Dad eased his chair back and I hopped onto his lap. He held me close to him and laughed so hard that he nearly knocked me to the floor.

The animals of the Rain Forest Café came alive at the strike of darkness, and they were all engaged in their characteristics.

A wall of vines slid open and a gorilla moved out of it. The gorilla made its entrance so fast that I thought it had flown out from behind the wall. The gorilla beat its chest. Its roars cut through the hurricane sound that the monkey made.

A monkey threw fist at the air. The Rhinoceros' mouth opened and closed. There was so much noise and roars threatening my hearing, that if the Rhinoceros was squeaking or snorting, I did not hear it.

The zebra nodded and shook its head. The dinosaur head moved from left to right at a snail's pace. I tossed my head back and stared up at the snake. Since the other animals were alive and making noise, I figured the snake was up to something, and it was.

The snake's tail rattled and its head moved like a wave.

"Excuse me, Sir, can you put the boy down please?" I heard a deep voice in back of me. I turned and looked back at Dad, who was straining his neck to see who was behind us.

Two tall police officers with the Anaheim Police Department hovered over him. They were dressed in all black with their uniform shirts adorned with gold and silver pendants.

"What's going on?" Dad asked them. "Wait!" Dad yelled after one of the officers snatched me from his arms.

"No!" I screamed. "Let me go."

The officer tried to run off with me, but I put up a fight. I kicked over one of the chairs at our table and scratched the officer's face.

"Daddy," I cried.

"Let go of my son," Dad yelled. He leaped to his feet and was quickly subdued by the second officer.

The animals stopped moving. The lights spilled over onto the darkness, one section at a time, until everyone in the Rainforest Café could witness my father and I being separated once again.

Blinded by tears, I glanced around the café and into the eyes of the men, women, and children who watched us. My tears and my fight to be with my dad frightened the other children.

"Sir, you are under arrest for kidnapping Michael Tyson," the officer that held my dad's arms behind his back told him.

"I did not kidnap him," Dad yelled. "He's my son."

"Daddy!" I cried. I squirmed out of the officer's grasp and fell to the floor. The officer crouched down in back of me, wrapped his arms around my waist, and held my back against his chest. He stood and tried to grab my swinging arms.

I reached for my dad when I made eye contact with the waitress that had served us. She was standing across the room with her back against a tree. She dabbed at her eyes like she was crying, but I can't say for sure that she was. There was a great distance between us.

To this day, I do not know how the police knew exactly where to find us.

"Look in my wallet." Dad breathed, out of breath. "His birth certificate is in my wallet. I'm his father."

Dad must have put the birth certificate in his wallet after learning from Big-Mama that Mama had called the police on him for kidnapping. A parent couldn't kidnap their own child could they? I guess that's what that birth certificate was to prove.

"Stop resisting, Sir." The officer pulled Dad's hands behind his back. As he was removing handcuffs from the holster on his belt, Dad snatched an arm out of the officer's grasp and reached for his back pocket. The officer released Dad and backed away from him. He pulled his revolver from its holster and released its clip. He then pointed the gun at Dad's face. "Put your hands where I can see them."

I guess he didn't care about a birth certificate.

Chapter 24
Please Help Me
Sunday @ 10:00 a.m.

I walked into church as slow as a baby learning how to walk for the first time.

"Baby, don't cry." Big-mama reached down and wiped my face. She would have to run her hand over my face over a dozen times before my heart would give my eyes a rest.

"I want Daddy," I wept. Tears streamed down my face. As they rolled past my nose, mucus joined in on the sorrow and drained from my nose to my lip. I freed my lips of the evidence of my pain and wiped the tears and mucus away with my tongue.

"What's wrong, Michael?" one of the ushers held on to my shoulder and looked at Big-mama.

"He's okay," Big-mama assumed. I won't say that she lied, because Big-mama was not in the business of lying. I'll just say that she probably didn't take my pain seriously. Either that or she dismissed me as being a cry baby.

I was not okay. I was hurt and overwhelmed with sadness. My tears carried over from Saturday into Sunday, with nightmares being the cause of most of them.

My dreams rested at the Rainforest Café. When I turned over in bed, my tears soaked my sheet, and all I could see was

Daddy. I brought my legs up to my chest, tucked my hands between my knees, and tried to force myself to sleep, but all I could see was Daddy.

I remembered my dad yelling, "The cuffs are too tight." I turned over and cried. Dad looked in my eyes. Giving up the fight, he sighed. "Michael, I'm sorry." And they took him; the police took my dad away. They took me too, only they didn't take us together.

I stretched my legs and turned over onto my stomach. I blinked past tears and forced my eyes closed. Behind my closed eyelids, I watched Big-mama walk into the police station and stop at the desk.

"Big-mama," I yelled from behind her. I had been sitting in a chair near the entrance waiting for Big-mama to pick me up.

"Michael." Big-mama stooped to my level and put all of her energy into hugging me. Her breasts against my chest were smothering me she was holding me so tight.

Big-mama bore no signs of having had a stroke. Her face was normal and both sides of her body functioned normally.

After showing proof that she was my grandmother and signing on the dotted line, Big-mama and I headed to her house.

I ran straight for my room and dived onto the bed. I kicked off my shoes and cried until my eyes hurt to touch.

"Michael, you want to talk to Big-mama?" Big-mama said as she walked into the room and sat on the bed next to my head.

"No," I mumbled. "I want my daddy."

Big-mama rubbed my back and ran a hand over the back of my head. "You will see your daddy again."

"I want to see him now." I sulked.

"Big-mama will see to it that you see him, but I need some

time."

"Okay," I sobbed.

"Come on, let's get you out of these clothes." She started to pull my shirt over my head when I rolled out of her grasp.

"No, Daddy gave me this." I pouted.

Big-mama smiled and said, "You can wear it to bed, but just this once. You know Big-mama don't like you sleeping in dirty clothes." She reached for my blanket. Once again, I stopped her. I was comfortable and did not want to be disturbed.

Big-mama kissed my cheek and headed for the bedroom door. She looked back at me before walking out of the bedroom and closing the door behind her.

"Daddy, come get me," I cried. And I was still crying as Big-mama and me were in church.

After making it past the hugs, kisses, and what seemed like a dozen of, "What's wrong with Michael," Big-mama and I made it to our seat.

"Go on up in the choir, and remember, don't give them folks a hard time," Big-mama told me for the thousandth time.

"I don't want to sing," I whimpered. "I want to sit with you."

"Oh Lord, help me," Big-mama said, throwing her hands into the air. It hurt my feelings when she threw her hands up into the air as if she was getting frustrated with me. Despite my tears, she obviously did not know how much pain I was in.

Big-mama twisted to her right and made room for me to slip past her. I sat down next to Big-mama and leaned my head back against the pew. My eyes wandered to the ceiling, and in less than five minutes, I was fast asleep.

"Michael," A faint, male voice called out to me. I looked around in the darkness caused by my closed eyes, but could see nothing.

"Michael, it's Daddy. Look to your right at the light. I'm here."

I looked to my right for the light, but all I saw was darkness. Seconds later, a light appeared with my dad standing in the midst of it. He lowered himself to the ground and held his arms open.

I ran toward him. I could almost feel his arms around me before I even reached him. With less than five feet between us, I leaped into the air for him to catch me, when the same officer that whisked me away at Rainforest Café stepped in front of Dad and caught me instead.

"No-o-o, Daddy," I yelled.

"Michael."

I heard Big-mama calling my name, but did not see her.

"Daddy! Daddy!" I cried. "I want my daddy."

"Michael, wake up." Big-mama's voice surrounded me, but I still could not see her.

"Michael, it's okay," Dad said. "I'm coming back for you."

Two officers walked out from around the darkness and stood in back of my dad. One officer fought for his left arm, while the second officer fought for his right arm.

"Let me go." I shot straight up in my seat and yelled, "Daddy!"

"Michael." Big-mama pulled me close to her and held my head against her shoulder. She tried to rock me into silence, when I pulled away from her and searched the congregation for my father.

"Where is my daddy?" I wept.

All eyes were on me and they were filled with sadness. I searched for a dad that no one knew existed.

I had started attending that church when I was two, and was baptized right before my third birthday. Thanks to Big-mama, everyone in the church knew me as her grandson with a mother who was strung out on drugs and a father that had abandoned me when I was two. To hear me cry for my father, they probably thought that I was going through a phase.

"Sister Love, is he okay?" Pastor Kidd asked. He placed a hand above his heart and looked as sad as I felt.

"Yes, Pastor." Big-mama smiled. She took me by the hand and led me down the aisle and out of the double doors to the lobby.

I could not control my tears, not even when Big-mama shook a finger in my face and said, "Michael, get yourself together, right now." Her scorn sent me to my knees in a stream of tears. I now had Big-mama fussing at me to add to Dad being stolen away from me. It was just too much.

I don't know why my dad's arrest affected me the way that it did. It's not like I knew him all that well. I knew my uncles better than I knew my dad. Did I feel some type of father and son connection with my uncles? At times, yes. Uncle Nard treated me like a son when his hands were not behind Mama's needle.

A child should not grow up without a father. As young as I was, I was happy with any man that was willing to show me attention. It did not matter whether we shared the same blood or not. I think I was upset because I'd had fun with Dad and did not want to see him go. Then the way he was taken away from me; it was traumatizing. I won't ever forget that day for the rest of my life.

Big-mama dropped my arm and placed her hands on her hips. She glanced at the closed double doors that led into the church. She rolled her eyes back into her head and lowered her eyes to me.

"Get up, baby, let's go. Big-mama about to put a smile back on that face of yours."

I peered up at Big-mama and wondered why her eyes were closed.

"Dear God, it hurts me to see my grandbaby hurting," Big-mama prayed. "Bring his daddy back to him. This boy done been through a lot with his mama and all them uncles she keeps bringing around him. He deserves to have his real father in his life. I don't know how much more of his tears I can take. Heal his little heart, Father. In Jesus' name. Amen."

"Amen," I mumbled.

Chapter 25

Tears No More
Sunday @ 11:00 a.m.

Big-mama held firmly to my hand as she paid for our pizza, wings, French fries and drinks.

"Place this number in the middle of the table," the cashier told Big-mama. She handed Big-mama a silver stand with a white card that held the number 29 sticking out from the top of it. The cashier took a white plastic cup, filled it with tokens that were kept beneath the counter, and handed it to Big-mama.

Big-mama gazed around John's the Incredible Pizza. "Let's find a table."

While searching for an empty table in the crowded restaurant, we passed by a merry-go-round, a pinball machine, and several arcade games. Big-mama nearly broke her neck when we passed in front of the all-you-can-eat salad bar. The salad bar offered four different kinds of pizza. It also offered wings, French fries, cinnamon rolls, brownies, cake, and ice-cream.

"I should have got the salad bar," Big-mama huffed.

"I want cake and ice-cream," I added.

Big-mama pointed to a table near all of the games. She

placed the number in the middle of the table and slid into the booth. "Here is four tokens," she said, taking four tokens from the cup. "Go on and play."

I cupped my hands together and held them out to Big-mama. "I need more," I told her. I leaned forward and looked into the cup.

"You can't even hold them four tokens in your hand," Big-mama grumbled. "Play those then come back for more."

"More, please?" I pleaded.

"Boy." She counted out four more tokens and dropped them into my hands. "You not getting no more, now go play. And don't talk to strangers."

I ran to the middle of the floor and looked in awe at all of the games that surrounded me. I wanted to play every last one of them until I overheard two boys and a girl arguing over tokens, tickets, and prizes.

"How did you get all of those tickets?" a red-head boy with dark freckles against his light skin asked the boy that stood in front of him.

"I got every ball in the forty point hole on the Skee-ball machine," the boy answered. He pulled up the bottom of his navy blue and white shirt, and then stuffed his tickets into the back pocket of his navy blue pants. While looking from a girl standing to the left of him, and to the right of the red-head boy, he scratched his arm and left dry streaks on his dark skin.

"He's lying. He took my tickets out of there." The girl ran over to the Skee-ball machine. Green and white lights flashed within two clear bubbles on the heels of her pink and white *My Little Pony* tennis shoes. The ruffles at the bottom of her pink, knee-length dress fluttered, and her two pigtails swung back and forth as she ran.

The girl pointed to a quarter-sized slot at the foot of the machine. "My tickets came out of here and you took them,

Mory."

"No, I didn't." Mory stomped over to the girl and pointed to the Skee-ball machine that sat to the right of the one that she was standing in front of. "I kept hitting forty, forty, forty." He pointed to the backboard of the machine.

The Skee-ball machine was made similar to a bowling lane, only it was elevated at the end where the pins would have been, and there were no pins. Five holes, surrounded by solid white, plastic covers with numbers on them replaced the pins. The covers were to keep the small, hard balls from bouncing out of the holes once they made it inside.

The first three holes held the numbers 10, 20, and 30, and they were lined one above the other. The hole in the upper left corner had 40 written on its cover, while the hole in the upper right corner had 50 written on its cover.

The boy with the freckles walked over to them and laughed. "I'm going to get more tokens so I can win a lot of tickets like Mory." He walked off laughing at his friends.

"Give me my tickets back," the girl whined.

"Tracy, I did not take your tickets," Mory tried to convince her. "I was standing right here playing my game at the same time that you were playing your game. We were talking. If I took your tickets you would have seen me."

"I want my tickets." Tracy crossed her arms over her chest and stuck out her bottom lip. "Now I can't get a prize."

"Come on, we can share my tickets." Mory smiled. He ran around games and ducked out of the path of other children and adults with Tracy following on his sneakers. They stopped at a glass counter with three shelves full of hand games within the glass. The wall behind the counter was covered in stuffed animals of every size.

"I want a prize," I uttered to myself. I rushed over to an empty Skee-ball machine and inserted a token into a slot. Six balls rolled out of hiding and filled a rack above the slot.

I picked up one of the balls, took two steps backward, and tossed the ball up the lane. The ball bounced off the ramp and landed inside of the 50 point hole. "Yay!" I jumped up and down and reached for a second ball. I tossed the ball, but this time I put more strength into it. The ball landed in the 40 point hole.

I tossed ball after ball, hitting the 40 and 50 point holes every time. Once I was all out of balls, I looked down at a string of tickets that spilled from the machine. "Yay!" I snapped my tickets off of the machine and stacked them on top of each other until I could hold all of them in one hand. I then ran back to the table where Big-mama was filling her face with salad.

I reached for the cup of tokens, but Big-mama was faster. She snatched the cup up from the table and placed it closer to the wall away from me. "Sit down and eat something," she told me.

I wanted more tokens, but I was hungry too. The games were not going anywhere. And seeing the food caused my stomach to growl.

I placed my tickets on the table next to the pizza and watched them spread out of the stack. I reached for a slice of pizza when Big-mama tapped my hand away from the pizza.

"Your hands are dirty," she said without checking to see if my hands were clean or not.

Big-mama placed a slice of pizza, three wings, and a few mojo potatoes onto a small plate. She pushed my drink to the middle of the table next to the pan of pizza. "Don't touch that soda until you eat some of that food," she instructed.

"Okay." I looked around John's Incredible Pizza as I broke down the food in my mouth. Every time I stuffed my mouth with food, I glanced around at the people that were playing the games. I stopped chewing when my eyes rested on a little boy standing at the counter of prizes. He was accepting a large Spiderman stuffed animal from a lady behind the counter. The lady was dressed in dark blue pants and a dark blue shirt. A dark blue hat trimmed in red covered her hair.

I took a bite out of a piece of chicken and grabbed my tickets. I held on to the back of my seat and the table, and then pushed my way out of the booth.

"Michael," Big-mama mumbled through food in her mouth. "Get back over here." Big-mama's order was too late. I ran to the counter and slammed my tickets down on the counter.

"I want that Spiderman." I pointed to one of two Spiderman stuffed toys on the wall. I then turned to the boy with the Spiderman. He stood staring at me with Spiderman down at his side.

The boy and I stared each other down while the lady counted my tickets. We were not staring at each other like enemies before a fight. Our innocent eyes wandered over each other like two kids at a park, right before one asked the other if they wanted to play.

"You have seventy-five tickets," the lady behind the counter told me. "What would you like to get?" She broke the silence between the boy and me.

"Spiderman." My mind had not changed since the first time I told her what I wanted.

"You don't have enough tickets," the lady said. "You need way more tickets."

"I don't have any more tickets." I crossed my arms on the counter and lay my chin on top of my hands.

"Here, I have a lot of tickets," the boy with the Spiderman offered. He pulled a wad of tickets from the front pockets of his jeans and placed them on the counter next to my tickets.

"Aww, how cute." The worker looked happier than me. I think her eyes even got a little moist. "Aren't you going to tell him thank you?" the worker asked me.

I turned to my blessing. "Thank you," I told him.

"You're welcome," my new friend replied

Without counting my blessings, the worker freed Spiderman from the wall and placed him on the counter in front of me. I took the Spiderman toy by its head and walked backward until his body fell to the floor.

I stood Spiderman up at my side, amazed at how tall he was. Spiderman was almost as tall as me. I looked at my new friend and smiled. He placed his Spiderman next to mine and held a hand above his Spiderman's head.

"My Spiderman is taller than yours," he said and laughed.

"They are the same size," I pointed out to him. I held my free hand over my Spiderman's head. I then moved it to the right and stopped above his Spiderman's head.

"They are the same." My new friend agreed.

"See, I told you." I chuckled.

"Come on, Michael, time to go." Big-mama walked out from behind me with two white bags in hand.

"I'm not finished eating," I told her. I looked past Big-mama at our former booth. There was a man clearing the table and tossing napkins and paper plates into a black bin.

"I have your food right here." Big-mama held up the two white bags. "You can have some for dinner and eat the rest when you get out of school tomorrow."

"Bye." I waved good-bye to my new friend. I trotted behind Big-mama until I caught up with her. "I'm coming home with you?"

"No, your mama wants you."

"No," I gasped. "No." I never wanted to go home with Mama. That wasn't anything new. But this time, I had a really bad feeling about what awaited me at home. A feeling much worse than ever before.

***

Saved by Death
Sunday @ 1:30 p.m.

Big-mama did a good job of taking my mind off Dad. I had fun at John's the Incredible Pizza and could not take my eyes off of my Spiderman. He was my new friend, someone I could play with at home. At home . . .

I pleaded with Big-mama to take me home with her. After a day of fun, I did not want to go home to darkness. All of the arguing between Mama and my uncles, drugs, Mama beating me, the filth . . . My stomach was loose with fear as I thought about the horror that awaited me.

Big-mama pulled in front of Mama's apartment. She stayed in the car, as usual. "Go inside. I'll call to check on you later."

"I want to go home with you, Big-mama," I whined.

"I have to be at Kaiser in the morning." She took one of the bags of food off the passenger seat and passed it to me. "You got school in the morning, and I won't have time to take you."

I accepted the bag from Big-mama and dropped my eyes to my fingers on my lap. I then heard Big-mama release a long sigh.

"I'll pick you up from school tomorrow and see if your mother will let you stay with me for the week." Big-mama smiled her heartwarming smile.

"Yay! Yay!" I opened the door and took Spiderman by the leg. I bunched the handle of the bag up in my hand and hopped out of the car. I looked from my hands to the door, trying to figure out how I was going to close the door.

I pressed my back against the door and walked backward until I heard the door click close. I walked as fast as I could to the front door of our apartment. Spiderman was slipping out of my hand, and I did not want to drop the food to save Spiderman. Yes, I would have saved Spiderman before I saved the food.

I placed the bag on the ground, opened the front door, and picked up the bag. I turned and peered through the lowered passenger window at Big-mama. "Bye, Big-mama. See you tomorrow."

"Go on in the house so I can go," Big-mama said.

I walked into the house and closed the door behind me. The house was quiet. Either Mama was in the room sleep, or one of my uncles was feeding her veins. It was one of the two, because anything right would have been uncivilized, at least in Mama's case.

I stopped at Mama's closed bedroom door. I turned the doorknob and quietly pushed open the door. I raised my right foot to step inside when Mama and I made eye contact.

Urine rolled down my legs. My body felt numb and limp, like life wanted nothing to do with me. It felt like all life had drained from my body, and I could no longer control my limbs. Spiderman met the floor with a thump.

Mama's eyes were wide open, and her pupils were a shiny blue. Her pupils reminded me of the marbles that Big-mama once bought me from the dollar store. White foam spilled from Mama's mouth and down the sides of her face. That same white foam, mixed with blood, trailed from Mama's nose onto her top lip.

With tears crying to be released, I walked slowly into the room to get a better look at Mama.

Mama was lying on her back with her right leg folded beneath her, and her left leg at an angle. Her right arm was lying across her chest, while her left arm hung off the bed with a rubber tie around it. The rubber tie cut off Mama's blood circulation and exposed her veins to the now empty needle that dangled from her arm. An empty needle punctured Mama's left arm.

"Mama," the words escaped quickly from my lips. I was calling out to Mama, but something told me Mama wasn't going to answer me. Her eyes looked nothing like they had when I'd walked into her room days earlier during her feeding time. That day, although her eyes were wide open and her body as lifeless as a dead rose, Mama was alive. Her pupils were of their birth color, and I could see her chest rising and falling. But on this dreary Sunday evening, Mama's pupils were blue, her mouth was capped with foam and dried blood, and her chest stood still.

God lied to me. Mama was dead and would not be joining me and Big-mama in heaven.

I closed Mama's eyes. Death was not supposed to look scary. Big-mama had always told me that when a person passes, they are at peace. With Mama's eyes looking as shiny as marbles and her hair all over her head, she did not look at peace.

I first stood back and ran my eyes over Mama's delicate body. Mama was really dead. All of my prayers were in vain. I believed everything that Big-mama and Pastor Kidd had preached about God hearing our prayers and answering them. I believed God healed the sick and fed the hungry. I believed the Word, but wondered why God looked out for everybody but me.

Big-mama, my savior, who always spoke of being powered by Jesus, continuously drove me into the arms of Mama, while knowing Mama was beating me. My uncles, who were once little boys themselves and who knew how ornery boys could be, allowed Mama to beat me, and right in front of them.

Despite being taken to the same hospital and seeing the same social worker both times my arms were broken, the social worker failed to see a pattern and allowed me to leave the hospital with Mama. Then my dad, my real father, was taken away from me. Seeing Mama lying there dead, I felt hopeless and faithless.

Then again, maybe God hadn't lied. Maybe He'd taken Mama to heaven first. If I went to heaven, maybe I'd see Mama again. She'd be better. She'd be happy. Maybe heaven is where Mama was at peace. Yes, that's it! Mama had finally found peace in heaven. I could too.

I removed the needle from Mama's arm and placed it on the bed next to her. I slipped the rubber tie from Mama's arm and placed it next to the needle. My eyes roamed Mama's drug lab. I picked up a spoon and the small bottle of liquid cocaine. I allowed four drops of the liquid cocaine to circle the center of the spoon. I set the liquid cocaine back down on the drug lab and picked up a lighter. I moved the flame beneath the spoon until small bubbles formed within the cocaine. I had watched Mama and my uncles get high so many times that I was as experienced in preparing Mama's medicine as they were, only this time it was for me.

I dropped the lighter back down on the drug lab. I picked the needle up from the bed and placed the tip of it on the spoon in the pool of cocaine. I drew cocaine into the needle like I did Big-mama's insulin. Once the needle was filled, I placed the spoon on the drug lab and the needle on the bed.

I picked up the rubber tie and used my teeth to help tie it around my left arm. I picked up the needle and climbed onto the bed next to Mama. I looked from the rubber tie around my arm, to my very visible veins. I then put the needle to my arm.

Maybe Mama's drugs hadn't been the devil. Maybe they'd been an angel in disguise trying to get Mama to heaven.

My lips smiled, knowing that just like Mama, for once in my life, I was about to have some peace too. My prayers had been answered after all. I was about to see Mama in heaven just like I'd prayed for.

Amen.

Reader's Question Guide

1) What type of effects can having multiple women/men in a child's life have on the child?
2) What type of negative effects can instability in the home have on a child's development?
3) How would you describe the relationship between Michael and his mother?
4) Why do you suppose Michael was infatuated with the sound of his mother's love-making?
5) Complex trauma describes a child's exposure to multiple traumatic events and the wide-ranging, long-term impact of exposure. What are some of the traumatic events that Michael experienced in the home? Do you believe they will have an impact on how he functions as an adult?
6) What are some of the problems associated with children who witness domestic abuse in the home?
7) Big-mama was a witness to both the physical and psychological abuse that Michael was forced to endure at the hands of his mother. Why do you think she did nothing to save him?
8) Michael had known his father for less than twenty-four hours, yet the impact of his father being taken away from him was as traumatic as the physical and psychological abuse he experienced. Why do you think that was so?
9) Did the hospital staff and the social workers fail Michael?
10) What laws, if any, should be passed to ensure a child's safety and well-being in the home?

ABOUT THE AUTHOR

Pernitha Tinsley is a graduate of California State University Los Angeles, where she obtained a Bachelor of Science Degree in Criminal Justice Administration. Miss Tinsley is also a Fingerprint Classification Expert, and is currently working toward becoming a Crime Analysts.

Born and raised in Los Angeles, California in one of the most troubled and dangerous areas of South Central LA, Miss Tinsley was not only forced to watch families grieve over the death of loved ones killed at the hands of gun violence, but she also painfully watched a close childhood friend endure child abuse at the hands of both her mother and stepfather, prior to her passing in a car accident. Marked by emotional and psychological scars from all that she witnessed as a child, Miss Tinsley grew to become an advocate against child abuse.

Miss Tinsley aims to bring awareness to child abuse by publishing novels that confront the issue and can be used in the classroom, as well as in training programs in institutions that work with families of children who are being abused.

You can visit the author at www.pernithatinsley.com.

Child Abuse Resources

https://www.childhelp.org/hotline/ or call 1(800) 4-A-Child (1-800-422-4453)

https://www.childwelfare.gov/topics/responding/reporting/

http://www.nationalcac.org/

http://www.kidsmatterinc.org/for-families/abuse-and-neglect-resources/